HELEN FORRESTER

The Moneylenders of Shahpur

HarperCollins*Publishers*

HarperCollins*Publishers*
77–85 Fulham Palace Road,
Hammersmith, London W6 8JB

www.fireandwater.com

This paperback edition 1999
1 3 5 7 9 8 6 4 2

Previously published in paperback by
HarperCollins 1994
Fontana 1987
Reprinted seven times

A hardcover edition also published by
Collins 1987

Copyright © Jamunadevi Bhatia 1987

ISBN 0 00 617354 3

Extracts from The Panchatantra translated by Arthur W. Ryder
Copyright © 1956 Mary E. Ryder and Winifred Ryder
Published by the University of Chicago Press. All rights reserved

Set in Sabon

Printed and bound in Great Britain by
Caledonian International Book Manufacturing Ltd, Glasgow

To Dianne, with love.

You are worried when you hear that she is born;
Picking husbands makes you anxious and forlorn;
When she marries, will her husband be a churl?
It is tough to be the father of a girl.

At her birth she steals away her mother's heart;
Loving friends, when she is older, fall apart;
Even married she is apt to bring a stain:
Having daughters is a business full of pain.

The Panchatantra,
trans. by Arthur W. Ryder from the
Kashmiri version 1199 AD.

PROLOGUE

'They'll think I'm mad,' muttered Dr John Bennett to himself, as he waited for the station porter to load his luggage into a tonga. 'To come back to India, when so many Indians are trying to settle in the West. It won't make sense to them, even though I was born and brought up here.' He smiled wryly to himself. 'Mad dogs and English-men . . .'

For over a year now, he had been thinking seriously of returning to India. He was bored by his job as lecturer in Asian Studies. He was tired of Liverpool, its cold, its dampness, its depression; he longed for sunshine. Suddenly, he could stand it no longer. He had his Air Force pension and some savings; he had no family. At the end of the 1949/50 university year, he packed up his books and joyfully took a boat out to India.

Now he stood unsteadily at the top of the imposing steps of Shahpur station, a thirty-four-year-old Englishman, whose war wounds in his legs ached abominably, and wondered if he would still be welcome; India had, after all, fought very hard to rid itself of the British, and it had had its freedom for only two years.

People pushed and shoved past, their luggage perilously poised on the heads of porters. Where once there would have been a number of white faces amongst them, now there was none. Amid the crowds of Hindus and Muslims, a fair sprinkling of Jains stood out, distinguished by their plain white clothes and their more sedate movements.

Looking across the railway lines, he could see the Chemical Works which his father had managed until his death. He observed from the neon sign that its name had been altered to the Star of Asia Chemical Company, and a large addition had been built. The smell of sulphur and other chemicals from it far outweighed the more traditional odours of horse manure and open drains.

He shifted his weight off his wounded legs and on to the two sticks with which he supported himself. God, how the heat made his wounds throb – but at least here he would not have to stand on them while he lectured, he consoled himself. He would try to find his old friend, Dr Ferozeshah, and get him to prescribe a pain reliever for him.

A dignified, elderly Jain came slowly up the steps, his quiet, saintly face lit by a smile, the palms of his hands held together in greeting.

'John, I am pleased to see you. I'm sorry I'm late. Your letter arrived only an hour ago.'

He paused for breath, and then looked aghast at John's sticks. 'You've not been cured?' he asked, a quaver in his voice.

John was sharply reminded that Jains regard physical disability as a punishment for misdemeanours in previous lives, and his heart sank a little.

'No,' he replied, as he watched his father's old friend trying to overcome his repugnance. 'But I can manage quite well with my sticks – and on a bicycle.'

The older man recovered some of his composure.

'I am very relieved to hear that,' he said, looking again uneasily at the offending legs, then averting his gaze to look round the station yard. 'We must get a tonga.'

'I have one,' said John, as he slipped a coin into the eager palm of the hovering porter.

They moved slowly to the little carriage, which was

weighed down with a trunk, a bedding roll and three suitcases.

'Thank you for coming to meet me, Dr Mehta.'

'I was most happy to come,' replied Dr Mehta with conviction. 'Since the death of your dear father and mother in that dreadful aeroplane accident, I have felt as a parent to you – and I hope you will regard me as such.'

John warmed to the kindly old man, and he felt sad that someone so gentle should have aged so much. The once upright figure was bent and thin, the face fine drawn. The voice which he remembered so well from many a lecture on English literature had lost its richness and was faded.

'You are very good,' he said.

He struggled into the carriage after Dr Mehta, using a firm grip on either side of the door at the back to swing his awkward legs up and over the difficult steps. He cursed under his breath as he hit his knee.

'And how is little Anasuyabehn?' he inquired, as Dr Mehta and he settled themselves on the side seats. 'She was about to be married last time you mentioned her in your letters.'

Dr Mehta arranged his white dhoti neatly round his legs before he answered. His ascetic-looking face registered an uneasy frown. Finally, he said, 'Her betrothed died, so she is not yet married – being motherless makes life a little more difficult for her than it should be – but I shall arrange another marriage for her soon. She must have time to recover.' He did not mention a grave shortage of suitable young men in his caste or that he had left his child's marriage rather late, because he found it hard to part with her.

John nodded politely.

'She's getting into touch with your father's old servant, Ranjit. We felt sure you would like to have him to serve you. He went back to his village after your father died.'

11

John was delighted. 'I'd like to have him very much,' he said. Ranjit was a Hindu, and he remembered the happy hours he had spent nestled against the strong, kindly peasant, listening to his harsh country dialect as he told him tales of the great Arjun, and of Ram and his faithful Sita. He also remembered suddenly his gentle, easy-going Ayah who had taken him with her to pray in Jain temples; he could almost feel again his offering of flowers clutched in his hand.

The carriage jogged along the narrow streets. Women were standing in queues to draw water from street taps, to carry up to their families who lived over the open-fronted shops. From behind white saris or red veils they peeked shyly at the strange Englishman.

In the Moneylenders' Quarter, the sweepers were busy brushing the pavements with small rush brooms. They worked their way phlegmatically in and out amongst the beggars, who sat on their heels with their backs against the high compound walls surrounding the moneylenders' communal family homes.

The carriage swept through the ancient Red Gate and John caught a glimpse of the temple to which his ayah used to take him when he was a little boy. It had a double row of lepers lining its imposing steps from top to bottom. Then, within a few minutes, they were engulfed by the overwhelming perfume of the Hindu flower bazaar.

The bazaar marked the end of the city. Dr Mehta raised his hand to point towards a group of fine, modern buildings, fronted by well-kept flower gardens.

'Our new Government University,' he announced with pride. 'You can just see our original college – which you'll remember – through the trees.'

Indeed, John assured him, he did remember – he had been happy when he had attended it. Many of his fellow scholars had been the sons of merchants and moneylenders from the Jain community, sent to the college to obtain a good command of English.

He had always been interested in Jains. They were so determined not to kill anything, not even an insect or one of the souls they believed inhabited the air or crowded into root vegetables and unripe fruit. Their desire not to commit violence meant that they could not use any implement, be it plough or typewriter; so they were usually moneylenders or merchants, though there were many monks and nuns amongst them and a fair number of scholars like Dr Mehta.

'My bungalow is one of those facing the campus, along that lane over there,' said Dr Mehta. He clutched the side of the carriage as it bumped suddenly off the gravel road and into the rutted lane he had just indicated. Then as it began to trundle more safely along, he asked, 'I'm not sure, my dear John, what your plans are . . .?'

John's voice was a little defensive, as he replied, 'My *History of India* is selling so well in the States, and in Britain and India, that I thought I might follow it with a history of the Gujerat – approaching it, perhaps, through the story of the Marwari Gate temple here in Shahpur.'

Dr Mehta nodded, and directed the driver to his bungalow.

'An old bachelor like me doesn't need a great deal,' John said. He did not know how to explain to Dr Mehta his desperate need to rest and be quiet. England had been as alien to him as to any other immigrant; his upbringing in India had not prepared him for the difference in its way of life. The struggle to earn a living when crippled had also been exhausting.

After the war, he had expected to marry the girl to whom he had become engaged before being taken prisoner, but she had looked with undisguised distaste at his torn legs and viewed with horror his tentative proposal that they should live in India. She had left him sitting in a wheelchair in a military hospital and, a month later, had married someone else. This unhappy experience had tended to make him brusque and defensive with women and he had never proposed to anyone else. He never considered that in spite of his damaged legs he was still a fine-looking man, with his brush of black hair lightly touched with grey, and blue eyes which normally twinkled cheerfully from under straight, bushy eyebrows; he had never really examined himself in a mirror for years.

As they descended from the carriage, Dr Mehta murmured gentle agreement with John's plans. The driver began to unload the luggage and dump it into the sand.

The compound gate was opened by an excited boy servant. Behind him, fidgeting nervously, was Dr Mehta's sister, who kept house for him, an old lady in white widow's garb, her cunning face creased with anxiety about her English visitor, whom she remembered as a precocious, ever curious young man.

Anasuyabehn, small, plump and passive, stood half behind her aunt, peeking at John through thick fluttering eyelashes.

John whistled under his breath. It always defeated him how Jain women could look, at the same time, so prim and so seductive. No one looking at a Jain, he thought, could guess at the passions raging beneath their placid exteriors.

Smiling, both women advanced timidly, putting the palms of their hands together in salute.

As John bowed and said how pleased he was to see them again, he was thinking that if he were Dr Mehta, with a twenty-four-year-old daughter like Anasuyabehn, he would marry her off fast, before she got entangled with someone unscrupulous.

CHAPTER ONE

The office of the Vice-Chancellor of Shahpur University was extremely hot. It seemed as if the white walls of the Arts and Science Building had, that September morning, absorbed all the heat of the surrounding desert, and it had then become concentrated in the Vice-Chancellor's usually pleasant room overlooking the carefully cultivated gardens in front of the building.

The Vice-Chancellor, Dr Yashvant Prasad, drummed his fingers irritably on his desk and tried to concentrate his attention on the papers before him, but the fan kept fluttering them and finally he closed the file and handed it to the Dean, Dr Mehta, who was standing by the desk.

The Dean's gnarled brown hands shook a little as he took the file from his superior. Today was a fast day and he felt suddenly very weak and weary and thought wistfully of his retirement, still twelve months away.

He flicked over the pages of the file, which was neatly labelled *Dr Tilak, Zoology*, and said, 'Dr Tilak should arrive this afternoon. I'm giving him two rooms in the students' hostel for the present.'

'That will do very well,' agreed the Vice-Chancellor.

'There's a small room next to the Botany Museum which has water laid on, and I have arranged for him to have it as a laboratory.' The Dean paled a little. He had long considered the requirements of Dr Tilak, the first staff member to be recruited for the new Department of Zoology. Would he, for instance, pin dead insects on to boards, as they had done in the Bombay Museum? Would

15

he dissect animals? Perhaps, knowing how sacred life was in the Gujerat, he would teach with the aid of pictures and diagrams. Dean Mehta fervently hoped so, as he continued, 'I – er am not sure what his research involves, but doubtless a little money will be forthcoming for equipment for him?'

'I doubt it,' said the Vice-Chancellor glumly. 'It was difficult enough to squeeze his salary out of the provincial government.' He chewed his lower lip thoughtfully. 'I'll try again,' he promised.

Several flies were buzzing round the office, so the Vice-Chancellor banged the bell on his desk and called to the peon outside the door to shut the window.

The peon, a thin wraith of a man clad in crumpled khaki, slipped down from his stool and trailed languidly across to the window, skilfully palming his small brown cigarette as he passed the Vice-Chancellor's desk. He banged the window shut and returned to his stool.

The Vice-Chancellor leaned back in his wooden revolving chair and fretfully pulled at his long straight nose. He thought longingly of his native Delhi and wondered why he had ever agreed to come to the Gujerat to head this struggling university at Shahpur. He had, he thought despondently, only two fellow mathematicians on the staff – poor company for a Harvard man like himself.

The peon brought him a cup of lukewarm, oversweet tea, and, momentarily forgetting the Dean's presence, the Vice-Chancellor viciously swatted a fly about to descend upon it. Flies all winter, roasting heat all summer; then the humidity before the rains, then the rains themselves with their following of cholera, typhoid and typhus. When the rains stopped there were clouds of mosquitoes carrying malaria to contend with. Really, Shahpur was only fit to live in for about two months of the year.

16

The Dean tucked the file on Dr Tilak under his arm and said anxiously, 'I hope that a Maratha like Dr Tilak will fit comfortably into our Gujerati ways.'

'I am from Delhi and I am managing to do so,' responded the Vice-Chancellor tartly.

'Ah, yes, indeed, my dear sir,' said the Dean, realizing his slip immediately. 'You are, however, *so* understanding.'

The Vice-Chancellor bridled and said jokingly, 'Well, well, at least the British left us a common language, so that it makes no difference that Dr Tilak's native tongue is Marathi, yours is Gujerati and mine is Hindi.'

'Oh, yes,' agreed Dr Mehta hastily. But his mind revolted at the idea than an alien tongue united his beloved Gujerat with the cocksure southerners and the stupid northerners. His thoughts began to wander.

Although he was a professor of English, knew the plays of Shakespeare nearly by heart and had bookshelves crammed with the latest works in English, his heart lay in his little glass-fronted bookcase amongst his sacred Jain writings, laboriously collected over the years, some of them manuscripts written in Gujerati or Prakrit or Magadhi. Before this bookcase he would sometimes put a little offering of rice; and he would carefully take the writings out and dust them at the appropriate festival.

Vice-Chancellor Prasad glanced up at the Dean's thin, lined face, clean-shaven except for a moustache, with its drooping eyelids and calm, firm mouth. The Dean saw the glance and came back to earth immediately. He pulled his watch out of his trouser pocket; it was a fine gold one which had belonged to his father, and he flicked the lid open carefully.

'Dr Bennett is coming to see me for a few minutes at about twelve o'clock. He wants to go over the Marwari Gate temple; so if you will excuse me I'll go now.'

'Certainly. I should like to see Dr Tilak as soon as he arrives — I'm particularly anxious that our new Department should start off properly.'

'I, too,' replied the Dean with more fervour than he felt. He had advised against a Department of Zoology and he had an uneasy feeling that Dr Tilak could find himself on a collision course with Jain members of the staff.

That same morning, a very bored Anasuyabehn Mehta had been to the library to change her books. Domesticated and obedient as she was, she trusted implicitly her father's promise to arrange another marriage for her. But in the meantime, she seemed to be living in an empty limbo, too old to associate with other single girls, yet without the advantages of matrimony.

Her aunt frowned at her as she entered and put the library books down in a corner. 'Go and wash yourself, child, before entering the kitchen,' she instructed. Then she turned to chide the boy servant for putting too much charcoal on the fire. 'Savitri is waiting on the roof,' she shouted, as Anasuyabehn trailed off to the bathroom.

Her friend, Savitri, knew her well enough to wait a little longer, thought Anasuyabehn, as she filled the bath bucket. Before commencing to wash herself, however, she went to the bottom of the stairs and called to Savitri that she would be up in a few minutes.

Savitri, comfortable in the shade of a tree taller than the bungalow, shouted that she had not to be back at work for an hour.

Anasuyabehn quickly bathed, washed her hair and changed her petticoat, blouse and sari. Then, taking a towel and rubbing her hair as she went, she climbed the stairs to the roof, promising herself that she would go down to help Aunt in the kitchen after a few minutes' gossip with her friend.

Savitri lived such a full and interesting life, she thought enviously. She actually earned her living as a chemist. She herself had never been able to persuade her father to allow her to work.

'Have you had lunch?' she asked Savitri. Her voice was solicitous and deferential. It rejuvenated the other girl's self-esteem, which always sank when she saw Anasuyabehn.

She turned her thin, heavily bespectacled face towards her friend and said she had eaten. She thought mournfully that she had a university degree and competed successfully in the world's hardest labour market; but when she and Anasuyabehn walked together in the evening it was at Anasuyabehn that young men cast longing glances. Savitri's needle-sharp wit might enliven a party, but it was to Anasuyabehn's shy acquiescing answers that men really listened — negative, obedient Anasuyabehn — so obedient, thought Savitri grimly, that it was just as well that she had few opportunities to meet young men alone. Savitri herself had haughtily repelled her father's offers to find her a husband and yet she craved for a man of her own.

She sighed, and watched without interest as a tonga loaded with luggage rumbled down the lane beneath her.

A thin, sharp shriek of 'Niece!' up the stairs broke into their conversation and reminded them suddenly that a caustic-tongued old lady awaited Anasuyabehn's ministrations.

The girls grimaced at each other.

'I wish I were married,' they said in chorus and then dissolved into laughter. They were still laughing and joking when two gentlemen walked down the lane.

19

CHAPTER TWO

John Bennett had found the peace he sought in a high-ceilinged, stone-floored room in the house of a retired teacher, a few doors away from Dr Mehta's home. The room was light and airy and austerely furnished with a wooden couch for sitting and sleeping, a big desk and a chair, and a table from which to eat; there was also a large cupboard for his books and other possessions. On a veranda behind the room, Ranjit camped contentedly among the cooking pots; and on another veranda, to the front of the room, were comfortable basket chairs.

Since his arrival, John had immersed himself in his new history and was almost happy. Though he could not trace any of his former English friends, he had met some Indian ones again and found that none of them held any rancour against him for being English. He had visited his old friend, Dr Ferozeshah, at his surgery, where he was introduced to his head nurse, an English lady of quiet, professional demeanour, Miss Armstrong; Ferozeshah told him that she had previously served in a medical mission north of Shahpur.

As time went by, he was able to discard one of his walking sticks, though his legs still caused him pain occasionally.

While Savitri and Anasuyabehn chatted on the roof of Dean Mehta's bungalow, John took the record of Beethoven's Fifth Symphony off his record player and dusted it carefully.

He opened the cupboard and laid the record on the top

20

shelf, put the record player on a lower shelf, and closed and locked the door.

'Ranjit,' he called, as he began to unbutton his shirt, preparatory to changing.

'Ji?' responded his servant. He put down the tray of wheat he had been cleaning and creaked slowly to his feet. Though elderly, he was a powerful-looking peasant. He had come to Shahpur from United Provinces forty years before, when only a boy. Except when the Bennett family was on leave in England, he had never left them. He had made a close study of Shahpur and was well known for his profound knowledge of exactly where to place a bribe to hurry officialdom or obtain a favour.

'Put those papers into my briefcase, while I change my shirt. I've an appointment with Dean Mehta.'

Ranjit wiped his seamed face with the dish towel draped over his shoulder and, with surprisingly deft movements, he packed the briefcase. He turned a toothless smile upon John. 'Will you be in for lunch?' he asked.

John buckled his belt, and, balancing himself by holding on to various pieces of furniture, he went to the bathroom in search of a comb.

'Yes,' he decided, as he combed vigorously at his hair, which never would lie down properly. 'I won't go to look at the temple until tomorrow.'

When he was ready to leave, Ranjit preceded him through the shady compound, in order to open the gate for him.

'Sahib, there's a tonga here.'

John presumed that the occupants of the carriage had come to visit his landlord. He viewed with interest, however, the tall, slim man who sprang down into the dusty lane. An elderly woman and a thin young girl still in the carriage peeped at him from behind their veiling saris.

'Excuse me,' said the man in good English. 'Can you tell me where to find Dr Mehta, the Dean?'

'Certainly. His house is the eighth one from here, down that way,' replied John, indicating the way the tonga had come.

'I'm really looking for his office.'

John looked thoughtfully at the man. Definitely not a student, he decided.

'I'm going to his office now,' he said. 'Would you like to come with me?'

The young man glanced up at the two ladies, who were whispering to each other, and seemed undecided. The tongawallah, on his high perch, started to fidget and began to mutter about people who made him wait forever and lose business. It was apparent that, at any moment, he would demand an increase in the agreed fare.

'I don't know what arrangements have been made for us. Mother is tired after our long journey.'

John's perplexity must have shown on his face, because he added, 'I'm Tilak from Bombay. I'm to teach Zoology here. In which department do you teach?'

'I'm not a member of the University staff,' John replied. 'But Dr Mehta mentioned that you were coming. I hope you'll like it here.' He extended his hand to the newcomer.

Though Tilak's fingers looked slim and delicate, his grip on John's hand was firm. 'Thanks,' he said.

'Perhaps the ladies would like to rest in my room,' John suggested. 'My servant would look after them, while we go to see the Dean.'

The offer was accepted with alacrity. With Ranjit's help and with much puffing and blowing, Mrs Tilak and her daughter were installed in John's room. John left to Ranjit the task of offering refreshments to the ladies. He had no idea of their caste or orthodoxy. If they were very orthodox, they would refuse all refreshment, in spite of the fact that Ranjit was himself a Brahmin.

Dr Tilak and he walked down the line of flat-roofed houses and bungalows before turning into the path which led to the Arts and Science Building. Tilak looked about him in a brisk, almost military manner which proclaimed his Maratha forebears, in marked contrast to the stolid, slower movements of Gujeratis. He seemed excitable and full of life, and remarked enthusiastically upon the green lawns and little flowerbeds which had been conjured up out of near desert.

Tilak had the beauty of face and form, thought John, which had made Indians famous for their looks, though he was gaunt and very dark-skinned. Though he did not know who John was, he was respectful to him, and he soon drew from him some details of his writings, in particular, about his new book on the history of the Marwari Gate temple and the surrounding district.

But Tilak's expression lost some of its exuberance, as they chatted. Finally, he said, 'I wonder what these Jains will think of my subject?'

'Why? I expect there is a demand for Zoology courses here. Otherwise, it would not have occurred to the University to appoint you.'

'There's a demand – probably from Hindus. However, it may not have occurred to anyone that I'll require small mammals to dissect for the benefit of my students – and fish to dissect for my own research.' He turned to John, his face very earnest, 'One can never be sure with Jains.'

John smiled at the ominous tone in which he pronounced his last sentence. His eyes twinkled, as he replied, 'The Vice-Chancellor is a graduate of Harvard – I'm sure he'll understand the requirements of modern research. We

23

have some old diehards here. A few staff fought against the establishment of a Science Faculty. Dean Mehta is, himself, quite orthodox in his personal life – but I've never noticed his trying to impose his views on anyone else.'

Tilak relaxed a little and was about to make some further remark, when his attention was caught by a flutter of pink on the roof of the Dean's bungalow, which they were approaching.

John, also, had noticed Anasuyabehn on the roof, her pink sari almost obscured by her long, black hair which she was drying in the sunlight. She was generally a very retiring girl and, presumably, imagined that she could not be seen from below or she would undoubtedly have dried her hair indoors; her Western education had failed to rob her of her modesty or dignity. Now, she stood, in all innocence, shaking out her wonderful tresses, and laughing and chattering with her friend, Savitri, who was seated on the low parapet which guarded the edge of the roof.

John thought what a contrast the two women made. Anasuyabehn had an inborn winsomeness, and, as she raised her arms to rub her hair, her fine figure was readily apparent; yet her laughing face and cheerful voice had all the ingenuousness of the carefully protected woman. She was no beauty; but he knew that when she felt at ease with people, she could be quite charming.

Savitri – well, Savitri was Savitri. Thin as a camel after a desert journey, hair cut short and permanently waved last time she had been in Bombay, large, horn-rimmed spectacles; an assertive woman, whose violent efforts to be modern sometimes had results which left her acquaintances gasping. Yet she and Anasuyabehn were old friends, products of the same school and the same college – but different parents, thought John. Though Savitri's parents were Hindus, their home was almost completely

European, while in Dean Mehta's house, despite his study of English, many of the old Jain ways still lingered.

As he and Tilak came level with the bungalow, Anasuyabehn approached the parapet, and, parting her waterfall of hair with her hands, she looked out across the compound straight at Tilak.

Tilak stopped in his tracks, fascinated by the gentle, fair face, made stronger looking by sweeping black brows, and by the marvellous hair rippling down past the girl's knees. In that unguarded moment she did, indeed, look very different from her usual modest self. Behind her, the leaves of an overhanging tree rustled and cast a dappled shade over her, guarding her from the searching rays of the sun.

She stood for a moment, as if captivated, and then, suddenly realizing her dishevelled state and the impropriety of staring at a man, she whipped away across the roof to the staircase.

Tilak continued to stare at the spot where she had stood, as if the shabby, white parapet had mesmerized him.

'Heavens,' he breathed in English, and then blinked and turned his face away, as he realized that he was being insolently scrutinized by Savitri, who was still seated on the low wall.

Embarrassed by this merciless examination, he turned to John and said in his stilted English, 'What were you saying about the Vice-Chancellor and the Dean?'

John was also acquainted with Savitri. He gravely lifted his stick in salute to her. She smiled acknowledgment and he turned his attention again to Tilak.

Though Tilak had reopened the conversation, it was obvious that he was not really listening to John's reply. His face was rapt as they walked along, the eyelids narrowed, the lips parted, and John felt uncomfortably that this lean, attractive newcomer was probably far too emotional to slip quietly into the life of the University. An intense man, thought John, with a difficult subject to teach, in a district where the life of every crawling bug is sacred.

In the middle of a story being told to him by John of how local villagers refused to spray a locust invasion, because of their beliefs, Tilak asked suddenly, 'Whose was the bungalow where the two girls were up on the roof?'

As they climbed the steps of the Arts and Science Building, he looked up at John, impatient for his answer.

A quizzical gleam in his eye, John glanced back at Tilak. 'It was Dean Mehta's bungalow. Why?'

Tilak flushed at the query and did not reply at once. Then, with a burst of inspiration, he said, 'It is helpful to know exactly where various members of the University staff live, and so on.'

In the hall, he saw the name of the Dean on a door facing him, and he promptly changed the subject, a slight grimness in his voice. 'Well, here I go. Now we shall see what effect Zoology creates in a Jain world!'

But Dr Tilak was received with quiet courtesy by Dean Mehta and his fears were allayed. The Head Peon was instructed to help him remove his mother and sister and luggage from John's room and he left to do this, while John arranged with the Dean to visit the Marwari Gate temple with him the following morning.

26

CHAPTER THREE

The Marwari Gate temple had been built by an emperor as a sacrifice for the sins of his teeth. John had visited it on a number of occasions, but this time he wanted to arrange to see some of its sacred manuscripts.

The next morning, with clean handkerchiefs held politely over their noses, he and Dr Mehta followed their amiable guide, a monk, through the courtyard and into the halls and sanctuary. He marvelled again at the lacelike carving of canopies, roofs and figures of Tirthankaras, all in white marble.

It was explained to him that some of the manuscripts he wished to see were kept in the Treasure House and no stranger could be admitted to that. He was allowed, however, to examine the outside of the Treasure House. It was covered with finely engraved silver. The engravings told the story of the fourteen dreams of Trisala, the mother of Mahavira who was the founder of Jainism. John asked if he might make sketches of these.

The monk was reluctant to agree to this, and called several others to consult them. John remembered again that a limp is considered punishment for past sins, and, from the conversation, he thought he would be turned down because of this.

They finally agreed, however, and John arranged to visit them again in a few days' time.

Dean Mehta wished to remain at the temple with his religious teacher, so John wandered off by himself.

A few minutes' walk brought him to the flower bazaar

and to the big, frowsy cinemas; the latter were tawdry with electric lights and hand-painted posters showing languid, suffering film heroines.

Near one of the cinemas, he stopped to buy some hot sweetmeats from a man clad only in a loincloth, who had a tiny stall tucked into the angle of a wall.

While he slowly ate his sticky sweets out of the palm leaf in which they had been wrapped, he watched an artist in the cinema entrance painting a poster to advertise the next film. Crowds of people pushed impatiently around him. A beggar woman, clutching a naked, swollen-bellied child, squatted at his feet and whined hopefully. He put a coin into the child's hand and the woman blessed him, while the starving child stared unseeingly over its mother's shoulder, giving no sign of life, except to clutch the coin firmly in its mouselike hand.

Although such sights were familiar to him from childhood, a sudden wave of pity swept over him as the woman crept away. With an irritable gesture, he threw away the dripping palm leaf, and made to move out into the crowd.

'Bennett Sahib!' exclaimed a cheerful, feminine and very English voice. 'How could you?'

Startled, he looked round.

Diana Armstrong, Dr Ferozeshah's head nurse, was standing half behind him. Down her rumpled khaki skirt was a spreading splash of sugar syrup, where the palm leaf had struck her. Her freckled face, brick-red with heat, was crinkled up with laughter. Her red hair was plastered down against her head by perspiration and her khaki shirt was equally soaked and clung to her slim figure.

John's first thought was that he had never seen a more bedraggled-looking Englishwoman. Then he hastily collected his wits. She was, after all, his doctor's head nurse.

'Miss Armstrong!' he exclaimed. 'I am so sorry.'

28

He looked around him helplessly.

'Can I get you a tonga in which to return home? Or perhaps the restaurant across the road would find us something to wipe it with.'

'The restaurant, I think,' replied Miss Armstrong. Her voice had suddenly lost its laughter and was rather quavery. 'I think I'd be grateful for a cup of tea as well.'

John looked at her sharply. The flush was ebbing from her face and he saw the blue smudges of fatigue under the clear green eyes. Poor woman, he thought. Why on earth does she work as she does, for an Indian doctor who probably pays her in annas?

He put his free hand under one of her elbows and, marshalling his stick, he guided her firmly across the street to the restaurant and into the gloom of a family cubicle at the back of it. He took her little black nurse's bag from her and sat down. He knew her quite well as Dr Ferozeshah's efficient shadow, but had never wished to know anything more of her, except to wonder idly how she came to work for Ferozeshah; and he was now quite surprised at his own temerity. She was, however, English like himself and obviously not feeling too well. He would not admit to himself that he wanted to speak English to somebody English.

'Tea,' he told the white-shirted, barefoot waiter, who was goggling at the rare sight of an English couple in his humble café. 'English tea with sugar and milk separate – boiling water for the tea. And a clean cloth to wipe the Memsahib's dress.' He pointed to the sugar stain.

'Would you like something to eat?' he asked. 'They make nice kabobs here.'

She smiled, showing uneven, very white teeth. 'No, thank you,' she said. 'Just tea.' She leaned back and closed her eyes for a moment, looking, in her exhaustion, soft and vulnerable.

29

The waiter departed, not too sure how to make English tea, but hoping the cook would know. He brought a cloth to sponge the skirt, and Miss Armstrong removed the worst of the stickiness.

'It doesn't matter,' she said. 'I'm a wreck anyway.'

John was inclined to agree with her but had sufficient diplomacy to stop himself saying so. He just twiddled his cold pipe which he had taken out of his pocket, and wondered what to talk about.

Miss Armstrong leaned her head against the wall of the cubicle and hoped she would not faint. She had certainly walked too far and too fast that morning. This John Bennett, though he was something of an oddity, was very kind and she was overwhelmed with gratitude at his bringing her into the restaurant and his concern at her spoiled skirt. She wished suddenly that she was beautiful, charming and amusing so that she could really entertain him with witty conversation. The ceiling gave a sudden swoop and was obliterated by a cloud of darkness for a second.

'I think you had better sip some water.' His voice came from far away, though he was bending over her and holding a glass, clinking with ice, to her lips.

She sipped gratefully and the faintness receded. John's lined, red face, topped by its unruly brush of dark hair, came into focus.

'Thank you,' she said with a wobbly smile, 'I am all right now.'

'Perhaps you're working too hard,' ventured John. 'Surely Ferozeshah doesn't expect you to work all the hours God sends?'

'Oh, no. He's very reasonable – though he works like a machine himself.'

She leaned forward and put her elbows on the stained,

battered table, and ran her fingers across her eyes. Her shirt was open at the neck. John found himself a little flustered by a glimpse of lace barely masking full, incredibly white breasts. It had been a long time, he thought depressedly.

Unconscious of the stir she had caused in her companion, Miss Armstrong relaxed in the welcome gloom of the restaurant. The dark, varnished wood partitions and the smoke-blackened ceiling gave it an air of shabby, homely comfort.

'There's so much to do here – for a nurse,' she said, a note of compassion in her voice.

John sought uneasily for a further source of conversation. Finally, to bridge the growing gap of silence, he asked abruptly, 'Were you visiting someone sick, just now?'

'No – this is my spare time. I don't have to be in the operating room until eleven, today. However, some of the big Jains here are trying to do a real survey of the city. They want to find out how many people live in each district, what water supplies they have, what parks or playgrounds for children. It's an awfully difficult job. I've been counting refugees from Pakistan camped out on the pavements round here.'

John's bushy eyebrows shot up in surprise.

'That's a departure – for Jains. They've always believed that suffering is brought upon oneself. I didn't realize they cared how the other half lived. What's the idea?'

'To raise funds to provide some amenities in the worst slums.'

Miss Armstrong rubbed absent-mindedly at a water ring on the table. She looked up at John's strong, calm face.

'Humph,' grunted John. 'Times they are a-changing!' His wide, thin mouth broke into a grin. 'Jains are usually more interested in protecting animals than humans — charity is simply giving to monks and beggars.'

'I know,' replied his companion. 'That's why I want to help them.'

She removed her elbows from the table, so that the waiter could put down the tea tray. When he had gone, she seized the teapot in a small, strong hand and poured out the tea.

John took the proffered cup and himself added sugar and milk, while Miss Armstrong sipped eagerly at the black brew in her own cup. She sighed. 'That's better. Mind if I smoke?'

'Not at all. Do you mind if I smoke a pipe?'

Miss Armstrong dug a packet of Capstan out of her shirt pocket. After he had given her a light, she began to look a little less flushed and her skin took on its more normal appearance.

'Cream velvet powdered with freckles,' reflected John in some surprise. 'She can't be much over thirty.'

He told himself hastily to stop thinking like a naive youth, and he dragged his mind back to the prosaic subject of the proposed map. 'I know Shahpur quite well,' he told her. 'I was actually born here, and I think I could draw a map of most of it. I'm sure that a proper one doesn't exist, particularly since the influx of refugees — they've built all kinds of shanties — I've watched them go up.' He laughed a little grimly. 'I bet the postmen are the only ones who really know Shahpur.'

'You're right.'

'It would save a lot of time, if you had a map — and, believe me, I could fill in a great deal of detail — mosques, temples, ruins, fountains — what few gardens there are . . .'

'Would you *really* draw one?' Miss Armstrong asked eagerly. Her face was alight, the mouth a trifle open to show the tip of a tongue as narrow as a cat's. 'Could I tell Lallubhai – he's the Chairman – about your offer?'

'Certainly,' replied John, and wondered what possessed him to undertake such a monumental piece of work. 'Do you want a wall-sized map – or sections?'

She looked doubtful and then quickly glanced at her watch. 'I'm not sure. Look, I've got to be in the operating room by eleven.' She picked up her bag. 'Could we meet somewhere to talk about it?'

John was immediately appalled at this complication. There was not a single European restaurant in the city. He could not very well ask her to his room. A vision of Ranjit's horrified face floated before him – an English Memsahib in his room would probably ruin her reputation. He had no idea where she lived or with whom. What a fool he was to get involved.

He fumbled with his pipe, matches and stick, at the same time trying to open the swing door of the cubicle for her. She waited patiently while he sorted himself out and thought of an answer to her question.

'Perhaps you should first talk to your Chairman, Mr Lallubhai,' he temporized, as he finally managed to push the door open with his elbow. 'If a student or artist would volunteer, I'd be glad of a little help. Any map I draw is not going to be technically perfect, but it'll save your Committee a lot of work.' He paused outside the cubicle, and then asked, 'I wonder if Mr Lallubhai has thought of asking the City Engineer for a look at his maps. He'll have some showing drains, waterpipes . . .'

Miss Armstrong's little white teeth flashed in a quick smile. 'I'm sure none of the Committee has thought of it. I'll suggest it. I'll write to you – your address is in Dr Ferozeshah's file.'

As they moved through the crowded restaurant, customers paused in their conversation to watch them pass. At the bottom of the narrow entrance steps, they were besieged by beggars. Miss Armstrong ignored them. She looked up at John, and said, 'You're a brick to offer to help – it's a big job – are you sure you want to do it?'

She looked anxiously at him, and he could not say to her that he wished he had not volunteered, and said instead, 'I shall enjoy it – it will be a change for me. Now, can I get you a tonga?'

She was dismissed and, in spite of his affirmative reply, felt unaccountably a little hurt.

'No, thank you,' she muttered, 'I'll walk. Goodbye – and thank you.'

She turned stiffly on her heavy, flat-heeled shoes, and in a moment was lost in the jostling crowd.

John waved at a passing tonga, and the driver drew into the pavement.

'University Road,' said John, 'How much?'

'Eight annas, Sahib,' said the driver outrageously.

'Four annas and not a pice more.'

'Sahib,' the voice was full of reproach.

'Four annas.'

'Six annas,' said the driver, 'and not a pice less,' and he lifted his whip to start his horse, to indicate that he would rather go without a fare than reduce his price further.

'All right,' said John, and clambered in through the door at the back of the carriage. A little boy, who had been sitting by the driver, scrambled down, ran round the tonga and locked the door after John.

John smiled at the boy and gave him an anna. But behind the smile he felt cross. In two days two new people had entered his life, if one counted that Miss Armstrong had previously been only a pair of hands passing papers to Dr Ferozeshah. They both seemed to be people who would disrupt the peace of his life; Dr Tilak appeared likely to seek his advice quite often and Diana had momentarily disturbed his usual composure.

Since his dismissal by his fiancée, he had tried to avoid women, swearing that he would never let himself be hurt again. Almost every time he walked, he was reminded of the repugnance in his fiancée's eyes, when she saw how crippled he was; and then he would damn all women.

He told himself not to be ridiculous. Nevertheless, by the time he was deposited at his compound gate, he had worked himself into a thoroughly bad temper. When Ranjit saw him, he scampered out to his own veranda, from which he did not stir until he had listened to the typewriter pounding steadily for more than half an hour.

Later, when he crept into the room to ask the Sahib what he would like for dinner, he was surprised to find him leaning his head disconsolately against the typewriter, looking as miserable as he had when first he returned to Shahpur.

'Sahib?' queried Ranjit, his wizened face full of concern. 'Are you well?'

The Sahib did not raise his head from its hard resting place, but he smiled up at Ranjit out of the corners of his eyes, and with a jolt Ranjit was reminded of the small boy John had once been who wept and raged his frustrations out of himself.

'I am all right now, Ranjit. Sometimes I get fed up because I don't walk very well.'

Ranjit scratched his jaw, and wondered if that was the only trouble. He decided, however, that this was not the time to probe further, and said, 'Your legs improve daily, Sahib. Don't get depressed.' Then in a cheerful managing voice, he asked, 'What would you like for dinner? I have some good lady's fingers, succulent and green.'

'I'd rather have them smooth and white,' said John with sudden spirit, while Ranjit looked at him aghast.

CHAPTER FOUR

It was about three weeks later that John was again re-minded of an uneasy sense of unwanted change in his life.

Ranjit came in to tidy his room and, seeing that he was not working, sat down on the floor to gossip.

He regaled John with a detailed description of the con-tents of Tilak's baggage, Mrs Tilak's disgruntlement at the poor lodgings provided for her son by the University, Dr Tilak's hot temper and, by comparison, the quiet character of his sister, Damyanti. Mrs Tilak was a widow, he said, and she and her daughter normally lived with her elder brother-in-law in Bombay.

John lay resting on his wooden couch and laughed at Ranjit. He lay on his back, with one muscular arm curled round his head, and Ranjit, as he watched him, thought that he must be much taller than he seemed when standing. When on his feet, he tended to stoop and put a lot of weight on his stick. A strong man, however, and very virtuous, though, in Ranjit's opinion, he was too young to live in quite the sagelike manner that he did.

'It defeats me, Ranjit,' remarked John, 'how you manage to find out all these things.'

'Sahib,' replied Ranjit primly, 'I do but listen to the conversation of others. Ramji told me himself that Mrs Tilak upbraided him personally because, she said, the lavatories were filthy, and, you know, Sahib, that he does his best to clean them.'

John thought of Ramji's apathetic efforts at cleaning, and snorted.

36

'And anyway, Sahib, what else does one expect a lavatory to be except very dirty?'

'Ours is clean,' said John, yawning and stretching like a cat.

'You clean it yourself, Sahib,' said Ranjit disapprovingly.

'If I left it to you and Ramji it never would be clean.'

He rolled over to face Ranjit and his eyes were suddenly a little flinty.

'Why should one not clean one's lavatory, may I ask? Gandhiji set everyone a good example by taking a sweeper's broom and doing a sweeper's work.'

'I am a Brahmin, Sahib, and well versed in the scriptures.'

'You cook for me.'

'True, Sahib – but times are changing and I must change with them,' said Ranjit huffily, fingering the little shikka on his head. His grey hair was thinning rapidly, but he cultivated carefully this precious tuft of hair by which God, in due course, would pull him up to Heaven.

John abandoned what he knew to be a useless argument and swung his legs down to the floor.

'Let's look at the account book,' he said. 'It's time we did.'

Ranjit heaved a sigh and produced from his shirt pocket a much thumbed notebook, in which were entered in Gujerati characters the various expenditures of their small household. John ran an experienced eye down the list, to make sure that not overmuch of any one item was being used; occasionally, Ranjit's hospitality to his family extended to gifts of tea or sugar out of John's store, as well as free meals.

Meanwhile, Ranjit took out of his shirt pocket a dirty screw of newspaper and from this extracted three rupee notes and a handful of small change, which he carefully counted out on to the floor in front of the couch. John checked the amount with the book and found it balanced. Satisfied, he returned the housekeeping book to Ranjit, heaved himself up and unlocked the almira, took out his cash box and went back to the couch.

Without thinking, he sat down cross-legged and was surprised that he could arrange himself in that position without pain. Ranjit held out an incredibly wrinkled brown hand and John counted his wages into it. He then gave him money for a week's supply of food and fuel.

The servant folded the notes up carefully and stowed them away in a grubby handkerchief, after which he sat looking rather gloomily at a small line of ants marching across the floor, until John asked him, 'What's the matter, Ranjit?'

'Sahib, you have thousands of rupees in the bank and yet you live like a monk. It is not fitting, Sahib, for an Englishman to live so. You should have a pukka bungalow with a compound – and a mali to cultivate the garden – and a kitchen boy to help me.'

'Ranjit,' said John with a sigh, 'you should be in the Secret Service. Do you by any chance know the exact amount of my bank balance?'

Ranjit flushed under the implied reproof, though he answered steadily, 'Yes, Sahib. Rs. 40,581, As. 3.' He cleared his throat, and went on, 'Further, Sahib, you will soon get another letter from Wayne Sahib, your book man in America, with more money; and you have two wealthy students to coach here – more money!'

John leaned back against the wall and roared with laughter.

'You know more about my finances than I do,' he said.

'The Statement from the bank lies on your desk,' replied Ranjit blandly.

The idea of launching out on to a sea of housekeeping

appalled John; he liked his present existence. It was comparatively uncomplicated, he had plenty of learned men for company, and for a change he could take an occasional trip to Abu or Delhi or Bombay, without having to worry about the cost of it. Already Tilak and Miss Armstrong had stirred in him a faint premonition of unwanted change, and here was Ranjit lecturing him about rearranging his life. A sharp reproof rose to his lips, but he stifled it hastily – Ranjit cared more about his wellbeing than anyone else.

'I'll think about it,' he told Ranjit gravely, and dismissed him.

He sat down at his desk and commenced reading the notes he had made on the Marwari Gate temple.

The evening was approaching and there was a comfortable clatter of saucepans from Ranjit on the veranda. Behind it John could hear the wind whining among the bungalows and University buildings. He rose and stretched. Balancing himself by holding on to the furniture, he went to the door and opened it. The sky was flushed with sunset, the pinkness dulled by the threat of storm in it.

His landlord's grandchildren were playing, as usual, in the compound, and the smallest child was in the act of unlatching the compound gate. As he watched, it managed to heave the gate open and peep through it, and then ventured outside. John called to it to come back but it did not, so he got his stick and walked as quickly as he could to the gate.

The toddler was sitting in the middle of the lane cooing to itself, while a small black carriage, drawn by a single horse, bowled smartly towards it.

As he went to retrieve the child, he shouted a warning to the driver. He pulled the youngster to its feet and, with a pat on its behind, sent it back through the gate. He paused himself, because the awkward bending had hurt his legs. The mangy horse drew up by him, and its owner leaned down from beside the driver.

Mahadev Desai smiled and bowed. 'Good evening, John. Can I give you a lift anywhere? Nice to see you.'

John surveyed the plump speaker through the dust engendered by the carriage. He had known Mahadev casually for most of his life. He was the son of a powerful moneylender and jeweller; but today he wore, like any fairly prosperous businessman, a plain white cotton shirt, jacket and trousers. A white Gandhi cap surmounted a moonlike, though not unhandsome, face. Shrewd eyes stared unblinkingly, while he awaited John's answer. Behind him, sat his younger brother and sister-in-law, who murmured 'Namuste' in greeting.

'No, thanks,' replied John. 'I called to you, because I wasn't sure if your driver had seen my landlord's grandchild – the little tike had strayed into the lane.'

'I saw him, Sahib,' the driver interjected hastily, lest he be blamed for carelessness.

John nodded, and inquired after Mahadev and his family. The cadences of the man's voice, he thought, had not changed over the years. He knew the nervous respect with which Mahadev was treated in the city. The Desai Society in which he lived was nearly in the centre of the old town, and from it, financial tentacles stretched out into the mills and homes of half the city, even as far as Delhi and out to Europe, it was said. Nobody held more mortgages and family jewellery in pledge. Nobody could put pressure on a hapless debtor faster than the Desais, or produce a bigger bribe when needed. Their knowledge of invective, that priceless asset of any Indian moneylender, had not been lost as their business became enormously expanded. John had heard Mahadev himself, before he had taken charge of their business in France, screaming in the bazaar at some unfortunate businessman, while a crowd gathered to see the fun, and the police vanished.

Desai was speaking to him.

'I am going to catch the Delhi Mail, after calling on Dean Mehta,' he confided in a slightly pompous whisper.

'Indeed,' said John absent-mindedly, his thoughts already wandering back to his book. 'A pleasant journey.'

'Thank you,' replied Desai graciously. 'A-jo.'

'Goodbye,' said John, stepping back as the driver, in response to a gesture from Desai, whipped up the horse.

John went slowly back into the bungalow. The children had gone in for their evening meal. The wind still whined its threat of a dust storm.

He went back to his desk and looked again at his sketches of the Dreams of Trisala, so often meditated upon by Jain women. He saw instead the ivory-coloured face of Mahadev.

The wife of one of his father's old friends on campus had told him that the well-known moneylender was considering remarriage; as one of the richer men in Shaphur he was of interest. His first wife, she said, had died in childbirth and, soon after her death, he had been sent by his father to Paris, presumably in connection with their business in fine jewellery. Rumour had it that he had opened an elegant jewellery shop there, where they sold silver filigree and other Indian-designed ornaments. By all accounts, this venture had thrived well.

Now Mahadev was home again and, perhaps because of his hairstyle, looked rather Westernized. He was not so influenced, however, that he had lost the ancient instinct of a moneylender to hide his wealth; he was still dressed quite humbly and drove a half-starved horse.

John smiled to himself, as he remembered Ranjit's description of why Mahadev Desai was being encouraged to look for another wife.

'It is well known, Sahib,' Ranjit had said, 'that the older Desais fear greatly that Mahadev may take a French woman to wife – France is next to England, isn't it, Sahib? And there has already been enough trouble in the Desai Society.

'The Society was quite happy when ruled by Mahadev's mother and father, and his little daughter blossomed in spite of the lack of a mother. But when the old lady died and that shrew of a younger sister-in-law became the eldest lady, then, Sahib, trouble seemed to spread from house to house inside their compound. The cousin brothers went away because their wives would no longer stand the ceaseless nagging. Then the wretched woman complained to all the neighbours that she was worked to death, because there was no other woman in the house – though they do have a number of servants, Sahib.'

Ranjit had stopped to blow his nose into a corner of his handkerchief which was not knotted round the housekeeping money, and had then gone on disparagingly, 'Trust them to think of the most economical thing to do – they are persuading Mahadev that he must marry again.'

CHAPTER FIVE

As Mahadev continued on his way to visit Dean Mehta, he mused on the charms of his possible future wife.

He wished to marry for reasons other than economy. He had discovered, to his cost, that a well-to-do Indian jeweller, alone in Paris, could be quite popular amongst women; and their bare legs and tight dresses had been a constant temptation, to which he had, too often, succumbed.

He thought that an educated Indian wife might keep him out of further mischief; he could take her on his travels. He also passionately desired a son. He was fond of his little daughter, but, all too soon, she would grow to marriageable age and leave him, whereas a son would be a joy to him all his life.

For different reasons, the older Desais were of the same mind. Mahadev had hardly distributed the gifts he had brought from France several weeks before, when, with sly hints, the matter was broached. Girls of suitable caste and orthodoxy were suggested; Mahadev found fault with all of them.

'It looks as if our French investment will flourish,' he reminded his father, 'so it is important that I should have a wife able to mix with French ladies.'

'French women!' exclaimed his father. 'She'll live in this house. She doesn't have to go with you to Paris.'

Mahadev felt the perspiration trickling down his back. He did not know how to explain to his father the witchery of the women he had seen in France. The amount of sin he had accumulated during his visit appalled him; somewhere, sometime, it would have to be expiated.

'It's the custom in France to travel with one's wife,' he lied in desperation. 'It's expected of one.'

His father digested this information in silence. He was aware of the pitfalls of travel. There was the temptation to eat meat, for example.

As if reading his thoughts, Mahadev said, with a burst of inspiration, 'It's extremely difficult to eat properly without someone to cook for me.'

'Ah,' exclaimed his father, satisfied at last. 'Most of the

43

girls whom your uncles mentioned can read and write. They'd be docile enough and do whatever you asked.'

Mahadev mentally dismissed the whole solemn, dull collection of them. He had seen a woman walking, with her boy servant, near the University. He had known her for years by sight. He remembered her long plait of hair swinging softly over pretty, rounded shoulders, her delicate ivory skin, her demurely lowered eyelids. Swallowing hard, he inquired of his father, 'Did Dean Mehta's daughter ever get married? Her father's with the University – you may remember him.'

Old Desai looked at him. 'She's not one of our people.'

'I know,' replied his son, rather crestfallen. 'But she *is* a Jain.'

Desai Senior pursed his thin lips, and considered the merits of the match. Finally, he said uneasily, 'She's not a lucky woman – she's been bereaved even before being married – and her horoscope may not be correct.'

Mahadev dared not show the irritation that he felt, neither could he describe the subtle seductiveness of Anasuyabehn or say that he had thought her beautiful long ago, when he was a young man and she was a quiet school girl travelling to and from her lessons. He had never questioned his father's choice of his first wife, who had been a good, obedient girl, but now Mahadev was no longer young – he was a rich, experienced man who hungered for a woman of his own choosing. He wanted Anasuyabehn, the sight of whom made him tremble. And of what use was being rich if one could not buy what one wanted?

The elder Desai listed a multitude of reasons regarding Anasuyabehn's unsuitability as a wife, but they only hardened Mahadev's determination to wed her.

'Perhaps eldest aunt from Baroda could inquire discreetly

about the horoscope,' he said, trying to keep his face impassive.

His father looked at him penetratingly. Mahadev seemed set upon this woman, and he himself was very anxious to see him safely married. Mahadev was his favourite son; in comparison, his younger son was a dunderhead – and the boy's wife was an avaricious shrew. He wondered what kind of a temperament Anasuyabehn had; something about her evidently pleased his son.

'Have you spoken to this girl?'

'No, father.'

'Have you seen her?'

'Yes, father. Many times since childhood. She used to go to a school near the Red Gate and I would see her getting off the bus at the flower bazaar with the other girls.'

'Hm,' murmured his father, thinking that young men did not change much from generation to generation. 'I'll consult your uncles.'

The elder man waved his hand in dismissal, and Mahadev knew intuitively that he had won. He got up from the mattress on which he had been sitting, bowed and made for the door.

'Wait,' said his father, and Mahadev turned apprehensively.

'You realize that a man in your position can choose almost any girl in our caste – parents would happily approve of you.' He paused, and then went on, 'You should consider this carefully, for I do not know whether the Mehtas will be so happy. Dean Mehta presumably has had other offers for his daughter.'

Mahadev, secure in his family's financial empire, had never thought of being snubbed by Dean Mehta and he was nonplussed for a moment, and then said, 'Would Baroda aunt cause inquiry to be made on this point first?'

He is quite determined, thought his father fretfully. I should be firmer about it – and yet the other boy is very unhappy with his witch of a wife.

'Very well,' he said grudgingly. 'Here, take these photographs and have another look at them – you might change your mind about one of them – Baroda aunt's young sister-in-law looks quite nice.'

Mahadev reluctantly took from him the half dozen or so studio portraits of prospective wives, promised to consider them and made his escape.

A man of thirty-four, who had seen the world, he fumed, should surely be allowed to choose a wife; and yet, beneath his resentment at his marriage being arranged for him, lay the knowledge that his father was being extremely patient.

He wandered into the compound, round which were ranged dwellings dating back a hundred years or more. How crowded and dirty it looked! Its smoke-blackened stone verandas with their steps hollowed out by generations of feet, its rotting woodwork, its lack of paint, depressed him. Later on – he would not admit to himself that he meant when his father and his Partner Uncle died – he would build a new Society in a more salubrious neighbourhood, and leave this compound to his brother.

Now that India had settled down after the horrors of 1947, others, less rich than he was, had moved out; he would, too. He sighed, and looked at his watch. Time to go into the office and relieve his brother.

In the gloomy, dusty office, his brother was haggling superbly with a rather cowed local landowner about a loan against his next crop. Mahadev went to stand quietly by him.

His father might consider Younger Brother dull and commonplace, but Mahadev was fond of him and felt he

46

would make an excellent junior partner, completely reliable in all routine matters, and, as far as the family was concerned, painstakingly honest. It was a pity that his father was so hard on him.

Gradually, Mahadev was drawn into the argument, and in a very short time he was engrossed in squeezing a higher interest rate out of their client.

The would-be brides soon had an account book banged down upon their neatly photographed features – and were forgotten.

CHAPTER SIX

Anasuyabehn's widowed aunt had made her home with her brother and his daughter because she had no sons and disliked the idea of living with one of her brothers-in-law. She had constantly berated the old scholar about his neglect of his daughter in respect of finding a husband for her. The only reply she had been able to obtain from him had been, 'We should wait a full two years from the time of her betrothed's death – it is not judicious to hurry the girl.'

As a result of this, Aunt had almost given up hope of ever seeing her niece married, since the older a girl became the harder it was to marry her off. Aunt felt that her own abilities as a matchmaker were simply withering away.

She had, therefore, been delighted when, by devious routes, it was made known to her that the Desais would make an offer for Anasuyabehn, if they could be sure of not being snubbed. This was an opportunity which could not be ignored, a real test of her matchmaking skills, which would benefit dear Anasuyabehn immeasurably. She consulted nobody, but assured the lady from whom this indication had come that such an offer would be well received. She was overwhelmed by the idea of being the instrument by which such a wealthy alliance could be brought about; it would crown all her previous successful efforts on behalf of other relations. After this, all her female relations with children to marry off would crowd about her, begging her favours on behalf of their offspring. Her thin, hooked nose quivered at the anticipation of her future importance in the family.

She conveniently forgot the difference in caste. She thought only of the Desai bank balance and willingly became the mediator between the two fathers. Two other offers for Anasuyabehn from the parents of poverty-stricken scholars were left to die from neglect on her part.

When she first broached the subject, Dean Mehta looked up from his book, said flatly, 'No,' and returned to his studies.

Undeterred, she continued to sit in front of him, chewing her thumb. He again glanced up, and added, 'I'll advertise for a husband for her in early spring.'

'The girl is already twenty-four years old.'

'I know, I know,' said the Dean testily, 'but Desai is not a Mehta.'

'He's near enough,' said his sister, 'and he's rich, healthy and in love with her. What more could we want in these changed times?'

'Does Anasuyabehn know Mahadev?' asked the Dean suspiciously. It would, he thought, be quite easy for her to carry on an intrigue without his knowledge – after all, she occasionally went shopping or to visit a friend by herself.

'No,' said Aunt decisively. 'Someone would have seen her and told me, if she had ever spoken to him.'

48

The Dean sat silently at his desk for a few minutes, staring out of the heavily-barred window and idly twiddling his fountain pen. He reviewed carefully all he knew of the recent history of the Desais, the hints he had heard of their holdings in many new enterprises, their influence amongst Government officials, Mahadev's travels. At last he said, 'Discuss the Desais with Anasuyabehn. She's old enough to be consulted.'

His sister hid her satisfaction at this reply, and merely said, 'All right.'

Her bare feet made a soft brushing sound on the stone floor as she shuffled off to the kitchen, ostensibly to consult Anasuyabehn.

The Dean continued to think about the Desais. Except on grounds of caste, there could be no reasonable objection to the match, and for years he had been preaching that Jainism had originally been a revolt of the Kshatriya military caste against their overbearing Brahmin priests; there was no caste among the original Jains. Young Desai was reasonably educated, had a good, though old, house and was certainly rich; his trips to Europe would have broadened his outlook and, indeed, these days, the family seemed to be financiers and jewellers rather than orthodox moneylenders.

It was said that Mahadev's father was ailing and his uncle was very old, so it would not be long before Mahadev became the head of his communal family. Further, in less than twelve months Dean Mehta would himself retire, and he dearly wished to give himself to a life of contemplation – to become a monk; he had for some years been quietly directing his life towards this goal by study, fasting, confession and the taking of those vows permitted to a layman. To have Anasuyabehn settled now might mean that he would see a grandchild before he severed all earthly relationships by taking his final vows.

He re-opened his book and composed his mind again for work.

'We'll see what Anasuyabehn has to say,' he decided.

Aunt, meanwhile, had sat in a corner of the kitchen and helped to prepare vegetables, while she considered what to say to Anasuyabehn.

The kitchen was quite modern. It had a water tap and beneath it, on the floor, had been built a low, stone enclosure to confine the splashes from it and guide spilled water down the open drain. The walls were whitewashed and, on a built-in shelf, glittered the brass cooking utensils. A watercooler reposed on a stand in a corner near the casement window, and huge double doors, which led on to a veranda, stood open to let in the morning freshness before the real heat of the day began.

'Take the new box of charcoal outside,' Anasuyabehn said to her little servant, 'and brush it.'

The boy picked up a small handbrush and the box and obediently went out into the compound, where he could be heard happily talking to a squirrel, as he gently went over each piece of charcoal with the brush to make sure that no insect was accidentally burned when the fire was lit.

Aunt seized the opportunity to say, 'I saw Mahadev Desai this morning.'

'He's been away a long time,' said Anasuyabehn. 'I don't suppose many people will be glad to see him. He drives even harder bargains than his elders, I'm told.'

She was sitting idly on her kitchen stool waiting for the boy to come in with the charcoal. A neat pile of prepared vegetables, flanked by a tin of cooking fat and her spice box lay on the well-scrubbed floor beside her. The empty charcoal stove was out on the veranda and soon the servant would light a cooking fire in it and bring it to her, carrying it gingerly with long pincers so that he did not get burned.

'Tut,' said Aunt. 'You listen to too much gossip.'

Who's talking? thought Anasuyabehn grimly.

'He's concerned mainly with the jewellery side now — opened a shop in a place near England.' As she snipped away at the vegetables, she tried to think of aspects of Mahadev which might appeal to a young woman, and added, 'He had a Western suit on this morning. I saw him driving through the cantonment, when I was on the bus — on my way to Mrs Patel's.'

'Did he?' murmured Anasuyabehn politely, and thought absently that she must buy some more glass bracelets next time a bracelet seller came round.

Aunt had no intention of discussing matrimony with Anasuyabehn, but she did want to obtain from her some words of approbation in respect of the Desais, which she could carefully misinterpret as assent to a proposal. Mistress of domestic intrigue, dedicated matchmaker, she had no intention of giving Anasuyabehn the opportunity of refusal, and she was certain that a man with the taint of moneylending about him would be refused. She, therefore, said no more that day, but during the weeks that followed Anasuyabehn was regaled with quite a number of stories of the nobility and kindness of Mahadev Desai.

Anasuyabehn should undoubtedly have realized what was in her aunt's mind, but she was entirely absorbed by ideas of marriage elsewhere. The memory of the beautiful, intense features of Dr Tilak staring up at her, as he walked past her home with Dr Bennett, had occupied her thoughts recently, and she only half listened to her aunt's chatter.

Aunt, meanwhile, luxuriated in the thought of bringing off such a superb alliance in spite of the difficulties of Anasuyabehn's advanced age and partly Christian

51

education. If only her sons had lived, she thought sadly, how much more interesting life would have been to someone as skilled in matchmaking as herself; there would have been grandsons and granddaughters to marry off. Why the cholera should strike at her sons and leave her daughters was beyond her; and what trying daughters she had – always complaining because they had been married off to brothers who lived in Bombay, so far away from Shahpur. They were lucky, she thought bitterly – at least they ate twice a day, which was more than she had done in the first days of her marriage.

How good her brother had been, she reflected, to give her a home. Anasuyabehn, too, was a charming, respectful girl; Aunt would enjoy taking an interest in her children, though, of course, she would not see very much of them – once a girl was married she belonged to her husband's family, not to her father's family.

First, however, Anasuyabehn must have a husband.

If I can get my brother so enmeshed in marriage arrangements that it would be difficult for him to retreat with dignity, he also will press Anasuyabehn towards the marriage. And I must prepare Anasuyabehn, so that at least she does not immediately object when the offer comes.

Lucky women went to and fro between the parents' houses, and it was curious how, every time a visitor was expected at the Mehta house, Aunt thought of something which was required from town, and Anasuyabehn and her boy servant were dispatched to purchase it, whilst the horoscopes of the proposed bride and groom were discussed and compared.

Anasuyabehn was not a gossip; she had no reason to suspect anything. Even Savitri, her best friend, who might have told her, knew no one else amongst the Jain community and, busy with her work as a chemist in a cotton mill, heard nothing.

Skilfully the old lady spun threads of praise and flattery between the unsuspecting fathers – the wily old moneylender, who was busy trying to rid his family of most of the taint of moneylending and to gain instead a reputation as a jeweller and financier of integrity, and the absent-minded scholar, who, having inspected and spoken to Mahadev, liked him very much. There were times, not so long since, thought Dean Mehta ironically, when neither of them would have dreamed of speaking to the other, but many things were permissible nowadays – the walls between the castes were crumbling down, and Dean Mehta was quite prepared to give them a helping push.

Once Dean Mehta asked his sister, 'Is Anasuyabehn content about this marriage?'

'Oh, she has all the foolish ideas of a young girl – but she will appreciate a good man. She agrees that the family in this generation is becoming a most worthy one – and she has been most interested in my stories of Mahadev.'

'Ah,' said her brother, a little relieved. 'I'm content, as long as she has no antipathy to the match.'

'None at all, none at all,' said Aunt, with considerably more conviction than she really had. She hoped fervently that all her propaganda directed towards her unsuspecting niece was having sufficient effect to ensure an affirmative answer when the time came.

As she became further committed, the horrid thought of how other women of the family would snigger behind their hands at her, if she failed, began to haunt her – they might even suggest that she was, with advancing years, losing her skill, and that would be hard to bear. She put these thoughts firmly behind her; dear Anasuyabehn should have a wonderful marriage – and all through her aunt's sagacity.

CHAPTER SEVEN

The day on which Mahadev would make a formal visit to his prospective bride's family drew near. Unfortunately, his aunt had to return to Baroda to nurse a sick son, so it was understood that Mahadev would be accompanied by his brother and sister-in-law.

That morning, Anasuyabehn's aunt hinted to her that her father had a well-to-do and charming suitor in mind for her. Anasuyabehn, who had done little else but dream about the new, unmarried Professor of Zoology, ever since she had seen him from the roof of her father's bungalow, asked with interest, 'Who is he?'

'Ah-ha,' responded Aunt, all cheerful coyness. 'Your father will tell you in due course.'

Anasuyabehn could not think of any particularly eligible man who had swung into their orbit recently, other than Tilak, and she smiled happily.

Aunt had informed her brother that all was now arranged. The first gifts had been exchanged, and Aunt explained, 'I locked them in the almira, so that they will be a nice surprise for Anasuyabehn, when you tell her that the final arrangements have been made.'

The Dean smiled. He liked the idea of giving his daughter a pleasant surprise. He had been extremely busy, because the enrolment in his Faculty had increased markedly that term, and he had hardly exchanged a word with his daughter for weeks. He felt that he really must now talk to her about her marriage, though his sister, he was sure, would already have discussed everything with her.

54

He opened his study door, and called, 'Daughter, come here.'

'Well,' he greeted her, as she entered a little apprehensively. 'This is a happy day for us, isn't it?'

'Yes, father,' she answered submissively, masking a tumult of anxiety in her heart.

Aunt shuffled in behind her and sank on to the couch.

Dean Mehta sat down in his desk chair and took his daughter's hand. 'Well, now, are we quite happy at the idea of leaving our old father and going to a fine, young husband?'

Anasuyabehn did not know how to reply, and raised her heavily kohled eyes to her father.

Finally she said, 'I don't want to leave you, father – but I know it *is* time I was married.'

'Good, good. You won't be going far from me, anyway.'

He contemplated his daughter benignly. A placid, obedient girl, educated and yet without the flighty ideas of some of the women students on the campus. He beamed at her with satisfaction, while she waited with as much patience as she could muster. Then she said, in reply to his remark, 'That will be nice, father.' After all, Tilak would probably remain for years at this university.

Dean Mehta dug his key chain out of his pocket and selected a key, which he handed to his sister, while he nodded his bald head in amiable agreement.

'Get the parcels out of the cupboard,' he instructed her, and Aunt creaked to her feet to do so. Anasuyabehn watched her with pleasant anticipation, willing to go along with their desire to tease her gently.

'The Desais have sent some beautiful gifts,' said her father, as he watched his sister bring out a number of bundles.

'The Desais?' Anasuyabehn looked at him with blank incomprehension.

55

Dean Mehta glanced quickly at her, startled by the surprise in her voice. She was looking at him as if she had suddenly discovered a corpse.

'Yes – Mahadev,' he said.

Anasuyabehn sank into the visitor's chair by her father's desk, dazed by the shock. Far away, she could hear her father's voice, but the only word she really heard was Mahadev. She was so aghast that it seemed to her that she never would take breath again; however, her aunt evidently turned the fan towards her, because she felt the breeze on her face. Gradually, the world took shape again. Out of the mist loomed her father's face, full of anxiety, and his voice boomed into her ears.

'Dear child,' he said, full of self-reproach. 'I kept you standing too long on this hot day. Let Aunt give you some water.'

Aunt had already poured a glassful from his carafe, and she held it to the girl's lips. For once, the old woman could not think of anything to say.

Anasuyabehn sipped obediently, and life flooded furiously back into her. All her aunt's gossip of the previous few weeks came back to her and fell neatly into place.

'Marry a moneylender?' she gasped scornfully. 'Oh, no, father. No!' The last word came out in a wail.

Dean Mehta looked at her in some astonishment.

'He's hardly a moneylender, child. He's a big financier. Desai Sahib and his associates put up no less than half the money for the new chemical works at Baroda. Anyway, I thought you wanted to marry Mahadev.'

'Why should I think of marrying him?' Anasuyabehn asked, through angry tears.

'Your aunt assured me that you wanted to.'

'When I spoke of him,' interposed her aunt hastily, 'you agreed what a nice family they were. You made no criticism whatever.'

'I never thought of marrying one of them,' retorted the girl. She dabbed her eyes with the end of her sari.

Dean Mehta looked at his sister, and demanded sharply, 'What've you been doing? Didn't you ask her?' He seemed suddenly fierce.

Aunt looked uncomfortable. Her mouth opened and shut, as she searched for a reply. She had not expected serious opposition from Anasuyabehn, once her father was committed to the match. She thought the girl would accept fairly contentedly the prospect of such a fine, rich bridegroom.

Anasuyabehn's faintness had passed and she glared at the old woman, whose white widow's sari served only to remind her of the troubles of early widowhood, the likely result if one married a man much older than oneself. Only a lifetime of training stopped her from screaming with rage at her aunt.

Aunt mustered her forces. She said indignantly, 'I've talked of little else for weeks. I told her all about the family and about the return of their eldest son. I was sure she understood.'

'Marriage never occurred to me,' Anasuyabehn defended herself, through gritted teeth. 'They're not the same caste. I just thought you were telling me the news – gossiping!' The last word came out loaded with rage.

'Sister!' Dean Mehta's voice was full of reproach. 'Now we are committed. You stupid woman!' Mentally he reviled himself for leaving so important a matter to her.

'It's a good match,' said Aunt defensively. 'Mahadev could marry anyone he chooses round these parts – and he chose Anasuyabehn.'

'*Chose* me?' exclaimed Anasuyabehn. Since she never even spoke to Mahadev she had assumed that his father was arranging the marriage.

57

'Yes,' replied Aunt quickly. 'He's admired you for years. However, you were betrothed. But now he finds you are free, and dearly wants to marry you.'

'Oh,' said Anasuyabehn, surprise for a moment overcoming her anger.

The Dean, thoroughly exasperated by his sister, nevertheless saw his chance, and said to his bewildered daughter, who was agitatedly running her fingers through her hair, 'My daughter, your aunt is right. It is a good match in these troubled times.' He pursed his lips, and then went on, 'Certainly she should have talked it over thoroughly with you – I regret not asking you myself, but I've had so much on my mind lately – however, here we are committed to it, and before we do anything more, I want you to consider it carefully.'

Anasuyabehn looked at him helplessly. She felt, as her father pressed Mahadev's suit, that her last Court of Appeal was being closed to her, and she sat like a silent ghost while her father extolled Mahadev's virtues. When he produced an exquisite sari which had been brought, as a token of the engagement, by one of the ladies concerned in the negotiations, she sat with it half opened in her lap, and hardly heard his voice.

'Child, it was sad that your betrothed should die – I know you liked him. And, unfortunately, it made you look a little unlucky in the eyes of parents . . .' He tailed off.

'Mahadev is a handsome man,' put in the old woman, her voice almost wistful, only to be crushed by an icy look from Anasuyabehn.

'And a generous and thoughtful one,' added her father, cheering up a little, as he picked up a small box from his desk.

Mahadev had often been impressed by Anasuyabehn's quiet and dignified demeanour when he had watched her in the streets; she walked with the perfect foot placement and timing of an elephant, he had many times told himself. Older and wiser than most bridegrooms, he greatly desired to win the favour of his wife-to-be. He had, therefore, insisted that the traditional bags of white and brown sugar be sent to her home, burying in them, instead of the usual two rupees, a small silver box with which to surprise her. It was this box which her father now handed to her.

Though she was very dejected, Anasuyabehn's curiosity was aroused by the unexpected token. She took the box from her father and opened it.

On a fluffy bed of cotton reposed a small nose ring consisting of a single diamond set in gold. Exquisitely cut, it flashed in the sunlight with a delicate blue radiance, a beautiful ornament which spoke, with fabulously expensive eloquence, of its donor's wealth, and of his interest in her as a person. With an odd quirk of humour, Anasuyabehn saw the mental agony with which a close-fisted, traditional moneylender must have parted with such a valuable gem. He must be in love to the point of insanity, she thought grimly.

Fascinated, she lifted the ornament out and laid it on the palm of her hand, a hand that began to tremble with a deep fear of the unknown. Here was proof positive that her suitor would not take a negative answer easily. The gift was really valuable and quite unnecessary at such a time.

Until her father had handed her the little box, she had taken it for granted that, somehow, she would be able to escape from the marriage agreement. But now fear seemed to creep out from the blue stone and wind itself round her heart. A man who loved passionately was not going to be fobbed off so easily – nor was his powerful family, who seemed to be bent on rising socially as a caste. She knew what it was to be in love, she admitted, in love with a strange Maratha from Bombay, and, as she met Tilak on various social occasions, she had begun to feel the white heat of it. What might a powerful man like Mahadev do, if he felt the same?

And deep down inside her was a little worm of added fear, nesting in her Gujerati respect for money, that, because of Mahadev's undisputed wealth, she might be tempted to be unfaithful to the new unnourished love which possessed her – though Tilak was not a bad match; a professor had everyone's respect and a steady, if not large, income.

She could feel fresh grief rising in her, in belated mourning for her original betrothed. If he had lived, she would have had a family by now and would never have lifted her eyes to Tilak – and Mahadev would have looked elsewhere for a wife. She had not cried at the time of her fiancé's death – one rarely does about someone seen only once; but now she wished deeply that his thin, tuberculosis-ridden body lay between her and the fires of passion and fear now consuming her.

I'll object, she thought, and her inward sense of weakness made her outwardly more belligerent. She gritted her teeth and glared furiously through her tears at her aunt.

Her father took her silence for reluctant acceptance, and said quite cheerfully, before her defiance could be expressed verbally, 'Well, daughter, now you can see how highly Mahadev thinks of you. I think well of him myself and I believe you would learn to, too. Come, let us make him happy and give him a marriage date.'

Toothless and shrivelled as a dry orange skin, her aunt squatted on the floor, nodding her head and smiling amiably.

'An astrologer should arrange it,' she said, taking out her betal box and scraping round in it for a suitable piece of nut to chew. 'Though first there should be some parties, so that my niece may meet her future husband.'

'I don't want to be married,' said Anasuyabehn in a small tight voice.

Anasuyabehn's rage gave way to panic; she sprang to her feet as if to fly.

Her father and aunt got up immediately, and her father said kindly, 'Don't be afraid, child. Would you like to see him?'

'No!' said Anasuyabehn fervently, while her aunt exploded, 'Tush, what are things coming to?'

'All right,' said the Dean a little testily, and, turning to the servant, he told him to bring Mahadev into the living-room.

Anasuyabehn fled to the kitchen veranda, picked up a basket tray full of millet which she had been cleaning earlier, and began feverishly to pick the small bits of stone and the insects out of it. When she was sure all the insects were out and carefully deposited over the side of the veranda, she tossed the grain up and down on the tray to bring to the edge any other impurities. She picked these out and then emptied the millet into a shopping bag.

'Bhai,' she called to the servant, 'take this to the miller.' Her voice still shook, but she had gained some comfort from her domestic task.

The boy shouted that he was making tea for the Sahib, and she waited quietly until he had finished and had taken the tea to the study.

He came slowly back to her, his bare feet dragging, and took the bag from her. He did not leave her at once. He stood first on one foot and then on the other, his grubby face as woebegone as Anasuyabehn's. In the moment or two he had been in the study his world had crumbled; from the conversation he knew that Anasuyabehn, whom he loved as much as his mother, far away in his native village, was going to marry the terrifying Mahadev Desai. He was only ten, and he could not visualize life in a house which held only a tart, old lady and an absent-minded old gentleman.

'Well?' asked Anasuyabehn.

'Bahin, are you really going to be married?'

Anasuyabehn nearly choked, as sobs rose in her and were hastily crushed down.

The boy looked frightened, and she took his hand and pulled him to her. 'I'm not sure,' she said. 'But you mustn't worry. Your work will be here just the same.'

He was not satisfied; a child's instinct to sense trouble was with him, and he feared change.

'Can I come with you to serve in Desai Sahib's house?'

'I don't know, boy. I will ask. Do you want to come?'

The boy fell to his knees and touched her feet. He would have lifted her foot and touched his head with it, but she restrained him. Such devotion from so small a person hurt her. 'My cup is full,' her heart cried. 'My cup is full.'

'There,' she said comfortingly. 'If the marriage is finally arranged, I'll ask the Sahib. Go and get the clean shopping bag, to put the flour in – and remember to feel the flour as it comes out of the chute. Last time you brought back half of someone else's rubbish which was already in the machine. The miller is a rogue.'

Her gay tone made the boy laugh. He crammed his round, black cap on to his head and was soon on his way.

Anasuyabehn sat stonily on the veranda. The first panic had ebbed from her and she felt tired and exhausted. Furthermore, she had no idea what to do. She was no fool; she knew that by worldly standards an alliance with the Desais was desirable; the difference in caste troubled her not at all – she had gone to school with many different castes – but the possible Bania orthodoxy of the Desais' home life did. It was an orthodoxy which forbade more than a minimum of communion between husband and wife, judged success in life by the amount of money buried in the floors of the house and regarded its acquisition as a religious duty.

Then there was Tilak, whose burning, narrowed eyes

sought her out from among the other women at the tea parties and badminton parties given by the University staff, so that she blushed and had to put her sari up over her head to hide her confusion.

In angry revolt against her father's wishes, her tired mind sought frantically for a solution. She could become a nun, she considered desperately, and gain universal respect thereby – but the Jain religion offers little of true comfort for a woman.

She could run away – to what?

There is no place in India for a woman by herself, she thought bitterly, no honourable means of earning a living alone.

She remembered mournfully those brave Jains who sought release from the cycle of rebirth by starving themselves to death. She thought of her soft, round body tortured by hunger, reduced to an ugly bundle of suffering.

'I couldn't do it,' she acknowledged miserably. 'I want to live – life could be so sweet.'

She thought of Tilak and the weight of disapproval that would descend upon him, as a result of her aunt's remark about his dissecting. What an old troublemaker she was. She wept.

As her weariness gained on her, fear receded. Eventually, half asleep, she began to dream of a real lover, someone who thought her beautiful in mind and body, someone who would give her a son like himself, tall, slender, dynamic, and a little girl to dress in frilly, Western dresses. But the fact that Desai obviously thought of her as a very desirable woman was forgotten.

Desai had stayed half an hour, listening politely to his would-be father-in-law and hoping to catch a glimpse of his betrothed. At last, reluctantly he took his leave, and it was arranged that he would call again more formally, bringing his relations with him to meet Anasuyabehn. The Dean gave no hint that his daughter might repudiate the agreement, because he heartily hoped she would not. Orthodox he was in much that concerned himself alone, but he was intelligent enough to know that his grandchildren were going to live in an entirely different world, and he felt that that world, as far as India was concerned, was going to belong to those with capital and initiative. The Desais had both. He knew that many might criticize his choice of a husband for his daughter; yet his instincts told him that he was right. Moreover, he liked Mahadev personally; the man was neither ignorant nor stupid and he heartily respected his future father-in-law's learning.

John had heard all these things from devious quarters. It provided him with considerable quiet amusement to listen to the sweeper, to Ranjit, to the milkman, the vegetableman, the washerman, all the horde of people who daily came up his veranda steps and took a tremendous interest in those they served. It was John's opinion that it was impossible to eat something different for dinner without all the neighbours being informed by their servants of the details of it. To John, it was like a play which he watched as an audience. His own life was so plain, so austere, that he cared nothing if his neighbours knew all about it; he gathered from Ranjit that it met with their approval, even if Ranjit himself felt that his lifestyle should be a little more suited to his station.

As John sorted out his sketches of the Dreams of Trisala and prepared to write captions for them, for his book, he wondered idly how Mahadev would get on at the formal family meeting in Dean Mehta's house; and whether Tilak was aware that his name was being coupled with that of Anasuyabehn. Did Anasuyabehn herself realize the fact?

CHAPTER EIGHT

John soon dismissed Mahadev Desai from his mind. After finishing the captions for his sketches, he began to draft a description of the enclosing cloisters of the Marwari Gate temple, with their fifty-two small shrines, each of which seemed to be the work of a separate person.

He did not hear the students shouting goodbye to each other as they left the badminton courts and the cricket pitch, nor Ranjit gossiping with the milkman when he brought the evening milk.

When Ranjit brought his tea on a small, brass tray, he forgot to drink it; and Ranjit took one look at the dark head bent over the manuscript and at the scuttling fountain pen, and turned on the desk light. Then he retired to the kitchen veranda and took a nap, knowing well that on such a day dinner would not be required until late.

A sharp rap on the outside door, however, forced John to lay down his pen and call, 'Come in.' He fumed inwardly at the interruption.

His irritation quickly turned to pleasure when he saw who the caller was.

'Why, Tilak!' he exclaimed. 'Come in.' He waved a friendly hand towards the couch. 'Sit down. How are you?'

It was odd, he reflected, that this excitable, tense man had found his way into his affections so quickly. Perhaps it was because his ability to be one minute exalted and the next minute cast down was almost childlike and one automatically consoled him as if he were still a youngster.

As Tilak took the proffered seat, he looked unsmilingly

67

at John. Then the door was flung open again by the wind, and a swish of sand flew across the stone floor. With a muttered exclamation, he jumped up to shut it. 'Sand storm coming,' he said, as he shot the great, brass bolt with unexpected force, as if to keep at bay something more than the whirling wind.

He plonked himself down again on the couch and sat there silently, pounding one clenched fist into the palm of the other. It was obvious that he was in a dreadful temper; his face was as grim as an idol of an avenging god.

John hastily abandoned all thought of his work, and asked, 'Anything the matter?'

'Everything,' said Tilak.

'Like to tell me about it?'

'Yes, indeed. I came to you . . .' he started and then stopped, realizing that he really did not know this monklike Englishman very well. The man was famous in the city and in the University, he told himself. Everybody spoke of him with admiration, and one of the first questions any member of the staff asked him was whether he had yet met him. Surely, he would understand. He looked at the face before him; a typical lantern-jawed English face, the skin made red and leathery by much exposure to the Indian sun, lines of pain etched deeply into it, yet with a long thin mouth as sensitive as his own and narrow, blue eyes, bloodshot with study, observing him sympathetically. Compared to Marathas, the English were not a handsome race, he ruminated with sudden pride. He sensed, however, that this eccentric Englishman had an integrity, a trustworthiness, which was rare enough anywhere, and he badly needed to talk to somebody outside the University.

John always seemed willing to give him time, time and a considered opinion when asked for it, so Tilak made a real effort to control his rage; but the words he wanted would not at first come to him in English.

John turned his chair so that he faced Tilak, took his

pipe out of his pocket and resigned himself to listening. Quite often he found himself consulted by irate members of the University staff deeply provoked by the petty politics of the campus – as if I were some antiquated guru, he thought ruefully, guaranteed to give impartial advice. He knew that all he had to do was to listen for an hour and then suggest a little moderation on both sides, and the men concerned went away comforted. Most of the squabbles were incredibly petty and he got some amusement out of watching them resolve themselves.

John offered Tilak a cigarette from the little wooden box which lay on his desk, and it was accepted eagerly. He struck a match for his guest, and watched him puff like a steam engine until he was wreathed in a cloud of smoke.

Since Tilak did not seem to be able to get started, John eventually asked, 'Well, how are things?'

'Things are very well, thank you,' said Tilak, grinding his teeth, 'except that it seems that I am not to do the work which I came here to do.'

'Really?' exclaimed John, rather puzzled by the intensity of rage in Tilak's voice.

Tilak scowled, his fine face distorted with anger, and ground the end of his much abused cigarette into an ashtray.

'These fools! These lunatics,' he muttered. 'These religious maniacs!'

John surveyed the bent and shaking shoulders. He was almost afraid of such intensity of rage – it appeared unnecessary and unseemly to him. But when Tilak buried his face in his hands, and muttered that he might as well be dead as in Shahpur, John got up and went to sit beside him, not even noticing that he had managed several steps without the aid of his stick. He put a kindly hand on Tilak's shoulder.

The friendly gesture calmed Tilak. He began to speak more coherently.

'After weeks of dealing with new students,' he said, 'preparing lectures, attending endless tea parties, fighting for the supply of a few magazines – at last, I tell you – at last it seemed that I might have a few hours for my own research; I'm doing some work on the gills of fish. So, off I went to the Muslim fish bazaar, and arranged for a small supply of the particular fish I wanted – you'll know that fish are shipped up here from Bombay in salt-water tanks, live.'

'Well?'

'Well,' responded Tilak. 'I took some fish back to my laboratory. They were dead but fresh, so I began work. I had three fish on a slab beside me, ready to put into formaldehyde, and one dissected. Then there was a knock at the door and the Dean came in.

'"Ah, good day, Dr Tilak," he greeted me, all charm.'

'He is a very pleasant man,' said John, a little on the defensive immediately.

Tilak snorted.

'Humph,' he said. 'He came close to the table and peered at what I was doing.

'"Whatever is this?" he quavered.

'"A fish," I said. "In fact, altogether four fishes."

'He went quite white and looked at me horror-stricken.

'"But, my dear sir, we cannot have this kind of thing in our University," he said.

'I didn't know what to say. I was not quite sure what part of my operations was disturbing him. He looked very shaken.

'"This is a Jain community, Dr Tilak, a Jain seat of learning. We cannot have life taken haphazardly right on our campus."

'I was so dismayed that I could only say stupidly, "They were dead by the time I got them here."

'He made a great effort to control himself, "I know that the sciences must be taught, but surely it can be done without taking life? Do you make a habit of this?"

'"I dissected a frog this morning for Zoology I," I said. Whereupon he was immediately violently sick all over my fish.'

John suppressed a desire to burst out laughing.

'What did you do?' he asked.

'I assisted him outside, and sent a servant across to his bungalow to get him clean garments. Anasuyabehn brought them herself. He did not address me further, and refused my help while changing in my office.

'After he was cleaned up, he went home, leaning on Anasuyabehn, while I walked behind him carrying his briefcase and the bundle of dirty clothes. I felt a complete fool.'

He got up and walked with three swift strides to the end of the room, turned and, with eloquent gestures of his hands, went on, 'When we got to the gate of his compound, he turned round and said, "I'll see the Vice-Chancellor tomorrow. In the meantime, please arrange to use only diagrams during your lectures."'

'What did you reply to that?' asked John, a twinkle showing in his eyes, despite Tilak's fury.

'I just said, "All right" and left them and went home. What could I say? While Anasuyabehn was there I couldn't quarrel with her father – such women as she are rare and I would not wish to trouble – and furthermore, he *is* the Dean, and I have only been here a few weeks.'

Tilak's rage was fizzling out and he looked haggard.

'When I went back to the lab. this afternoon, there was a different padlock on it – and that seemed the final insult. I couldn't even get into my own laboratory. I'm tired, Bennett Sahib. No Hindu will take life wantonly – but the situation here is absurd.'

He sank his head again into his hands and groaned, the drama of which was lost, as the veranda door burst open,

71

admitting three of Ranjit's grandchildren, who must have been visiting him. John knew them well. They liked to peep around the door and examine the white Sahib, unbeknown to him, they imagined.

Ranjit shouted to them from amongst his cooking pots to come back, but John held them with a smile.

'Tilak,' he said, 'stay and have your evening meal with me. We can send a message to your mother by the children, and we can talk about the Dean.'

Tilak looked relieved.

'Dean, Dean,' shouted the children like parrots.

John laughed, and explained to them what he wanted. Tilak wrote a note for them to carry to Mrs Tilak and gave them an anna each. They hitched up their ragged little pants and were away through the front door and were scudding through the gloom of the dusty lane, before an irate Ranjit was aware they had gone.

CHAPTER NINE

Anasuyabehn had been very frightened by the message from Tilak, asking for a clean set of clothes for her father. As she flew to the almira to get out the garments, she questioned the peon.

The man knew only that the Dean had vomited. A cold fear nagged at her that he might be seriously ill – he fasted so much.

She decided that she would herself take the clean clothes to the small corner of the University building in which the Zoology Department had been lodged.

Two silent, embarrassed men awaited her. The peon carried the clean clothes into Tilak's office, so that the Dean could change in privacy, and then sat down cross-legged outside the door, to wait. Except for him, she was alone with Tilak for the first time.

Although she had already met him at several parties, she felt very shy, and her eyes uneasily examined her toes peeping out of her sandals.

Tilak cleared his throat, and after two false starts managed to say, 'It's nothing very serious. Dr Mehta was a little upset.'

Anasuyabehn raised her eyes as far as Tilak's middle shirt button, became painfully aware of the fine, muscular body showing through the sweat-soaked shirt, and despairingly raised her eyes to the thin, black face at least a foot above her own.

'What upset him?' she asked.

The shy scrutiny to which he was being subjected was too much for poor Tilak. Unused to having many women about him, he was acutely aware of every detail of the small, plump person before him. He could not think how to reply; he was aware only of the turmoil caused in him by a pair of rather deepset eyes, carefully rimmed with kohl, looking anxiously at him. He had a frightening desire to touch her softly rounded cheek and tell her that all was well.

He turned abruptly and took a couple of steps away from her.

'I dissected a fish and a frog,' he said.

Anasuyabehn was shaken out of her shyness by this admission, and she asked with a faint trace of awe in her voice, 'Did you kill them?'

'Yes,' said Tilak defiantly. 'It's part of my work – it doesn't hurt them.'

73

'Oh,' said Anasuyabehn. 'I didn't attend the science courses at the convent – I don't know much about these things.'

She lifted her sari over her head, so that her long hair, now carefully plaited, was hidden. She held the sari a little over her face, so that neither the peon nor Tilak could see her trembling lips. She again examined her toes, while the peon smoked a cigarette hidden in his palm.

A shaken Dean emerged from the office. He accepted the support of his daughter's arm, and they walked slowly homeward, followed by Tilak carrying the neatly bundled dirty clothes.

She prevailed upon the Dean to rest in the big swing which hung on the veranda and brought him water and a bowl in which to cleanse his mouth, face and hands; she was grieved to see that his hands shook, as he washed himself.

She set her little servant to preparing rotis and herself completed the making of a light lentil soup, which task she had had to leave unfinished when called to the University.

The need to hurry with her household tasks steadied her; her heavy lower lip ceased to tremble. With quick, experienced hands, she relit the charcoal fire, selected spices and pounded them, and took out the shining brass talis ready for serving the meal, as if nothing had impinged on her quiet life with her father.

Only after the meal was over and her father had gone to lie down for a little while, could she retire to her own room and acknowledge the tumult within her. Her aunt had spent the last few days extolling the virtues of the Desais to her. She was sick of it and was thankful to lean her tired head against the cool stone wall by her bed. The old lady had, that morning, gone to visit another elderly gossip nearby, so presumably, by now, the whole neighbourhood would know that she, Anasuyabehn, was to marry a Desai.

Anasuyabehn cursed softly and fluently, as only suppressed, orthodox women the world over can curse.

She allowed her mind to wander back over the past few weeks. Her lips curved tenderly. Her pulses pounded, as she remembered the boring tea parties through which she had sat patiently with the other women in the kitchen, in the hope of glimpsing a certain tall, soldierly figure.

The advent of a new, high-caste bachelor on the campus had, of course, caused quite a lot of interest among the few unmarried girls in the families of the staff. They all agreed that, if he had not been so dark, he would be handsome – and he was so *Western*, that magical word vaguely associated with delicious licence and peculiar freedoms.

And the wonder of today. To stand alone, quite close to him, and actually speak to him. One by one, as if they were gold, she went over the words of their little conversation. He kills animals, she reminded herself, and was shocked to discover that she did not care whether he did or not. She, who had once hotly defended a scorpion against the thwacks of a University gardener's spade, found suddenly that anything done by Dr Tilak must be right, regardless of what the scriptures propounded.

Her aunt returned from her visit and crawled on to the end of her niece's bed, to sit cross-legged and reflective for a moment. Out of courtesy to the older woman, Anasuyabehn moved to get up, but with a slight gesture of one gnarled hand, she was told to remain where she was. Rheumy eyes regarded her kindly.

'Your future husband is calling again in the late afternoon,' she informed Anasuyabehn. 'Put on your best sari – he wants to see you.'

Cold commonsense flooded back. Who was she to dream?

'Yes, Aunt,' she replied sadly, doing her best to hide the

burning resentment she felt. She knew she had no right to complain. Parents decided who one married.

Aunt watched her, as she changed into a blouse to match her best sari. 'In my young days,' she said, 'things were much more formal. But, then, this is a late marriage.' She shifted the piece of betelnut in her mouth, and then added, 'I am glad you're seeing sense at last.'

She wiped her lined face with the end of her white sari, while Anasuyabehn, feeling very helpless, got her best sari out of the cupboard and unwrapped it. The bright orange silk spoke to her of many a wedding attended in it, and her depression increased.

'I ordered a basket of ladus,' said her aunt conversationally. 'Dadabhai will make and deliver them himself. One never knows how many people will come on these occasions, and one should have plenty to eat in the house. I bought extra vegetables last evening for pecawlis, and I was looking for the boy to prepare them. Where is he?'

'At the grain shop. He won't be long. I'll prepare some of the vegetables now, and put on my sari later.'

The habit of obedience to her elders was so strongly ingrained in her that her acquiescence and her offer to help to prepare the tea for her unwelcome suitor were automatic. Only much later did it occur to her that she could have refused to have anything to do with the visit.

She was still tying her sari when she heard the carriage draw up at the compound gate. There was the sound of strange voices mingled with those of her father and her servant. She hastily brought the end of her sari forward over her bosom and tucked it into her waistband; the soft folds failed to disguise completely the generous curves of her figure, and she wished heartily that she was fat to the point of ugliness.

She felt so afraid of the interview before her that she was tempted to shut herself in her room and refuse to come out, but Aunt came to inspect her and quickly swept her out towards the front veranda.

'You look very well,' she said approvingly. 'That dark green blouse shows off your pale complexion. Hurry up, now. Your future husband has to catch the Delhi Mail.'

'Oh,' said Anasuyabehn, 'I wondered why the visit was so late.'

To her nervous fears was added more resentment. So she was being sandwiched in between business, was she? Her lips closed tightly, and it was a very distressed young woman who followed her aunt out on to the shadowed veranda.

A woman was seated on the swing; she was very thin and her expensive, flowered sari drooped on her. Huge eyes looked insolently out at Anasuyabehn from a heavily-boned face. Her lips smiled, however, and she put the palms of her hands together in salutation.

A small fat man in spotless white, who was seated in a basket chair near her, sprang anxiously to his feet and also saluted her. The lady immediately frowned at him and he subsided obediently back into his chair.

Another man who had been observing her quietly from the shadows now rose and made his salute.

Anasuyabehn was terribly afraid and looked down at the floor as she put her palms together in greeting. Except for a crow squawking in a tree in the compound, there was complete silence; all eyes regarded her, and she knew what it must be like to be a slave on sale in a market.

The stillness was broken by a shrill giggle from the visiting lady.

Anasuyabehn bit her lips and slowly gained enough courage to look up at Mahadev.

Her first thought was that he was much bigger than she had envisioned him to be. In spite of his plumpness, he had a commanding presence. Though she had no knowledge of the business world, she understood suddenly why he might be successful in his work. There was a dignity about him which spoke of a man who would not tolerate any nonsense, and his bright, intelligent eyes gave indication of the quick wits which were essential to his caste. Today, however, he had put aside his business for an hour and was looking down at her with benign approval.

So great was her respect for male authority and her desire for male approbation, that she held down her fears and treated the moneylender like any other visitor.

Mahadev himself was very nervous. He was anxious to make a good impression, and that bitch of a sister-in-law with her arrogant laugh was too much altogether. He scowled at her, and she retired behind her veiling sari to sulk.

He turned back to his wife-to-be, and the scowl cleared from his face. From a distance, he had watched Anasuyabehn many times in the bazaars and on the campus, but seeing her closely he was enchanted. She had a skin like ivory and the innocent expression of a child. All sorts of ideas shot into his head. That piece of land they owned down by the river – he could build a house upon it – a house for his father, himself, his daughter and Anasuyabehn; a quiet haven by the water. And she should wear emeralds – he had some perfect stones which only needed cutting.

Behind his impassive expression, his quick brain was already circumventing for this charming little woman the ills which she must most fear, particularly the one now sitting on the swing. After his experiences in France, he felt restless and anxious to shrug off the collar and lead of custom and try himself in the new world evolving in free India.

Anasuyabehn looked down at the floor again, and he was disappointed. He felt that the lid of a box had closed just as he was about to discover the contents.

'Let's all sit down,' said Mahadev, and Anasuyabehn and her aunt obediently sat down on basket chairs a little way from the Desais.

A painful silence ensued, which was providentially broken by the arrival of another carriage. Everyone, except Anasuyabehn, whose head was swimming with fresh fears that she might not be strong enough to fight the match, got up and went to the veranda rail, while the servant danced excitedly to the gate to let the new visitors in. They proved to be a stout, middle-aged couple accompanied by two wide-eyed schoolchildren.

'My respected father's cousin-brother,' announced Mahadev. 'Father and Uncle were unable to come owing to business. Father mentioned it to you last time you saw him, Doctor Sahib,' he said to Dr Mehta.

The Dean nodded, and room was made for extra chairs brought by the servant. Everyone again sat down and stared at Anasuyabehn.

Aunt ordered the servant to make tea, and the children cuddled close to their mother, who turned an amiable, lined face to Aunt.

'It's so hot still,' she said. 'It should have cooled a little by now.'

She accepted a glass of water brought by the servant, who carried a tray as big as himself from one visitor to another until all were served, and then vanished into the kitchen.

Aunt smiled at her, and inquired the names of the children. This launched the fond parent on the history of her offspring, their misdoings and shortcomings.

Anasuyabehn excused herself and went to help in the kitchen. Mahadev watched her go with regret; he would have dearly liked to talk to her.

Dean Mehta was, however, talking about making a visit to Abu during the summer and he had, perforce, to give his attention to him, while in the kitchen Anasuyabehn deep fried savouries for him and wished he would kindly fall in love with someone else.

She was very bewildered. Her first fierce hatred of her suitor had died on seeing him; he did not strike her as the kind of man she could hate, nor did she despise him or his power. She felt like a mouse in a Gujerati cage trap; her thoughts rushed round and round and saw no way of escape. It is harder to fight an enemy one does not hate, she thought. Curse Aunt and all her machinations. 'Oh, Tilak Sahib,' she muttered, 'could you not make a move to save me?'

Why should he? asked commonsense; he doesn't know what you feel for him.

'I'll stall as long as I can,' thought Anasuyabehn, and then winced as the boiling fat she was using spat and burned her wrist. 'Time might offer some escape.'

She handed a dish of savouries to the servant to take out to the visitors, and then put a saucepan of water and milk on to the roaring Primus, for more tea.

She was sitting on her little stool, watching the mixture, when Aunt brought the two lady visitors into the kitchen. Though she stood up respectfully, she looked surly; then the heavy eyelids were again lowered.

The cousin-brother's wife was startled by the resentment apparent in Anasuyabehn's quick glance; it was unexpected, since the family had been assured that Anasuyabehn felt very honoured at the match. She sighed softly. She hoped that this new addition to the family would not cause more trouble; the thin stick of malice standing by her was a big enough trial. Mahadev should have looked in his own caste for a wife – this girl was too well educated for comfort. Mahadev's father had, however, agreed, so the good lady extended an invitation to the sullen girl to make a formal visit to the Desai household, in company with her father and aunt.

Anasuyabehn did not reply, so her aunt spoke for her. They would come in a week's time. She shot a reproving look at her niece, who ignored it. They could arrange her life for her – let them get on with it. She saw no reason to give them much help. She needed time – time to draw Tilak's attention to her. But how?

The gentlemen could be heard pushing back their chairs to leave, so the ladies put their hands together in farewell and an unsmiling Anasuyabehn did likewise.

The Dean saw his guests to the gate and afterwards walked slowly up and down the compound. A good, respectable family, he thought. And to think that Anasuyabehn had allowed her thoughts to stray towards that bloodthirsty horror, Tilak. The Dean shuddered as he remembered the murdered fish.

'Tomorrow, I'll talk to Dr Jain of Mathematics,' he considered, 'and together we can see the Vice-Chancellor. By this time even he must have heard about it.'

Indeed, by dinner-time most of the staff was debating the matter, the story having been spread by the peon who had overheard Anasuyabehn's and Tilak's conversation while they waited for the Dean to change his clothes. The story had lost nothing in the telling. The younger members of the staff laughed gleefully at the Dean's predicament. Despite persistent propaganda from the Central Government in Delhi that locusts, vermin and invading armies might be dispatched without sin, the older staff held strongly to the view that all life was sacred.

CHAPTER TEN

That evening the heat was still so great in John's room that he and Tilak decided to sit on the veranda, despite the occasional gusts of wind carrying sand. John propped his front door open in hope of cooling the room a little.

As he settled himself carefully in his basket chair, he tried to assure Tilak that he should not take Dean Mehta's fussing over his fish and frog too seriously. 'It may take a little time, but there are other, more worldly people on campus who'll prevail – don't forget that they want a medical school here one of these days.'

Tilak thought this over and then said, 'It isn't the Dean's being sick that troubles me – anybody unaccustomed to seeing meat or corpses might react in the same way. It's his assumption that everybody thinks the same way that he does – he's supposed to be Western educated and is a university man – he should have room for other people's ideas.'

'I know, but ahimsa is pretty well embedded anywhere in India, and especially so in the Gujerat.'

'If it were village people who had complained, I could understand it,' said Tilak, twisting himself round in his creaking basket chair. 'The village people here are Gandhiji's own people, and their belief in ahimsa – non-killing – was reinforced by him. It would be very hard to persuade them to kill anything, under any circumstances.'

'I think that's correct,' replied John. He remembered, again, the story Ranjit had told him about Government officials who had, a couple of years previously, tried in vain to get the local farmers to spray the locusts in their fields. They had faced starvation before they gave in, too late to save that year's crop.

'You know, Tilak, the Gujerat furnished both money and brains for Gandhiji's cause.'

'We all did,' sniffed Tilak.

'Kana,' shrieked Ranjit from the kitchen veranda, much to John's relief. He realized that they were both getting irritable from hunger, and he got up immediately and ushered his friend into his room.

A cloud of moths was dancing round the lamp and in the circle of light reflected on the ceiling, so he told Ranjit to move the table into a corner where they would not be bothered by falling bodies.

When they were seated, Ranjit went to the kitchen and returned with a bowl, a jug of water and a towel, so that they could wash their hands. Then, with a clatter of brassware, he brought in two talis laden with food, and the two friends ate ravenously in spite of the heat. Lentil soup, vegetables, fresh Indian rotis and curd vanished remarkably quickly, and Tilak looked considerably better when he finally accepted a cardamom from a carved box proffered him by John.

John took a clove from the same box, and they tipped back their chairs and grinned quite cheerfully at each other.

'I didn't eat much lunch,' said Tilak, almost apologetically.

'You would hardly feel like it.' John lit his pipe. 'Would you like a cigarette?'

Tilak accepted a cigarette, lit it and drew slowly on it.

'To someone like myself,' John remarked reflectively, 'Mehta is typical of all India – keeps his own customs, but is tolerant of other people's – except when it is a matter of killing something.'

'He's far too reactionary to be typical.'

'Not in everything,' John protested. 'He doesn't seem even to press his daughter to comply – she actually finished her education at a Christian convent school – and then her engagement – that's not a bit orthodox.'

'I heard that the boy died,' Tilak replied idly, as he blew a smoke ring.

'Yes, but I wasn't thinking of him. I was thinking of her new fiancé.'

'Her new one?' Tilak was shocked. His thin hands gripped the arms of his chair.

'Yes, she's going to marry the Desais' elder son – you know, the family which seems to have a financial finger in any pie round here. They're really moneylenders, but on a big scale these days.'

Tilak asked in a breathless voice, 'When is she going to be married?'

'In a month or two, I suppose.' John glanced quickly at Tilak. The Maratha's face was immobile, the lips compressed, the black eyes staring into the darkness, as if he saw, unexpectedly, something frightening. 'Why?'

'Because I want to marry her myself,' Tilak almost snarled between his clenched teeth.

'Well, don't bite me, old chap,' said John humorously. 'I didn't know you were interested – seriously.'

Tilak stood up and went to the veranda rail. 'I am most interested,' he said sadly.

'I'm sorry,' John said sympathetically, and wished suddenly that he, too, could feel as strongly about a woman. Now, however, he looked at Tilak with some concern. The man had seated himself on the veranda rail and was feverishly cracking his finger joints, pulling first one finger and then the other as if he would dismember himself.

'I've no father to advise me, and my uncle would not understand,' he said. 'Bennett, what can I do?'

John shifted about in his chair.

'Do you *really* want to marry her?'

'Of course I do. It's time I married and I want to marry her.'

'She's a different caste and religion.'

'Don't be old-fashioned, Bennett Sahib. Plenty of people are marrying out of caste now.'

'Surely your family would object?'

'Uncle will – and so will mother, at first – but mother I can persuade.' He spoke with all the certainty of a spoiled younger son. 'It's Dean Mehta who is the stumbling block.'

'And the girl? What does she think?'

Tilak looked startled for a moment, and then said, 'I haven't asked her.'

'Well, perhaps you should find an opportunity to know her better, and then ask her. You'll have to be quick, though.'

Tilak gave up cracking his finger joints and gnawed one instead. 'I feel that it is all right with her – I've seen her a number of times.'

'Have you spoken to her?'

'Twice. The last time was when she brought clean clothes for her father this morning.'

John marvelled at the speed with which Tilak had made up his mind. Yet was it so very different among English people? One saw a girl and sought to know more of her and, after a while, one realized one was in love; yet probably that love was present from the first moment, unacknowledged.

'Look,' John said, 'I can't see, really, how you can forestall the marriage arranged for her, without a concerted

85

effort on her part. Even then, I can't imagine how you're going to persuade the Dean to let her marry you – you're simply not popular with him, at present.'

'I'll do it, somehow.'

John whistled under his breath. 'Be careful, Tilak,' he warned him. 'It's not worth ruining your career.'

Tilak agreed, and then laughed sardonically. 'To have a wife and no food for her would be a disaster.'

'I saw Desai and some of his relations going to visit them, earlier this evening,' John told him, as he relit his pipe.

Tilak started to pace up and down, and John pushed his chair back, to give him more room. 'Don't do anything rash, old man.'

'Humph.' Tilak swung back to John's chair. 'I'll go home, Bennett Sahib. Come to visit me one day.'

'I will,' John promised, and escorted his friend down to the compound gate. 'Take care,' he said.

Tilak hardly heard him. He was already swinging swiftly down the dark lane, towards the hostel.

After he had vanished into the gloom, John stood for a moment holding the heavy compound gate ajar. It was not a pleasant night. A small crying wind was whipping up little whirls of dust. Families, who would usually be strolling up and down at this time, had obviously stayed at home because of the threat of a storm. Even the pariah dogs, who could ordinarily be heard rustling in the bushes or snarling at each other, seemed to have taken refuge. In spite of the puffs of wind, the heat was intolerably oppressive, and John took out his handkerchief to mop his forehead.

As he tucked the hanky back into his shirt pocket, he heard the sound of galloping horses approaching up the lane. Fools, he thought, to ride so fast in the darkness.

They were passing him almost before he could see them; four turbanned figures, their turban ends wrapped across their faces to protect them against the dust, naked feet thrust into high stirrups. He wondered who they were; there were few riding horses in the district, camels and oxen being the working animals. Horses were used for carriages.

Strangers, he guessed. Visitors of some kind, following the lane through until they would, eventually, strike the new road that had been built to connect more distant villages with Shahpur. It was a road which ran parallel with the railway and would, one day, be driven right through to Delhi.

Encumbered by a stick, it was not easy for him to shut the gate and shoot its great iron bolt. He felt tired and was thankful to reach his couch again, to lie down under the slowly turning ceiling fan.

CHAPTER ELEVEN

John rose early the next morning, with the intention of working steadily through the day. He felt restless, however, and found himself doodling idly in the dust deposited on his desk by the dust storm the previous night.

The storm had begun soon after Tilak had left. The wind had howled round the small bungalow, like a lonely ghost. It had stirred up a dust so thick that windows and doors had had to be shut tightly, to avoid near suffocation. This morning, every leaf on the trees in the compound had a thick coating of dust balanced precariously on it. Inside the building, a fine powder lay on every floor and ledge; food tasted gritty and hair and skin felt dry and uncomfortable.

'Ranjit!' John shouted. 'Come and clean this room – it's not fit for a dog. Get the chattya wetted, to cool the place.'

'Ji,' came a resigned response from the back veranda. Brass dishes clattered against the stone floor, as Ranjit stopped doing the washing up and found his duster. Then John heard him shriek across the compound to Ramji, the sweeper, to bring his broom; Ranjit himself would not touch a broom – he was high-caste.

Ranjit appeared at the veranda door and surveyed his fretful master. 'Sahib, do your legs hurt?' he inquired solicitously. 'When I go to the bazaar, shall I ask the Doctor Sahib to come?'

'It's not my legs this time, Ranjit; my brain won't work.' He pressed his hands over his eyes. 'I can walk fairly well now with only one stick. In fact, I think I'll go for a walk.'

Ranjit grunted agreement. So that he could dust, he piled all the books and papers on the desk into one tottering tower. Ramji came in silently and began to sweep, shuffling across the floor in a squatting position, the soft fronds of his broom making a sighing sound on the stone flags.

As Ranjit removed the cover from the typewriter and shook the dust off it, he remarked, 'That murder on the Mail train was a bad business.'

John was halfway into a clean shirt and his voice came muffled through the cotton cloth. 'What murder?'

Ranjit ran his duster along the window sill, and Ramji clucked as the dust fell where he had already swept.

'You haven't heard, Sahib?'

'I haven't been out today. How will I know if you haven't told me?' A flushed face emerged through the neck of the shirt. 'Who's been murdered?'

Ranjit paused in his work and twisted his moustache thoughtfully before he answered, 'An English lady travelling on the Delhi Mail.'

'Not Miss Armstrong?'

Surprised at the sharp concern in his master's voice, Ranjit hastened to reassure him. 'No, no, Sahib. That was not the name. She was going up from Bombay in the First Class – a stupid place to travel, Sahib. It's where thieves will go first – she should have gone in the Ladies' Compartment.'

John smiled, as he buttoned up his shirt. It was true that when trains were held up, the Ladies' Compartment, full of screaming women, all of whom would have sent their valuable jewellery ahead by post, was not usually tackled by thieves.

'Where did this happen?' he asked.

'About four miles up the line, Sahib. You know where the train curves into that cutting? – I think it's called Ambawadi.'

'A good spot,' said John.

'Yes,' said Ranjit, 'Harichandra says there were many of them, some on horseback, some travelling on the train, and they – '

'On horseback? I saw four men on horses pass, when I was seeing Dr Tilak out of the gate last night.'

Ranjit stopped dusting, and Ramji looked up and gaped at John.

'Did you, Sahib? It could have been some of the Sindhi refugees – some of them brought horses when they came, and have made a little business trading in them – but horses are not very commonly ridden here, Sahib, are they? They are mostly for pulling carriages.'

'Yes,' said John. 'Perhaps it was just some Sindhis taking horses to a customer.'

He ran his fingers through his hair to straighten it. 'Make something with puris for lunch,' he instructed. 'I'll go for a walk round the campus and maybe call on Dr Tilak.'

'Ji, hun,' agreed Ranjit. 'The campus will be the only place free of police today.'

'Do you think they'll scour round this district as well?'

'They will come bothering and badgering, no doubt, Sahib. Locusts!'

'Tut, Ranjit. They have to work fast, or the dacoits will be out of the province before they can say Jack Robinson.'

Ranjit opened the door and Ramji continued his sweeping across the front veranda. He grunted. 'Police – work?'

John laughed, and went out into the merciless sunshine. Although it was hot, the air smelled sweet after the storm, and he began to whistle cheerfully, as he wandered along the lane. From inside the houses he passed he could hear the lively chatter of women's voices and the thud-thud of spices being pounded. The dhobi, bent nearly double by the great bundle of washing on his back, saluted him. Children stopped their play to listen to his whistle, fascinated at the strange, sweet sound, and he called a cheerful 'Hullo' to those he knew. It was a pleasant morning and his spirits rose.

He found Tilak emerging from a lecture room, followed by a crowd of students who drifted down the corridor, their shirt tails wafting gently behind them. They were all talking at once, their voices as shrill as cockatoos'.

Tilak drew John into the welcome quiet of his small laboratory which, he informed him, he had found unlocked that morning. He bade him sit down on a stool, while he washed the chalk from his hands.

'My frog and fish seem to have sparked a great debate,'

he remarked, as he dried his hands on an old duster. 'The families of some of the students are really orthodox, and their relations are making a fuss. They don't want their children to take such Courses.'

'O, Lord,' groaned John sympathetically.

Tilak flung the duster into a corner.

'The old folk want the impossible,' he said. 'They want their young men to get enough training to put them into the better paid Government jobs, without their usual way of life being upset. It's the same everywhere.'

'Surely, it's only amongst the Jains that you would find it. And you have to remember that they are really a very cultured people. Seeking work outside their traditional occupations is new to them.'

'A pack of village moneylenders,' snorted Tilak.

John laughed. 'Come, Tilak,' he said. 'It's not so bad. They'll get used to you. After all, you must have had a battle with your family to get permission to take up research.'

'No. Father went to Cambridge,' replied Tilak tartly. 'He did physics.'

John felt snubbed, but he managed to say, 'That must have made your path much easier.'

Tilak caught the slight sarcasm in his friend's voice, and repented his sharpness.

'It didn't,' he said with a rueful laugh. 'He was insisting all the time that I take physics.'

John relaxed and laughed, too. 'Do you want to do some work now?' he inquired. 'If so, I'll leave you.'

'I prepare my lectures at home. Like to walk over with me? I can offer you some coffee.'

John assented, and they went out together and walked through the flower gardens in front of the building.

On the lawns, water-sprinklers slowly revolved, with an

opulence which always made passing villagers stop to gape, because they themselves were so short of water. Blackbirds hopped in and out of the gentle downpour and the flowers glittered with tiny droplets; their perfume in the desert air seemed strange and exotic to John.

Tilak interrupted his thoughts by saying, 'Mother and Damyanti went home to Bombay this morning. They caught the nine o'clock train.'

'Really?' exclaimed John.

'Yes. They missed the gaiety of Bombay – and the heat here was hard on mother. I suppose I must get myself a servant.'

'I can imagine their being homesick.'

'Can you? Is it that you are homesick for England?'

'No. When I was in prison, I used to be homesick for Shahpur!'

Tilak laughed, disbelievingly. 'That is not possible. I wish I had never seen the place. You were in prison?'

'I was a prisoner of war.'

'Ah,' said Tilak, highly interested. 'I once did three months for participation in a riot.'

'All the best people in India have been in jail.'

'True,' replied Tilak. 'How else would we have got Independence?'

They came on to the road which bordered the campus. Students were standing about in sullen groups, all apparently engrossed in shrill argument. On the verge, a group of villagers was squatting in a circle, resting for a while from their long walk to town. As they leaned towards each other and gave respectful attention to an old man haranguing them, their big, ruby-red turbans looked like great raspberries ripening in the sun. Their red-clad womenfolk sat placidly behind the men, gossiping amongst themselves, while their half-naked children, oblivious of the heat, darted about like minnows in a stream.

John paused and regarded the scene lovingly. So colourful, so sane.

'Arree!' shouted Tilak suddenly. He stumbled and clutched at one shoulder.

John jumped, and turned to him in astonishment. 'What happened?'

Tilak picked up a half brick. 'This,' he said grimly. 'It was thrown at me.'

John's eyebrows shot up. 'Good heavens!' He turned swiftly to look back along the road.

The groups of students were melting rapidly away; those who had bicycles had already mounted them and were pedalling hard into the distance.

The villagers had shot to their feet and were staring aghast at the two men. Except for squawking crows, there was a profound silence.

'Did you see who threw that brick?' John called to the nearest villager, a middle-aged man.

'No, Sahib.' His face looked like a dried raisin, and he fluttered work-roughened hands. John could well imagine the panicky fears of accusation going through the man's head; fears of arrest, of beatings, of a fine levied against his village. He would never open his mouth.

John turned back to Tilak, who stood looking down at the brick in his hand. With the other hand, he ruefully rubbed his back.

'Are you much hurt?' John asked, in some anxiety. 'Turn round. Let me see your back.'

'I'm only bruised, I believe,' Tilak answered, as he turned. 'My frog is avenged, I think.' He dropped the brick in the dusty road.

There was some blood on Tilak's shirt, so John said, 'Let's get back to your room, so that you can take off your shirt and I can see better what the damage is. Are you steady enough to walk?' He put his hand under Tilak's elbow, and they continued slowly towards the hostel. 'I don't think a villager threw that brick – they would not dare to,' John continued. 'It was a student, all right. We'll get the Dean to institute an inquiry – he'll find the young devil.'

'The Dean?' exploded Tilak. 'No, John. I'm grateful to the brick-thrower – he's made up my mind for me.' He stopped and faced John. 'I'd like to be alone,' he said, his expression sad and disillusioned. 'I'm not badly hurt.'

'Of course, if you wish it.' John bit his lower lip. 'Are you sure you'll be all right? Don't do anything rash, will you?'

'My friend, sometimes one must grasp life by its shirt tail. Otherwise, it flashes past before you realize it.' He raised his hand in salute and left John to ruminate over this cryptic remark, while he strode away towards the students' hostel and his empty rooms.

CHAPTER TWELVE

When John approached the gate of his compound he was surprised to see Ranjit squatting outside it, when it was reasonable to suppose that he would be on the back veranda preparing lunch. John quickened his step, and, as he approached Ranjit, he observed an unusually tense, tight-lipped look about him.

'What's up?' he asked in Gujerati.

Ranjit stood up, and his clean, white loincloth gleamed in the sun, as he set his legs belligerently apart.

'A Memsahib has called and is waiting in your room,' said Ranjit, rank disapproval apparent in every line of him. Never, in all the time he had served the Sahib, had a Memsahib called. Why, the Sahib hardly ever visited English people himself.

'A Memsahib! Who is it?'

'Armstrong Memsahib.' Ranjit had an excellent knowledge of English names.

'Oh,' said John. 'She's come about the map, I suppose.'

'Map, Sahib?'

'Yes, Ranjit, I'm going to help her and Lallubhai Sahib prepare a special map of the city – showing drains and playgrounds and parks.'

'I see,' grunted Ranjit, relaxing a little. One never knew, however, what happened when a Memsahib was made free of a gentleman's home – Ranjit could not imagine a worse disaster.

John knew fairly precisely what was running through Ranjit's head and the gossip which would sweep through the campus, and yet, as he hurried across the compound, he was full of pleasurable anticipation. He forgot Tilak and his frog and thought only about talking to someone English; he found it hard to admit this need but knew it to be true.

He paused at the top of the veranda steps to rest his legs, then approached the door more slowly.

She was seated nervously on the edge of the chair by his desk, her face turned expectantly towards the door. He smiled as he approached her and shook her hand. Behind the smile there was great surprise.

He had previously seen her only in her nurse's uniform and again on the occasion of meeting her in the bazaar, when she had been garbed in grubby khaki. Today, her red hair shone with washing as it fluttered in the breeze of the fan, and, though her green eyes still had rings of fatigue round them, they were oddly appealing in a face no longer brick-red from exertion. Like many English women in hot climates, she wore little makeup, and the natural gold of her eyelashes and the delicate pink of her mouth reminded him of one of his mother's beautiful china figurines.

The same artist's eye which could note and transfer to sketch book the incredible detail of Jain sculpture saw and realized the implications of her plain white dress, obviously made at home from the cheapest mill cloth, and the plastic chuppells on her feet. Propped against her chair was a black umbrella, the cheapest way to protect herself against the ruthless sun.

God, thought John, Ferozeshah must pay her in annas. Yet, in spite of her obvious poverty, she made a pleasant picture, sitting in his working chair.

She explained shyly that Lallubhai and his Committee had come to the conclusion that the housing needs of the refugees were very urgent, so the previous evening they had asked her to convey their thanks to John and to discuss with him the map and the data already collected by the Committee. As she handed him a file of papers, she added her apologies for descending upon him so abruptly, but she had only one day a week free, and this happened to be it. 'I didn't want to delay it another week,' she went on. 'We have only four months before the rainy season and we hope that the maps will show up small open spaces, which we can begin to beg from landlords in order to put huts on them.'

John smiled and soon made her feel at ease, and she continued by saying that they had enlisted the help of the reluctant, overworked City Engineer, who had agreed to let them have access to his records, inasfar as they touched on the mapping of the city. The Mayor was already on the Committee, so civic co-operation was assured, as long as it did not get bogged down in the usual inertia of Indian officialdom.

John listened with pleasure to the rather deep voice, slightly tinged with a Gloucestershire accent, as she made each point clear. Occasionally, he asked a question. They had no hope, she said, of compiling a properly surveyed map, but, using John's and the City Engineer's maps as a base, they hoped to fill in most of the blanks sufficiently well to discover the more pressing needs of the population.

John considered all this for a minute or two. Then he said, 'They'll have to watch that the funds don't get misappropriated somewhere along the line.'

'Lallubhai is incorrupt,' said Miss Armstrong, 'and so are some of the others.'

'Yes. It's a very good Committee. Jains are like the little girl with a curl in the middle of her forehead. When they're good, they're very, very good, and when they're bad they're horrid.'

Miss Armstrong laughed.

'Could you stay to lunch?' asked John, and he was amused to see her go faintly pink as she answered that it was her free day, and all she had to do was to visit an old woman in Pandipura later in the day.

John went to confer with Ranjit, who was grinding spices on a flat stone, with a stone rolling pin. He still looked as sour as old milk but agreed that he could feed the lady, if she could take the north Indian food he usually prepared. John said that he was sure that she could eat it, provided he did not put too many chillies in it.

John returned to his guest and explained the situation to her, and she confirmed that she enjoyed Indian food.

'I eat a good many meals with the Ferozeshahs,' she said. 'Mrs Ferozeshah is a friend of mine – she was trained in Edinburgh as a nurse.'

97

'Ah, I wondered how you coped in a purely Indian hospital.'

Miss Armstrong blushed at the implications of the remark.

'Oh, I've never had any trouble,' she said. 'Dr Ferozeshah and his hospital have an excellent reputation, and he's always treated me very well. He's an FRCS, you know.'

'I know. He's lucky, though, to have a State Registered Nurse to help him.'

She beamed at him, and fingered the tiny brooch pinned to her dress; its enamel and gilt indicated her nurse's status.

'I find the work very worthwhile. Doctor does a lot of work in the City Hospital – and a good deal in the villages round about. You should see his doorstep at Divali – people come from miles around to bring him thankofferings of flower necklaces or fruit – he won't take anything else from poorer people.'

John was enjoying this feminine company more than he cared to admit, and wanted badly to know more about her. He chanced a direct question.

'Have you been with Ferozeshah long?'

'About two and a half years – I was with the Mission of Holiness before.'

John had never heard of such an institution, and said so.

'They have a tiny Mission about twenty miles north of here – almost in the desert. There were two American nurses, besides myself, and an elderly doctor.' She hesitated, and then said, 'They do excellent medical work . . .'

'A bit "holier than thou"?'

Miss Armstrong grinned mischievously.

'Very,' she said. 'I couldn't stand it any more, and yet I liked India and was in no hurry to go home. One day, when I'd come to Shahpur to buy shoes, I met Mrs Ferozeshah also trying on footwear. She saw my nurse's brooch and spoke to me, and ended up asking me to have tea at her house. She

98

used to help her husband in his work, but now she has children she has not much time; and after another visit, when I met Dr Ferozeshah, I was offered my present post. The salary isn't much – a little more than he would pay an Indian nurse – but I can manage, and both of them are wonderfully kind to me, and I love their children, too.'

'You could nurse in England – and you must have friends there, also.'

'Yes, but the need there isn't so desperate. Maybe when I'm older and can't stand the heat so well, I'll go back home. My father would like to have me at home with him – he is a minister, a widower – and would like me to settle down at the parsonage and keep house for him.' She looked shyly out of the corners of her eyes at John. 'I simply couldn't face it,' she said with feeling. 'At least I'm alive here.'

'It can't be very entertaining for you, here, though. So few English people around.'

'On the contrary, I find I have quite a social life. The Ferozeshahs have introduced me to a number of their friends, and I get invitations to tennis parties and tea parties from all kinds of people. I feel very content. Nobody drives me in any way – I am free.' She unclasped her hands, which she had previously held tightly in her lap, and made a little opening gesture as if to show how her character had expanded in the wide latitude of Indian life.

John deliberated over this, and then said, 'You're right – I have the same feeling of freedom from social pressure. People aren't pressed so tightly into moulds here, are they?'

'No, they're certainly not.' She gave another of her low soft laughs. 'Is that why you stay here?' she asked.

'Me? I – er – well, after the war I just came back to the place I knew best.' Her question had confused him. He could feel an old depression creeping over him. 'To be honest, I felt after the war that we should be blown to hell pretty soon and, since there was not much I could do about it, I wanted to enjoy what time was left doing the work I like best. So I came home to Shahpur. After all, I was born here,' he finished up a little defensively.

The laughter went from Miss Armstrong's face and she stared unseeingly out of the window. His reminder of the menacing atomic shadow over the world brought back to her her reasons for taking up nursing. A desire to repair, to build in some small way in a destructive world, had become a dedication so that she had soon lost herself in her work. Now, she never thought further than a day or two ahead, and that mostly when she was arranging Dr Ferozeshah's tight schedule of visits, operating, and so on.

She glanced quickly at John. He had absent-mindedly taken out his pipe and was packing tobacco into it, and at the sight of this male refuge being prepared, she smiled.

'I'm told that your coming here has been very fruitful. I've read your book about the conquest of the Gujerat in the thirteenth century, and, frankly, I found it so gripping that I read it at a sitting.'

She wanted badly to cheer him up and see him laugh. Today they were alive and there was time enough to worry about other days when they arrived. She was delighted to have such a cultivated Englishman to whom to talk and wanted desperately to please him.

He was grateful to her for turning the conversation, and replied, quite cheerfully, 'Ala-ud-din the Bloody in 1297. He was nearly as thorough as present day conquerors.' And once launched, he kept her spellbound, while he told her tales of ancient Shahpur.

The door to the back veranda swung open. A frigid Ranjit, in clean shirt and dhoti, announced that lunch was ready.

Miss Armstrong ate neatly with her fingers, using pieces of bread as a spoon where necessary, as did John. Afterwards, he persuaded her to wait a little, in the hope that the heat would decrease, before she set out to see her patient in Pandipura; but it was still very hot when she announced that she must go, and firmly picked up her small, black bag. He looked at her uneasily.

'Would you like Ranjit to accompany you?' he asked. 'The police are supposed to be looking for the train robbers in this district.'

'I heard about it,' she said. 'But I shall be all right, thank you very much. The police know me and most of the villagers do, too.' She went to the door and opened the umbrella. 'Mr Lallubhai has promised to invite you to the next Committee meeting. I do hope you can come.'

'Certainly,' said John. 'Only too happy to help.'

He was rewarded by a quick smile from beneath the ugly umbrella, and he felt reluctant to let her go. The Indian countryside was not a place for a woman to walk alone, particularly when it was believed dacoits were in the district. He told himself that his disquietude was unwarranted, that she was obviously accustomed to going about by herself and that the robbers had probably made all haste back to Saurastra, their usual stronghold.

He saw her out of the gate and received again her thanks, then closed the gate and shot the bolt.

Back in his room, he surveyed with distaste its cell-like bareness; only the desk with its untidy piles of paper spoke of life and work. He sat down on his chair and thumbed idly through his notes, which represented months of research. Determinedly, he picked up his pen and began to write.

CHAPTER THIRTEEN

Tilak went slowly up the long, stone staircase which led to his rooms. His back hurt more than he had admitted to John, and his spirits had suffered an equal blow. He could still hardly believe that a student had stoned him.

He dropped his briefcase on to the cement floor of his living-room, shut the door quietly and locked it. His second room led off the first and had been used by his mother and Damyanti.

He peeled off his shirt and vest to examine the backs of them. They both had a little blood on them, so he took down the cracked piece of mirror which served him when shaving, to have a look at the wound.

By holding the mirror at an angle and peering over his shoulder he was able to see the nasty weal, raw in places, which the brick had caused. He put the mirror down on his work table, on which the remains of a hasty breakfast still lay.

Deeply depressed, unsure of what to do, he crawled on to his unmade bed and lay there through the long, hot afternoon until darkness fell, his thoughts wandering miserably backwards and forwards over the events of the previous few days.

Footsteps in the passageway stopped at his door, and a white envelope shot under it and across the floor. He sat up quickly, winced when his back hurt him, and went to retrieve the missive.

In a polite note, Professor Jain regretted that a tea party, to which Tilak had been invited, had been cancelled, owing to unforeseen circumstances. 'Arree,' grunted Tilak. 'Poor frog –

you are now called *unforeseen circumstances.*' Irritably he screwed up the note and flung it into a corner.

This letter reminded him of another, and he went to his briefcase and took it out. Delicately, he unfolded the two precious sheets of paper, and went back to his bed to sit down and read them again. The first page said:

Dear Dr Tilak, I am requested by the Committee of the Thomas Jones Foundation to inform you that they have considered your recent application and are pleased to grant you a Thomas Jones Fellowship, tenable at our laboratories in London from October 1st, 1951, for two years, after which consideration may be given to extension of this period by a further year. The scholarship consists of a grant of £700 per annum plus travelling expenses to and from England, and a small sum to cover visits to universities during your stay here. Kindly let me know when you expect to be able to take up the Fellowship.

Yours sincerely, Ian MacAngus, Secretary.

The second sheet was an informal and kindly epistle from Mr MacAngus, congratulating him and offering advice regarding travel and accommodation.

Tilak caressed the letters gently with his fingertips. The Head of the Foundation was Sir Andrew Diamond, a specialist in Tilak's field; and Tilak knew that, working under such a great man, he would expand his own knowledge and could hope for international recognition of his research.

Could he marry Anasuyabehn in a civil ceremony, get her a passport and whisk her out of the country, before her father could catch them? An elopement, that was the English word for it. The problem was that the Fellowship was not available until October and as yet it was only March; the Desai marriage was probably planned for sometime in the next two months.

103

'What the hell shall I do?' he fumed. 'What *can* I do?'

Would his uncle offer for her? No point in that; he would almost certainly be turned down politely, on the grounds that she was already betrothed. Alternatively, if he approached the Dean himself and begged a reconsideration of her present commitment, he would court an immediate rebuff. His dead frog would be enough to put the Dean off, never mind the problem of untangling himself from an agreed marriage. To add to the problem, there was always the argument that they were of different religions and different language groups.

While he stewed over the problem, he lit his Primus stove and made a cup of coffee. He took it over to the open window and sat down on the sill.

From the floor below rose the din of brass on brass as seven Brahmin students were served their dinner by the Brahmin servant they jointly employed to cook for them, and Tilak realized fretfully that the vegetable seller had not called on him that evening. This worthy, being the brother of the nightwatchman, was able to go through the hostel hawking vegetables, and he had never missed calling on Tilak before.

Perplexed, Tilak put down his cup and went out into the passage, in case he had failed to hear his knock and the man had left some vegetables outside his door. There was nothing. Three doors down, a wilting green leaf testified to his passing. Tilak's eyes hardened and he went quickly back into his room and banged the door shut.

The vegetable seller was a Muslim and it meant nothing to him that Tilak chopped up animals or fish for his research. It did, however, mean a great deal to him if some of the larger Jain families or groups of Jain students, who lived in or around the students' hostel, indicated that they would take their business elsewhere, if he continued to serve Dr Tilak on the second floor. Undoubtedly, the vegetable seller's memory would slip conveniently, and Dr Tilak would be forgotten. Tilak wondered if the milkman would also forget.

He surveyed the grain bins in the corner of his room and wondered if he should cook himself some rice and lentils. He decided that it was too much trouble. Instead, he took down a round brass tin from the shelf and extracted half a small loaf of bread from it. Dipping pieces of it into another cup of coffee, he wandered round the room eating it. Though the bread was very dry, the austere meal revived him and improved his ragged temper.

Tilak could hear the nightwatchman doing his first round, stumping his staff on the ground to warn thieves, snakes and scorpions of his coming. He went back to sit on the windowsill. The chatter of students returning from their evening walks subsided, and a later wave, returning from the cinemas, was also swallowed up by the great hostel, and still Tilak sat grappling with his problem – Anasuyabehn.

The parade to the communal bathrooms could be heard shuffling up and down the corridors and slowly sleep crept through the building. In that time, Tilak finally made up his mind.

CHAPTER FOURTEEN

While Tilak dozed the afternoon away and John worked, Diana Armstrong trudged through the blinding heat to Pandipura village. She wished she could have afforded a tonga, but she had already spent eight annas on one to John's house, and that was the limit if she were to be sure of eating for the rest of the month.

105

'You don't *have* to see this old girl at Pandipura,' she told herself, as she paused to wipe the sweat from her eyelids with her handkerchief. She had, however, volunteered to keep a watch on her, so, after a moment, she went on again.

The operation on the scrawny body had been a success, and it seemed as if the woman's excellent constitution would lead to her early recovery. They had not counted, however, on the stark fear of being cut open, nor on the fact that she had expected that such a cut would fester and that she would die.

Dr Ferozeshah had found her by the roadside near his house when taking his usual early morning walk. She and her niece had been on their way to the market with a basket of vegetables when the pain which had been bothering her for some days had suddenly flared up. The young girl was seated with the woman's head in her lap trying to soothe her. Though the old woman was doubled up with pain, it had taken the united efforts of the watchman's wife and Diana, hastily called by the doctor, to persuade her to come into the consulting room to be examined. Nothing would persuade her to remove her cotton skirts, so the doctor had to feel through them to find the source of the pain.

He diagnosed appendicitis and advised an immediate operation, which was enough to send the old woman nearly into hysterics. She tried to get off the examination table. Dr Ferozeshah, and the sharp agony within, persuaded her to lie down again, while he sent the watchman's son out to Pandipura to get her brother-in-law.

Once over her first panic, she gasped to Diana that she had been a widow for years and that her brother-in-law, with whom she lived, disliked her very much. It was better that she should die.

Diana suggested that this would be tantamount to suicide, since the doctor had the power to cure her. She took a cloth and wiped the sweat off the sick woman's face, and added,

'There may be work for you to do yet, respected mother. Grandsons or grandnephews to guide. Motherless children to look after.'

A gaggle of relations had come running, babbling with fear of the unknown. They had blenched when the doctor had explained what needed to be done. The brother-in-law, his small, bright eyes shifting uneasily from the doctor's feet to his face, had said, 'I remember, Sahib, that when the cholera raged, you and the city Doctor Sahib came to our village and put needles in us to save us. I do not forget this, Sahib – but a cut like that would fester and mean certain death. Why bother? A little opium may help her to get over the pain and recover.' He shrugged, as if to suggest that the woman's life was of little importance.

His sister-in-law had all this time been lying on the examination table, breathing heavily and trying not to moan. Suddenly she had spoken up.

'There is no particular reason why I should live,' she gasped, 'but let the Doctor Sahib assuage the pain in any way he can. If I don't recover, who will mourn me?' She turned her head and glared malevolently at her brother-in-law.

The brother-in-law spluttered about the cost.

'I shall not charge,' Dr Ferozeshah assured him, and before anybody could say anything more, he called the bearer to wheel the woman into the next room and told Diana to scrub up.

A cry of real fear burst from the forlorn little group behind the brother-in-law, but the doctor turned and said authoritatively, 'One of you stay here to cook for her. There is a veranda where you may sleep and cook, and a well in the yard. Bring in a little food to which she is accustomed.'

With much going to and fro and grumbling and fussing, it had all been arranged. After a few days, the invalid had been carried home on a stretcher borne by her nephews. She was

107

cheerful and had undoubtedly enjoyed being made a fuss of and the unaccustomed rest in a real bed with a cotton mattress. Not so many of her caste practices had been flouted, and she hoped that prayer and suitable ablutions, when she was well, would appease her caste brethren.

Diana reached the village and stood for a minute in the shade of a tree by the well, to recuperate from the heat.

How very quiet everything was. Though it was long past the hour of afternoon naps, there was none of the usual shouting back and forth between housewives across the lanes, no sound of scolding mothers, no sound of goatherds playing their flutes – or a cloud of dust on the horizon to herald the return of the buffaloes to be milked. A few men sat on string beds outside their houses. They were talking quietly, heads close together, not arguing loudly with lots of gesturing, as they usually did. When a woman with a small child on her hip came out of one house, crossed the lane and went into another house, Diana relaxed. It must be the heat, she decided. She walked briskly down the main lane and then turned into another, in which her patient lived.

The woman's brother-in-law and his sons rose from their string bed outside the hut door and greeted her politely. Two women came out and led her inside to the old woman. They watched quietly, as Diana checked and changed the dressing, and took the woman's temperature and blood pressure. It was obvious to her that her patient was far from well; yet the wound appeared clean and healing. The silence of the waiting relatives oppressed her – Indians were not a silent people. Diana slowly put her thermometer back into its case. She wondered if something had happened to the village as a whole; had a fine been levied collectively for some misdemeanour? Or were they afraid of some infectious disease? Or had they lost a crop?

The hut in which she stood was clean, she noted, its

earthen floor smooth and shining from a recent application of cow dung; the talis and other eating utensils twinkled on a shelf cut out of the earthen walls; the womenfolk's spare skirts and a couple of clean, unwound turbans hung neatly over a rope stretched across the hut, so as to divide it and give a little privacy; a figurine of the Elephant God, Ganesh, shone softly in a corner, a small offering of rice before it. Everything was as it should be, and yet she sensed that something was wrong.

The woman opened her eyes, knew her and tried to smile. Again, Diana took her wrist to check the faltering pulse. In slow, clear Gujerati, she teased the old lady that she would soon be up and making flower offerings in the temple in thanks for her recovery. Now she was going to give her a pill, something like opium, which would give her a good, long sleep, after which she should feel very much stronger.

'Radhabahin,' murmured the sick woman. 'Sister of God.' She trustingly swallowed the pill.

As Diana went outside to speak to the three men and the two older women who followed her, she was worried. She reiterated to the relations that the woman would live, if the family would help her. Perhaps the little niece could be delegated to sit with her, hold her hand, fan her, make her feel she was needed and respected.

'She's not easy to live with,' the brother-in-law said frankly.

Diana laughed, and responded, 'We all grow old and impatient, in time.'

The response was an absent-minded smile, instead of the light joke which she had expected. She snapped her little black bag closed and said she would return on the following day.

It's as if all their cheerful gossip has been turned off, by order, she thought crossly.

109

Across the way, she was almost relieved to see Miss Prasad, a volunteer who came each week to teach women to read. She was asking Jivraj, a member of the village council, if he could send a donkey to fetch her servant, who was sitting by the side of the track leading to the village, unable to walk because she had a thorn deeply embedded in her foot. After the lesson, Miss Prasad would like to retain the animal to take her servant home. She would see that it was returned the following day.

Jivraj was looking most uncomfortable. He was an old man and he walked with the support of a grandson, a quiet, wide-eyed boy, round whose shoulders he draped one arm. In his right hand he held a staff for further support. His short, frilly jacket hung loosely on him and his dhoti flapped against sticklike legs. Jivraj had faced many famines, many disasters, and Diana thought that life could hardly present him with a problem he could not solve; and, yet, the polite request for a donkey from a most respected lady had obviously put him out.

'All the donkeys are at work, Miss,' he was telling her. He dug his stick into the sand and looked around him doubtfully. 'They will be busy for several days.' Then relief dawned on the lined, tired face. 'My grandson can go and help her,' he said.

Miss Prasad's earnest face still showed some anxiety, but she agreed to this. His grandson helped the old man back to his seat on the string bed outside his house, and then skipped away to find the servant.

'Good afternoon,' Diana called as cheerfully as she could to Miss Prasad.

'Namuste,' responded Miss Prasad briskly, as she gestured to a growing group of women and children to follow her to the shade of a nearby neem tree. She set up a tiny blackboard, and, as Diana made her farewells to her patient's family, the women sat down cross-legged and began to chant the letters of the alphabet, as she wrote them on the board. Diana had seen her do this in many villages, and usually the women made a social event of the occasion and there was much laughter. Today, they kept their veils across their faces and sometimes their excellent memories slipped.

'I can't imagine what's up,' Diana thought irritably, as she waved to them in passing. 'But something is.'

CHAPTER FIFTEEN

Tilak waited patiently until the students' hostel had been perfectly quiet for over an hour. Then he moved swiftly.

He dug out a clean shirt and cotton trousers from his untidy cupboard. Taking a towel and a sliver of soap, he walked with his usual, quick, masterful stride down to the indescribably filthy bathrooms. He found a shower cabinet less disgusting than the others and made a hasty toilet. Back in his room, he put on his clean clothes and his chuppells and slipped his torch into his pocket.

Very quietly he opened the door of his room.

The passage was empty, except that at the far end a servant lay sleeping on a mat outside a door.

Tilak glided across the passage and down the ill-lit main stairs. Behind the last flight of stairs he found a narrow door, made originally for the entry of Untouchable cleaners. It creaked when he opened it and he waited for a second or two to make sure that the nightwatchman, sitting on his stool towards the front of the building, had not heard him. Then he slid silently through it and left it a trifle ajar for his return.

The moon had risen and cast a great shadow of the building. Tilak made full use of it. The ground was rough, undeveloped land, criss-crossed by tiny paths made by many student feet. He found one of these paths leading to the lane bordering the campus, and followed it. Once out of the shadow, he might be seen by a watchman, but he would be far enough away not to be recognized.

He began to breathe more easily. There was no curfew to prevent his taking a walk at night, but anyone observing him would undoubtedly gossip speculatively about his being out at such a late hour.

On the other side of the lane bordering the campus, grazing land stretched for at least a mile, and he could hear heavy beasts moving about and snuffling at the herbage. The herdsmen must be somewhere near, he thought, and he walked lightly, using the shadows of a few mango trees to mask his presence as much as possible.

He saw them before they saw him. They were crouched in a tight circle, their woollen blankets clutched around them against the night chill. When they heard him, they sprang to their feet and raised their staffs ready. Tilak lifted his hand in salute and passed on quickly; he did not know whether he was recognized or not.

He reached the row of bungalows in which many of the senior professors lived. Here he paused, beside a small Jain temple which lay a little to the rear of them. His head throbbed and his throat was dry. He had walked so fast that his breath came in short gasps.

He wanted the eighth bungalow from where he stood. He forced himself to think carefully. The Dean, he reasoned, would at this time of year probably be sleeping in the courtyard, the boy servant nearby; Anasuyabehn, with her sharp-eyed aunt, would be either on the inner veranda or on the roof. The problem was to get close enough to the girl to talk to her without waking her family. Would he have to get on to the roof? And thence, possibly down to the veranda? That, he decided, would be madness.

He began to move, rather uncertainly, down the field path that ran at the back of the bungalows. His heart sank when he realized that a bungalow emitting a great deal of light from its back window was that of the Dean.

'I'm crazy,' he muttered, and wondered if he should look for an opportunity to speak to Anasuyabehn when she went out to the bazaar or the library. 'But it could take days,' he told himself, 'and then she might have the servant with her.'

The lighted window was open and the thin curtains flapped sporadically in the night breeze. Was a late-working Dean behind the curtains? Or a sleepless old lady? Or Anasuyabehn?

The curtains solved the problem for him by suddenly billowing inward. Before they subsided, he caught a glimpse of Anasuyabehn sitting on an iron bed, reading. His mercurial spirits rose. What luck!

He crept forward to stand at the side of the window, so that he would not be silhouetted against the light. He had to find out if she were alone. When, eventually, the curtains obliged by flipping inward again, he could observe no one else, so he chanced anyone being in the corner outside his line of vision, and called softly, 'Bahin!'

The quiet voice calling 'Sister' through the window shocked Anasuyabehn. She dropped her book and jumped off the bed to slam the window shut before the impudent student or would-be thief had time for action, but again the voice came, 'Anasuyabehn!'

'Ramji!' she exclaimed, and gripped a window bar for

support. With the other hand, she parted the curtains slightly. The shadow of a neem tree dappled the side of the house and she could see no one. 'Doctor Sahib,' she whispered.

'Put the light out,' whispered the disembodied voice hoarsely.

In her agitation she vacillated.

'Don't be frightened,' urged Tilak, his usual irritability apparent in his tone. 'There are excellent window bars between us.'

Shakily, she went across the room and switched the light off. Then she wrapped her sari closer round herself and returned. A small plump hand timidly drew one of the curtains back. 'Bhai,' she whispered. 'What are you doing here? Go home before you're caught.' Here was romance straight out of a Western novel, but it was too scary.

There was no reply to her question, so she gripped the window bars to peer out, and gave a frightened squeak as a masculine hand closed over one of hers. 'Brother,' she gasped again imploringly, as she tried to free her hand.

Tilak was entranced and held her firmly. He could just see her face glimmering in the moonlight, despite the tracery of the tree shadow, and behind her was the immense shadow of her loosed hair. Though the folds of her cotton sari covered her completely, she was blouseless and petticoatless. He could feel the heat of her body and smell her perfume. He nearly choked with desire and leaned close to the unyielding bars.

As he put his arm through the bars and then round her shoulders, she sobbed, 'Bhai, please, please go home. You'll be caught – and I've enough grief to bear without any more.' She burst into tears. Without thinking, she laid her wet face on the arm which gripped her, and Tilak came to his senses.

114

'Don't cry,' he said softly. 'I'm sorry I frightened you.'

He had come to find out if his feelings were in any way reciprocated. Now he knew by the trustful way in which she wept in his arms that love was there. All the ancient love stories seemed suddenly to be true. He was going to fight for this woman.

The words came tumbling from him. 'Rani,' he said. 'All I want to do is to marry you and take you to England and make you happy. I'm going to England to study – I can take you with me . . .'

'I'm to be married to Mahadev Desai,' she interposed, her voice lifeless. 'Tomorrow some relations will arrive – the first guests – and Aunt has already sent for the astrologer to name the day. Desais have already sent the last gifts before the marriage. I am inundated with silken saris and jewellery.'

The jackals howled at the moon and the insects sang, while Tilak silently digested this information. In the distance, the nightwatchman called to his relief man to take over.

'I have to be quick,' he told her. 'When is the marriage likely to be?' He slipped his hand under her hair and ran his fingers along her neck. She shivered, and said, 'Two or three weeks, probably.'

'You must prevaricate – bribe the astrologer. Pretend to be ill. Defer it somehow while I make arrangements.' She was trembling under his touch, but she did not draw back, and he thought that few would let him come so near, bars or no bars. She loves me, he rejoiced.

Her deepset eyes searched the gloom to see his dark face. 'Father is so upset by you. He'd never give permission.'

'Nothing's hopeless,' he assured her passionately. 'We're old enough to decide for ourselves. Would you like to marry me?'

Her teeth flashed, as she smiled up at him, and the heavens rang with pure joy for him, before she even breathed out, 'Oh, yes, of course.'

With a curious prescience, Tilak felt that this was the happiest moment of his life, and he savoured it.

The fresh watchman's staff was plunking down the front lane. 'I must go,' he said. 'Meet me tomorrow. Where?'

She sighed helplessly. Then she said, 'I'll try to be at the Marwari Gate temple about nine o'clock. But how shall we manage everything?'

'Never fear. I'll arrange it all.' He stepped back reluctantly and bent to kiss the hand holding one of the bars, and then he was gone.

CHAPTER SIXTEEN

The following morning, preparatory to going to the Marwari Gate temple, Tilak wrote a note on the blackboard of his lecture room, telling the students that the lectures for that day were cancelled.

He had spent most of the night going over his financial position, a record of which he kept in a battered account book. He had some savings and a little money in Government Bonds left him by his father, but it was not enough. He wondered which of his relations could be prevailed upon to lend him some more.

He was certain that his uncle would be pleased about his Fellowship and would stand surety with the passport people, so that he would not have to find the considerable deposit which would, otherwise, be demanded of him.

Suddenly, he stopped writing. How was he to get a passport for Anasuyabehn?

His uncle would certainly not connive with him in the abduction of a young woman. He had planned to marry her and then take her straight on to the boat or plane for England. This would not give time to have her name included on his own passport; and to obtain a separate passport would take even longer. Speed was of the essence if they were to avoid her family's wrath breaking over their heads, not to speak of the anger of the mighty Desai clan.

He was standing staring with glazed eyes at the blackboard, when Dr Yashvant Prasad, walking along the corridor, spotted him.

'Ah, Tilak,' he called. 'I was about to send my clerk to find you. Will you come into my office for a few minutes.'

Tilak turned sharply, trying vainly to think of an excuse to evade the interview.

'Ji hun,' he assented, and followed the Vice-Chancellor with lagging feet. 'My murdered frog,' he thought glumly and correctly.

As Tilak sat opposite him, Dr Prasad's pleasant voice meandered on. Tilak said, 'Yes, sir,' and 'No, sir', wherever it seemed appropriate, and thought of Anasuyabehn loitering alone by the temple. He prayed that she had sought seclusion inside the building.

'I propose,' said the Vice-Chancellor, putting his fingertips together, 'to speak personally to each Jain member of the staff and urge tolerance.'

'Thank you, sir,' responded Tilak, seething with worry under his polite exterior.

'I also propose to call on the more influential and forward-looking Jains in the city, to seek their help. I hope through them to reach the more orthodox groups with whom we do not so frequently come into touch. There is a very powerful family of Desais here, for example – if one could get people like that . . .'

'Desai?' queried Tilak, jerked back from thoughts of the Marwari Gate temple.

'Yes. Big financiers – they live in the centre of the city.'

'I've heard of them,' responded Tilak. It dawned on him that it was probably one of these Desais who was to marry Anasuyabehn. He thought bitterly that it would be too ironical to lose Anasuyabehn to a family which might be able to influence favourably his own position in the community.

The Vice-Chancellor was continuing.

'It will be slow work, I fear. In the meantime, Tilak, lock the laboratory door while doing your researches.' He smiled conspiratorially.

Tilak felt despairingly that if the Vice-Chancellor went on much longer, all his anger at the Dean, all his worry regarding Anasuyabehn and his frustration in respect of his work would explode out of him. He took a large breath, however, and then managed to reply, 'Certainly, sir.' Now was not the time to precipitate his resignation.

Desperate in his general agitation, Tilak half rose, hoping that Dr Prasad had finished.

'Before you go, I would like to ask your opinion about establishing a postgraduate course,' Dr Prasad went on remorselessly. Tilak sat down in his chair again and commended Anasuyabehn to any gods who happened to live in the temple.

He emerged at lunchtime at a loss to know how to communicate with her. He strode across the campus through the broiling heat of the sun. Suddenly his legs faltered and he had to stop in the shade of a tree. He watched the tree ants make a detour round his fingers and continue their endless running up and down the tree trunk,

118

while the trembling in his legs eased. As the faintness passed, he remembered that he had not eaten a proper meal for over a day, and he wondered how to get one without travelling into town; he had only a little rice and lentils in his room.

He remembered John, ever kind and sympathetic.

'Perhaps he'd be kind enough to give me lunch,' he thought, 'and maybe Ranjit could find me a boy as temporary servant.'

A very exhausted Tilak again presented himself at John's door and was fed by a resigned Ranjit and comforted by John, who assumed that his friend's shaken appearance was due, largely, to lack of food and the long session with Dr Prasad about the murdered frog and fish.

CHAPTER SEVENTEEN

'I thought I might be able to pick up a little Delhi rice,' Anasuyabehn told her aunt that morning, in the hope of justifying a visit to the Marwari Gate bazaar in which the temple lay. They had both been busy, getting ready for the expected arrival of their relations, and Anasuyabehn would, ordinarily, have gone to the nearest bazaar for the day's vegetables. She watched the indecision in her aunt's face. She knew the old woman loved the long delicate grains of Delhi rice, so hard to obtain in Shahpur, even on the black market.

'Well,' the older woman said finally, 'perhaps I could spare the boy for an hour to go with you.'

'I'll be all right alone, respected Aunt,' Anasuyabehn assured her quickly.

'Very well, then. Be a modest, circumspect girl and keep your sari over your head. I hope no Desais see you.'

Anasuyabehn obediently hitched her sari over her head, seized her cotton shopping bag, checked that sufficient money was tied safely in a tucked-in corner of her sari, and fled before Aunt could change her mind.

The bazaar was packed with people. After she had made her purchases, including a seer of Delhi rice from under a stall, she paused apprehensively to scan the crowd for Tilak. A young man on a bicycle eyed her insolently and, as he approached her, began to slow down. She moved hastily closer to the stalls, only to be jostled by a group of millhands going off shift. They touched her obscenely and shouted ribald remarks, as, impeded by the heavy shopping bag, she tried to shrink from them. In a moment, they were past her and clambering into a bus, leaving her nearly weeping with humiliation.

A countrywoman shouted a stream of abuse at them and then called to Anasuyabehn to come closer to her. Anasuyabehn stumbled towards her, wiping her face with her sari and trying not to be sick, while a policeman, rifle on back, leaned against a door jamb and laughed at her.

The woman nodded her head towards the pavement beside her. 'They won't bother you if you don't stray on to the street. Stay here, near us.'

Anasuyabehn nodded and made her way quickly into the temple behind them. She went only as far as the outer cloisters, feeling that Tilak would be sure to find her there.

The building was cool and shadowy. Morning prayers were long since over. The cloisters, with their fifty-two small shrines, were almost deserted. Only at one end a man and a young boy sat together, cotton masks over their mouths, and told their beads. The boy looked up as she entered, but a reproving glance from his companion made him hastily bow his head and continue his prayers.

Anasuyabehn stood leaning against the wall and drank

in the peace of the place after the heat and hurly-burly of the bazaar outside. The minutes ticked by and her pounding temples and nausea eased.

Where was Tilak? He should have been there fifteen minutes ago. She went to the top of the entrance steps and looked out over the crowd. No sign of him. She retraced her steps inside and continued to wait.

When her watch told her she had been waiting half an hour, she turned reluctantly and sadly once more to the entrance. Perhaps he had regretted his impetuosity of the previous night and decided that his suit was hopeless.

Head bowed to hide her tears, she did not see, until she nearly trod on him, the monk who had been silently watching her from behind.

Tall, naked except for a tattered cloth covering his genitals, it seemed as if he had no flesh, that the skin was drawn straight over his skeleton. His body was ingrained with dirt and his bald head was covered with sores, where the hair had been painfully plucked out by hand. In one emaciated hand he held a peacock feather and in the other a begging bowl. For a moment, until he drew hastily back from her, her face was within a foot of his.

Her father's guru, his religious teacher, Anasuyabehn realized, with a sense of shock.

As if to pierce her soul, penetrating, bloodshot eyes had looked deep into her own, and made her shiver.

She recoiled from him, feeling as if her mind lay naked to the man and that he had divined her reason for being alone in the temple. She cringed with sudden fear of his supernatural power. Then she bowed low, to touch the horny bare feet.

He knew her. Mehta's daughter, a modern miss with no real respect for her religion. He had warned her father once that he had left her too long unmarried. For his own spiritual good a man must see his children married before he dies. Marry her into an orthodox family, he had counselled. He had heard, however, that he was marrying her, instead, into a monied one.

And now, what was she doing in the temple? She was obviously not there for worship; her clothes were not fresh and she had shopping with her.

He knew that he should not care, that he should turn away from her; but perhaps the child had, of her own accord, sought to return to her religious observances and was not sure how to accomplish this.

Perplexed, he surveyed her ashy face as she rose from her obeisance. She could not go out through the gate until he moved, and he had been so long cut off from any consideration of time, that he was unaware that he had kept her standing there, head bowed, for several minutes.

Anasuyabehn was frozen with fear, as she suffered an intense examination by serene, intelligent eyes, that had spent years looking for the Ultimate Truth, and seemed now to be able to look through her and past her.

She was suddenly acutely aware of her own pettiness compared to men like this. Though she might assure herself that she had discarded her religion, she knew in those scarifying minutes, that it could not be shrugged off like a Kashmir shawl; it was part of the warp and weft of her life, hopelessly woven into her thoughts and actions, and now showing its strength, by making her stand, so frightened, before this uncanny, withdrawn monk.

At last the monk spoke. His voice was soft, so as not to disturb the souls in the air. 'You were looking for me?'

'No.' The answer came in a whisper.

It was an essential part of a monk's creed that he feel no personal interest in anyone. It was laudable, however, and would gain him merit, to hear confession or to instruct in the scriptures. Furthermore, try as he might to conquer it, he was curious to know what had caused her to visit the temple and why she was so obviously terrified.

If he stares at me much longer, thought Anasuyabehn, I shall die at his feet.

The man saw her sway. A bad conscience, he diagnosed.

'You wish to make confession?'

'No.'

'I am here each day. Go home and examine your conscience. You may ask your father to bring you to see me, if you wish, and I will hear you.'

After this pronouncement, he seemed to forget about her, and he turned along the side of the cloister, slowly sweeping the floor in front of him with his peacock feather, so that he would not kill an insect by treading on it. Anasuyabehn tottered out into the blazing sunlight, to the shrieks of the bazaar radios and the vendors' voices.

The bustling crowd around her did little to dispel the mesmeric effect of the monk's frightful godliness. For, to her, godly he undoubtedly was, with a personality purged of all human desire. She felt he did not need to hear her confession to know all that was in her mind.

Hypnotized by the mystic, she forgot to look again in the bazaar for Tilak and the bus was well along the road to home before she remembered him.

CHAPTER EIGHTEEN

Mahadev Desai's father sat on the worn stone steps of one of the verandas that faced the courtyard of his home. Though the morning sun shone warmly upon him, he was shaking as if with cold. The hands that held the telegram, which his servant had just handed to him, trembled so much that he could hardly reread it, to assure himself that he had understood it.

'Send my brother and my son to me,' he snapped finally, his wizened face looking more than usually owlish as he tightened his lips under his large, hooked nose.

The scared servant flew to obey, while, with quivering fingers, old Desai smoothed the crumpled edges of the telegram.

His second son, his usually blank face full of apprehension, rolled across the courtyard like a billiard ball slowly into a pocket. His uncle followed him, still tucking in his flapping dhoti as he came.

They each read the telegram and, as its full implications sank into their minds, utter consternation made them both burst into speech. Yet the message was such an innocent one. It merely informed them that Mahadev had not arrived on the Delhi Mail and asked on which train he would be travelling.

'The diamonds,' wailed Uncle, his hawklike face blenched.

'The rubies!' exclaimed his nephew, a mass of dithering fat.

'My son,' gasped old Desai. 'My only intelligent son,' and he glared at his second son, who shrank visibly at the insult.

The smell of trouble had by this time brought others to the scene. A knot of servants and hangers-on had gathered at a little distance and were watching the conference speculatively. The daughter-in-law of the wicked tongue could be heard approaching, scolding Mahadev's daughter as she came. The child trotted in front of her, silent and sullen. Automatically, her grandfather hid his fears and called her to him and she thankfully nestled down by him on the step. She stuck her tongue out at her aunt, who mercifully did not see the impudent gesture.

'What's the matter?' the daughter-in-law asked in respectful tones.

'It does not concern you,' replied old Desai coolly. 'I must, however, go out on business.' He turned to his younger son. 'Have the carriage brought out.' His voice sounded as brittle as his frail limbs looked, beneath their thin cotton covering.

The man went obediently, doing his best to crush the rancour he felt at his father's unkind remark. 'It's unjust,' he muttered under his breath. 'I work so hard.'

Old Desai's waspish daughter-in-law hung on to every word, in the hope of obtaining a clue as to what was wrong.

'Daughter,' he addressed her. 'Get out a clean set of khadi and put it in my room. I must change. Your husband will accompany me and will need the same.' He motioned her away impatiently with his walking stick.

The woman's face fell. Her temper flashed out as she called to a servant to get the clothes requested.

'Brother, you must stay here. Several important people are coming in this morning. I'll go to see the Chief of Police immediately.' He sighed deeply, and then exclaimed in apprehension, 'Heaven help us! I hope Mahadev is all right.'

His brother nodded his bald head. 'I was afraid for him when we heard of the robbery,' he said.

'I thought he would be all right,' said the older man. 'He's so quick-witted. I should have sent him by plane – it would have been much safer – though very expensive,' he sighed.

'I've never known dacoits in this district take someone right off a train – usually they rob and murder on the train – or just by – in which case the Railway Police would have found him, and his death would have been reported at the same time as the white woman's.'

'Someone here must have betrayed him, either deliberately or by gossip,' said old Desai suspiciously.

'The dacoits must have been primarily concerned with the registered mail, as usual,' reassured his brother. 'They could, of course, have stumbled on Mahadev by accident.'

Mahadev's father rubbed his chin thoughtfully. 'I doubt if they could have done,' he said at last. 'There was nothing to distinguish him from fifty other Banias who must have been travelling on the train – the boy was himself so sure that he would not be picked out in such an event as this – that is why he carried the stones with him, rather than entrusting them to the registered mail – as you know, some of the stones are particularly good. Our honoured customer, the Maharaja inherited some excellent ones – and they were a good partial surety for the loan to start his factory. Now he's ready to pay his debt – and we have lost them – and our boy.'

He got up wearily.

'Brother, you had better arm me with some money – and a gift – a good ring, perhaps. Some presents are indicated to speed investigating feet. Arree! Shall I ever see my son again?'

His brother touched his arm comfortingly, and assured

him, with more confidence than he felt, that Mahadev was probably safe. The much maligned police were not really so inefficient. There would certainly be a dreadful row about the murder of the English lady and that would galvanize them into action.

The little granddaughter, still as a scared mouse, had all this time been sitting, forgotten, on the step beside them. Her father was a magical person to her, who was often away from home. But when he returned his suitcase was full of presents for her and he had wonderful stories to tell. She opened her mouth suddenly and howled.

Her grandfather and great-uncle jumped guiltily, and, until a servant came to say that the clothing was ready, they kept assuring the little girl that Papa would be all right. She must, however, say nothing about him until Grandpa came home again – and maybe he would bring her a gift from the bazaar when he returned.

'I'll keep her with me,' promised Great-Uncle, and swung her cheerfully up into the air, and carried her off towards the counting house. He stopped suddenly, and turned back to his brother. 'Shall I inform Dean Mehta?' he asked.

'Tell nobody,' replied old Desai. 'Let's first try to find out what's happened.'

Old Desai climbed into the little black carriage, and told his second son to drive fast. No servant went with them. This business had to be kept as quiet as possible, he reflected, if only because he did not wish the Income Tax collector to read in the newspaper anything of their rapidly expanding operations. There was safety in a fair display of poverty. Where riches are splashed about, there come the thieves, the spongers, the hangers-on, the tax collector. Better to hide behind the ancient walls of one's Society, deep in the older part of town. A story of valuable rubies and diamonds lost would alert every robber to the possibility of large quantities of valuables hidden in the floors of the Desai Society, he thought dismally, however poverty-stricken it looked. They would not realize that nowadays money was invested in ships, planes, factories and machinery, instead of being buried as gold.

The traffic was held up by the Red Gate, which was too narrow to allow the vehicles to flow through fast. Old Desai shouted to a toy seller on the pavement, and the man fought his way through the stalled vehicles to the middle of the road. Old Desai solemnly bargained for and then purchased a monkey-on-a-stick.

'Father's reached his dotage,' thought his second son gloomily, as he whipped up the horse again.

CHAPTER NINETEEN

Although the Income Tax authorities might not yet be aware of the extent of Mr Desai's fortune, the police knew of the plainly dressed old man. Doors were immediately opened to him, and it was not long before he was ensconced in a chair in the office of a police chief of gratifying eminence, a small, calm Bengali who had come down from Delhi, armed with instructions to solve the robbery mystery at all costs, before there was a diplomatic row over the death of Mrs Belmont-Smythe.

He sat quietly and listened, while Desai told him of his son's non-arrival at Delhi and his fears for the young man's life. Desai minimized somewhat the value of the jewels he was carrying, but indicated that it was sufficient to tempt a professional thief.

Desai had spoken in Gujerati, his knowledge of English being limited to being able to read it, and his son translated as he went along. There was a pause at the end of the recital during which time the Delhi detective removed his shoes and socks thoughtfully, so that he could sit comfortably cross-legged on his chair. At last he said, 'No body, other than that of the English woman, has yet been found; and these dacoits, as you know, rarely hold anyone for ransom. Perhaps he missed the train.'

These remarks did little to console Desai. 'No. My head book-keeper saw him on to it. Perhaps some of the other passengers saw what happened to him?'

The detective made a wry face and shifted the papers about on his desk.

'We still have in custody a few suspicious characters who were on the train, and we have, of course, the names and addresses of a number of passengers. The majority are untraceable.' His voice rose with decision. 'I'll cause further inquiries to be made, and will have the railway embankments searched again.'

Desai had already decided to obtain the help of his caste brethren in a private search round the scene of the robbery, so he took his departure.

He was conducted to the door, with painstaking respect, by a local inspector, who promised that he would himself again question the railway police who were aboard the train. 'They were overwhelmed by the force of the attack,' he said almost apologetically.

'They always are,' replied Desai dryly, and climbed wearily into his carriage.

As his younger son drove him deeper and deeper into the heart of the city, the old man's spirits sank lower. Why did one scheme and amass money, if it were not for one's sons and their sons? The boy must be dead, dead without leaving a son to tend his funeral pyre, he thought bitterly. The nincompoop beside him had two sons, satanic images of their mother, for whom he felt no affection. It had been Mahadev's sons he had wanted to see before he died himself.

'If he lives, I'll hasten his marriage,' he promised himself.

Hearing his father's mutter, his younger son turned to him. 'Ji?' he queried respectfully.

'Nothing, nothing,' replied Desai testily.

He had told neither Mahadev nor his brother about the opposition of older members of the family to the marriage to Anasuyabehn. The elders had argued that a wealthy girl in the Desai community could be found, a girl strategically placed to increase the power of the caste. Intercaste marriages, they said, dissipated wealth and weakened authority.

Desai had been tempted to agree. When he read the *Financial Times*, however, and when men of other castes planning big enterprises asked his financial help, he felt that to become a power in the new, free India, it was wiser not to emphasize caste.

No one, not even his trusted brother, had ever seen Desai's small private ledger with a swastika drawn, for luck, on its first page. In this, the final results of all his business were entered. He planned that most of what that ledger represented should pass to Mahadev, just as his own father had chosen him to head the business when he had retired. It was, therefore, a good idea that Mahadev have a modern wife, but a wife without bossy caste relations.

The carriage jerked to a stop in front of the plain wooden door behind which lay the Desai Society. Old Desai was helped down from his perch by his son, who handed the horse and carriage over to the care of a servant squatting on the step.

Old Desai went immediately to the counting-house. Partner Uncle was immersed in work, his little grand-niece playing contentedly at his feet with a piece of paper and the office's entire collection of rubber stamps. She received the monkey-on-a-stick with great glee.

'The police,' said old Desai, 'are doing their best, I'm convinced. However, so much is at stake – our reputation for reliability – and poor Mahadev – I'm worried to death about him – that I think we should attempt a search ourselves.'

'I suppose we could,' said Partner Uncle doubtfully.

'Of course, we could,' snapped old Desai. 'We can send for Brother-in-law from Baroda to help organize it, and we have plenty of servants and clerks to help.'

'What about the business?'

'The business can wait,' snorted old Desai, to which unheard of heresy his brother had no reply.

CHAPTER TWENTY

Diana and Dr Ferozeshah's sweeper wearily tidied up the operating room. Dr Ferozeshah, his legs shaking with fatigue, washed his hands and wished he could afford air conditioning. Perhaps next year, he thought. His reverie was broken by Diana's voice.

'. . . and so I promised to go over again today. Would that be convenient to you?'

He turned round, his hands dripping.

Diana was struggling out of her white gown.

'Go where?'

'To that old body in Pandipura. She doesn't seem to be doing very well.'

Dr Ferozeshah surveyed his employee. In spite of her lack of weight, she was plum-coloured with heat and exertion. Too thin, he decided; she needed more rest.

'She'll be all right for a couple of days,' he said, 'and you should rest for a while – we've had a busy morning.'

'I am tired,' admitted Diana, 'but I feel uneasy about her. If you don't want me this afternoon, I could go up on the bus.'

Dr Ferozeshah's perfectly modelled face broke into a mischievous grin. 'All right. Go to see this illustrious patient – and then take the evening off.' He picked up a towel to dry his hands. 'Mirabai can do the evening rounds with me – you've taught her very well.'

A whole evening off was a rare luxury. It sounded as if Ferozeshah was at last satisfied that Mirabai, the new nurse, and a new Sindhi dispenser were competent to undertake some of her work, and she heaved a sigh of relief.

She thanked the doctor, took her handbag from a locked cupboard, and went slowly through the waiting-room for high-caste clients and down the steps to the tree-lined road. She had a room in the house of a widow further down the road, and, as she strolled towards it, she looked back over the previous thirty months. She smiled a little as she remembered how the small private hospital had helped to fight epidemics, patched broken limbs after riots, done operations that in England would have been left to specialists, delivered babies and consoled the bereaved. Though the doctor was making money, much of it was spent on precious pieces of equipment – the X-ray machine, for example, what a help that had been – and the big sterilizer.

When she knocked, her landlady, Mrs Jha, unbolted the front door to let her in. She was a stringy-looking woman, garbed in a plain white sari, her grey hair clipped close to her head to indicate her widowhood. Though she was quite orthodox in her way of life, her grandson, Dr Ferozeshah's lawyer, had persuaded her to take in Diana.

The two women had become good friends and, quite often, Mrs Jha would cook some vegetarian delicacy for the girl and bring it to her. As a caste Hindu, however, she would not eat with her. The line was drawn there.

In return, Diana respected her caste rules and tried not to infringe on her privacy. She never entered her landlady's part of the house lest she defile it. With the aid of a tin bath in her room, she washed herself and her clothes. The sweeper came twice daily through a special sweeper's door into the cupboardlike bathroom, to clean her commode and remove her garbage. Mrs Jha's own servant, for a small tip, drew water from the well in the compound and filled her water-pots on the veranda, both morning and evening. It worked quite well.

Now Mrs Jha was full of news. Mr Lallubhai had sent his peon to ask Diana to attend a meeting at his house the following evening. The man had also brought more news of the train robbery. 'He said,' she commenced in a hissing whisper in case the dacoits might hear, 'that in the bazaar they are saying that this is no ordinary train robbery, and that they must have had local help.' She pursed her lips and glanced over her shoulder, as if expecting to see someone listening to her. 'They think it was not Saurashtrian dacoits who did it – and that makes sense, when you think of it. They wouldn't be foolish enough to kill an English Memsahib.'

She pushed her key ring more securely into the waist of her petticoat, as if to guard it carefully, and looked expectantly at Diana.

Diana, however, knew the value of bazaar rumours, and replied quite cheerfully, 'Except for the murder, the newspaper this morning didn't seem to think there was anything special about it. Just that they were after the registered mail.'

Mrs Jha refused to relinquish one scrap of her morbid excitement, and wagged her head slowly in negative fashion.

'We must be prudent,' she said earnestly. 'When my nephew comes home from work, I shall ask him to clean the gun. And he and his sister can escort you whenever you want to go out.'

Diana restrained the gurgle of laughter which rose in her throat. Mrs Jha's nephew was a huge, flabby, amiable youth and in a crisis, Diana was sure, his only thought would be to find a cupboard big enough to hide in. His shy young sister was hardly necessary to act as chaperon.

She thanked Mrs Jha and retreated to her room.

It was an airy, comfortable room, though, by Western standards, rather bare.

A divan, covered with a homespun bedspread, lay along a whitewashed wall, a few gaily coloured cushions piled upon it. Above this hung a carefully arranged group of family photographs in plain, black frames. There was a small bookcase, crammed with novels, a few travel books, the Bible, a Gita, English translations of the Upanishads and the Light of Truth; on top of it, by a brass vase of wilted wild flowers and grasses, lay some library books, including one of John Bennett's histories. Her few dresses hung on a rail set across a corner of the room, with her shoes in a neat row beneath them. A trunk, its careworn appearance disguised by a frilled cover, held her underwear and a precious tennis racket. On top of the trunk there was a workbasket in which lay balls of wool and knitting needles.

There was little else in the room, except for a small wooden table with its accompanying chair, and a locked cupboard for her modest stores of food, linen, clothing and other oddments.

Diana hurried to her veranda, where she kept her cooking tools and Primus stove. She quickly put together a pan of khicharhi and, while it was cooking, she washed herself and changed into a khaki blouse and skirt, relics of her Mission of Holiness days.

To eat her meal, she sat in a basket chair and looked out over the little courtyard, with its well in one corner and a drooping neem tree in another. Near the well, tiny flowers bloomed between the paving stones, watered by splashes from the water-bucket. A sacred, well-tended tulsi tree flourished in a stone pot in the centre of the courtyard.

Diana never trespassed into the courtyard, and now she thought how nice it would be to do so. 'I'd like a home like this,' she pondered a little wistfully.

'You could have it, if you took a nursing post with a European company here,' she told herself.

'And get caught up in the empty world of club life? Ugh!'

Marriage would also have brought her a home, but she always shrugged when she thought of it. 'I'm past it,' she would say quite philosophically. During her probationer days in Edinburgh she had dated other students, but her shyness made her boring. She had turned to her studies and had become a reliable, cheerful surgical nurse, losing her individuality behind her starched uniform.

It would not have been difficult for her to obtain a well-to-do Indian husband; her ordinary English prettiness was a thing of unusual beauty in Shahpur. She knew, however, that the adjustment to such a life would be too difficult for her.

Her mind wandered. 'What about your new friend, John Bennett?'

Tears stung her eyes. In a moment of honesty, she

realized that John had ceased to be only a patient to her and had become a special person, unlike anyone she had met before; a man of integrity, considerable physical strength and high intellect, she reflected wistfully.

She stirred her food around a little, to cool it. Perhaps, she thought rather pitifully, there was good reason for a quiet, older woman like herself to keep away from him, if she wanted to avoid being hurt. Absorbed in his work, he would hardly think about her.

He had an enviable war record and, amongst the University people, he was famous for his kindness – and his celibacy. No hint of gossip ever seemed to touch him, she had observed, not even the assumption, common enough in regard to a man who lived like he did, that he was a homosexual.

She pushed away her half empty dish, and wiped her lips on her handkerchief. 'It doesn't matter, anyway,' she told herself. 'Just because a man is courteous and thoughtful of you, doesn't mean much.'

She pushed back her chair, took a glass and went to a water-jar. She drank a glass of water and also filled a small water-bottle, which she put into her black, nurse's bag.

She picked up her black umbrella and went out to catch the bus.

CHAPTER TWENTY-ONE

In comfortable solitude, Diana swung along the meandering field path which led from the end of the bus route to Pandipura village. After the smell of the city, the air seemed sweet and heavy with the odour of drying foliage. Even the occasional goat she met stood comatose, the tiny goatherd usually fast asleep in the nearest patch of shade. She became aware, however, of an irritating hubbub further along the path. Loud cackles of laughter and birdlike shrieks smote her ears, increasing rapidly as she approached. When she rounded a bend an unlovely, though familiar, sight met her gaze.

The remains of a dead donkey, by now almost reduced to a skeleton, lay across the path, and though not much was left, four or five vultures still argued and jostled each other over the spoils. One bird had found a particularly succulent morsel and had it clasped in its beak, its bald head and neck bobbing as, with ungainly hops, it tried to find an opportunity to swallow its prize, while the others pushed and shoved around it in an endeavour to rob their companion.

'Blast,' muttered Diana, and drew back hastily.

The vultures ignored her, if they had noticed her at all; they are no animal's prey. They were big birds and Diana teetered uncertainly at the edge of the path, wondering how long it would take them to finish their revolting work and fly away. Finally, she decided to strike into the bush and make a circle round them. She had on heavy shoes and there was little danger from snakes in such heat – most of them would be hibernating. She followed a goat track in and out of the thorny bushes, taking her direction from a distant mango tree which she could see growing further along the path.

Except for an occasional glance at the mango tree, she watched the ground she covered, in case of scorpions. Because of this, she observed a scrap of clean paper clinging to the base of a cactus. Newspaper was not uncommon in the countryside, but any other type of paper was. This was not newspaper. It was linen-backed, with threads still attached to where it had been torn. At one point a light blue line ran across it. Small, unimportant, a piece of rubbish – but out of place.

Her curiosity aroused, Diana stooped to pick it up, and, as she proceeded on her way, she turned it over and over in her hand. Guessing at its origin provided an amusing little puzzle to ease the monotony of her walk.

She reached the mango tree and rejoined the path to the village. The tree gave welcome shade, so she paused to wipe her face free of dust and sweat.

'Namuste, Memsahib,' said a thin, cracked voice behind her.

Diana jumped, and turned towards the voice.

A very old man, who had been sitting in the shade further round the trunk of the tree, was struggling to his feet.

Diana knew him, and sighed with relief. She shoved her handkerchief and the piece of paper into her shirt pocket and picked up her bag and umbrella.

'Namuste,' she greeted the village bone-setter.

He grinned at her, his white-stubbled face dissolving into a mass of wrinkles, and, as she made to continue on her way, he accompanied her. His staff dragged in the sand as he described to her a boy's arm which he had just set. She had once admired an ankle he had set and she had, in consequence, added to his local prestige. He now regarded her as a medical colleague, much to her amusement, though she had to admit that he was surprisingly competent for one who had learned his art only from his father in the traditional way.

'Are you going to Virchand's house?' he inquired, naming the brother-in-law of Diana's patient.

'Yes.'

The bone-setter stumped along for a few yards, and then

gave his opinion. 'She'll live, Memsahib. She has been worrying about things which are no concern of hers. Sick people shouldn't worry – it makes them sicker.'

'It does,' agreed Diana.

'The Panchyat will worry about the village – it's *their* job.' His tone was vicious. He would dearly have liked to be a member of the village council himself, but saw no hope of it.

'What's the trouble in the village? I thought there was something wrong when I was there yesterday. Have they been fined for something?'

'Not yet,' replied the bone-setter. He looked up at her from under his grubby white turban, clamped his pinched mouth tightly shut, and refused to say anything more until they reached the village. Still wordless, he saluted her and left her outside Virchand's house.

Her patient was awake and tried to sit up as Diana entered. She made her lie down again, while she took her temperature, which proved to be normal. The deathly look of the previous day had also gone, though she was not very cheerful. The scar of the operation was knitting well.

She sat down on a mat by the bed and advised Virchand's wife how to get the old lady on to her feet again, while the patient herself occasionally put in a word. The young niece brought into the hut a shy mother with a little boy who had a boil, and asked advice. Tea was offered her. Everything was as usual.

Whatever was bothering them must have passed over, Diana decided. She had seen before how a caste group or a family would shut up like clams while they dealt with a domestic scandal or even a murder. Distrusting both police and lower courts, they tried their best not to seek help from anybody in authority.

Diana sighed. They were brave and resourceful, but,

because of their poverty, they were open to all kinds of bullying. She hoped, however, that her elderly patient was now safely on her way to recovery and that her brother-in-law would not aggravate her in any way for the next week or two.

The wind was rising, making the sand fly unpleasantly, so she said her farewells. 'If the patient does not seem to be improving, please send a message immediately to Dr Ferozeshah,' she instructed Virchand, sitting in his usual spot on the string bed outside the door.

'Ji, hun,' he agreed, and rose and saluted her.

As soon as she was clear of the village, she stopped to drink the bottle of water she had brought with her. Without water, she would assuredly get sunstroke, and she dared not eat or drink anything in the village for fear of dysentery.

The vultures had departed, leaving the small skeleton to the jackals; a rustle in the undergrowth hinted at their presence. The shadows were lengthening, so she stepped round the skeleton and increased her pace. In the distance she could hear the herdsmen shouting as they rounded up their charges, preparatory to driving them home.

Two red-clad milkmaids, with their big brass vessels of milk, were squatting at the bus terminus. There she hesitated. John Bennett lived not far from the following stop. If she picked up the bus there, she could call in to tell him of the meeting at Lallubhai's house, in case Lallubhai had forgotten to inform him.

She persuaded herself that Lallubhai could indeed be so inefficient, despite his pleasure at John's offer, and walked on. She was followed by the stares and giggles of the milkmaids; her flushed face and short skirts always caused amusement to village women who did not know her.

The compound gate was unbolted, and she pushed it

open and went in. John's light was already switched on and she could clearly see, through the open windows, that he already had a visitor.

As she stood uncertainly on the path, shyness over-whelming her, the gate swung slowly shut behind her.

John heard the gate click and turned in his chair to look out of the window. When he saw her, he waved, and a few moments later, he opened the door to her.

He was leaning on his stick, as she entered and stopped just over the threshold. Rather primly, she delivered her message.

'Of course, I'll come,' he assured her. He turned to Tilak, who had risen at Diana's entrance, and introduced him to her.

Tilak put his hands together in salute. What a weird-looking woman – her face was as red as burning charcoal.

She sat down in the basket chair indicated to her, and John sank on to the divan. The divan was low, and he winced; for the thousandth time, he cursed his inability to move properly.

The wince had gone unnoticed by his guests. He turned his attention determinedly to them and they were soon talking quite easily to each other. The story of the dead frog was told once more, and Diana was quick to sympathize. In return, she told them about some of the bigotry she had observed in the Mission of Holiness.

As her shyness receded, her face became more animated and her green eyes twinkled. She accepted a cigarette and smoked it slowly, enjoying the rare luxury of it. John apologized for Ranjit's absence and his own inability to manage the Primus stove to make tea for her. Ranjit had gone, he explained, to find a boy servant he thought would suit Dr Tilak.

The mention of tea brought back her former diffidence.

She said hastily that she had not intended to stay, and looked at her watch. 'I think I should catch the next bus,' she said.

Tilak surveyed her gloomily from under lowered brows. He had discussed with John the fine opportunity of the English Fellowship, and had been about to consult him regarding taking Anasuyabehn with him, when they had been interrupted by Diana's knock. Now the moment was gone, taken by this fool of a woman with her maps and her nursing. As he chewed his nails and tried to enter politely into the conversation, the insoluble problem of the passport whirled in his mind.

Diana was picking up her bag and umbrella and John was saying that he should see her on to the bus. But his legs were hurting savagely and his voice did not carry conviction.

Diana sensed his reluctance, though she did not realize the cause. She said stiffly, 'I shall be quite all right alone.'

Tilak had come to the door, too. He felt that John's interest had transferred itself to the woman, and that he would not give his full attention to Tilak's own problems. 'I must go, too,' he said sulkily. 'I have lectures to prepare. Ask Ranjit to let me know about the boy.'

'Certainly,' replied John absently. He looked at Diana a little coldly, feeling that she was, in some way, distancing herself from him. He hesitated, holding the door half open. 'I don't think you should go alone in the dark,' he said to Diana.

Tilak felt he would never escape and he suddenly wanted to get out of the hot little room. 'I'll take Miss Armstrong to the bus,' he offered.

Diana accepted the offer gracefully.

So Tilak found himself escorting an English lady down the sandy lane, past the Dean's bungalow. From the roof, Aunt observed him with astonishment.

At the bus stop, a group of children was playing Horses and Riders. The smaller boys were riding piggyback on the bigger boys, and they pushed and shoved in an effort to unhorse the riders. The fun they were having was infectious, and Diana laughed when one of the riders, with a deft push, caught another one off balance, and, to shouts of acclamation, horse and rider went down into the dust.

The bus arrived in a flurry of sand. Diana hastily thanked Tilak and eased her way into the crowded vehicle.

The little unhorsed rider rolled, puffing and laughing, to Tilak's feet, while, from a nearby house, a shrill voice shouted to the children to come in at once. Three children fled, leaving the fallen one sitting rubbing his back. He looked up at Tilak and grinned beguilingly. Tilak knew him, and his pulses jumped at his good luck.

'You're Mehta Sahib's servant?' he asked.

The boy scrambled to his feet, picked up his black pillbox hat and crammed it back on his head. 'Ji,' he replied respectfully.

'I want you to take a note to Miss Anasuyabehn,' he told the child. 'It is about a special secret with which she will surprise Mehta Sahib, so you mustn't show the note to anybody. Do you understand?'

'Ji.'

Tilak took out his notebook, tore out a page and scribbled a few words on it with his fountain pen. He fished a four-anna piece out of his trouser pocket and handed it, with the note, to the servant.

The boy put the note into his shirt pocket and the coin into the pocket of his ragged pants. He grinned at Tilak and ran happily across the road towards the Dean's house.

Meanwhile, Aunt stumped thoughtfully down the stairs from the roof, where she had enjoyed a short nap. She had just risen from the mat on which she had been lying, when she had observed, over the parapet, Diana and Tilak going to the bus stop.

Still feeling physically and mentally drained after her confrontation with the guru in the temple, Anasuyabehn was seated on the kitchen floor preparing dinner for the visitors. Two chattering female cousins were helping her. The parents were seated on the veranda, sipping lemon water.

The servant had been sent to the house of a neighbour with a full water-pot, the neighbour's tap having ceased to function, and Anasuyabehn said, as her aunt entered, 'I wonder where the boy is? He's been gone quite a long time.'

'Playing with the children down the road,' replied Aunt sourly. 'Saw him just now.' She sat down by a small charcoal fire, which one of the cousins had been tending. She took up a rolling pin and uncovered a pan of dough, which had been put ready for her by Anasuyabehn. The cousin put a pan of oil on to the fire to heat. As the older woman began skilfully to roll out puris on a small pastry board, she said, 'I saw something else, while I was on the roof.' She dropped a puri into the fat and pressed it under with a spatula, while the three girls looked up expectantly. 'That troublesome Dr Tilak was walking down the lane with an English lady — the one who visited Dr Bennett the other day!'

The Dean had put his head round the kitchen door to see how the dinner was coming along. The meal was late, and it troubled him to have to eat after nightfall — no Jain liked to do that. 'Indeed,' he exclaimed. 'You must have been mistaken.'

'My sight isn't that bad,' snapped Aunt. 'Perhaps,' she added cunningly, 'he asked Dr Bennett to introduce him.' That, she surmised, might damn him in Anasuyabehn's eyes. She glanced quickly at her niece, never ceasing the quick rolling of the bread she was making.

The girl sat as if turned to stone, her eyes wide, a lid in her hand poised over a saucepan of vegetables. Suddenly, within her, raged jealousy so raw that she could have spat like a fighting cat.

So that was why he had not come to the temple. Given the chance of an English girl in marriage, he had dumped her like a coolie dumping a bag of sugar.

Aunt smiled contentedly down at her frying puri.

'He would never allow himself to be seen walking with her unless he intended to marry her.' She flicked her sari back from her face and looked up at her brother. 'What do you think?'

The Dean lifted a hand in a dismissive gesture. 'I don't know,' he replied. 'It doesn't matter, anyway.'

Matter? Anasuyabehn nearly screamed aloud at him. It matters terribly, and I don't know how I can bear it.

CHAPTER TWENTY-TWO

The boy servant slipped silently into the kitchen. No one noticed him, except Aunt, who hissed out of the corner of her mouth, 'And where have you been, Maharaj?'

The sarcasm of the appellation made him cringe. He shrank into a corner, scared by the thought of the money in his pocket.

Consternation grew in him; supposing she found the four-anna piece? Its weight burned against his thigh, its delicious promise of sweets lost in overwhelming fright. If she found the coin, the old owl would shriek and nag at him until she discovered how he came by it; and, dimly, the little boy understood that this would cause not only trouble to himself but, possibly, to his dear Anasuyabehn as well. The fact that the note might be more incriminating than the coin did not occur to him – he regarded it merely as a piece of paper.

In a funk, the child moved to the charcoal bin. As if to make up the fire, he took a piece out and at the same time dropped the coin into the box. It fell with a soft plonk into the slack at the bottom.

At the sound, Aunt turned round. 'Don't make up the fire now,' she snorted.

His fear receded. She had not seen. Obediently, he put back the piece of charcoal and stood waiting for the family to finish their dinner, so that he could have his.

The Dean suggested a walk in the Riverside Gardens. Everyone agreed, and, with a swish of saris, the ladies rose and went to the bathroom to wash their mouths.

Aunt turned to the servant. 'Next time you're sent on a message,' she growled, 'come back at once, do you hear me? At once. Otherwise, I'll take an anna off your wages for every five minutes you're late.'

The boy skulked in a corner and hung his head.

'No dinner, tonight,' added the indefatigable crone. 'Now, clear up the dishes.'

The hungry boy hardly heard her. If they all went for a walk, he would be alone in this terrifyingly big bungalow, where the spirits in the air went *shush-shush* as they flew round the compound; and they rattled at the door bolts and made the curtains flutter at the windows.

As he stared at the discarded brass talis on the floor, they seemed to grow bigger, like staring eyes, too big for a little boy to scour. The littered kitchen floor stretched out before

146

him like the desert of Rajasthan, miles of it to be swept and washed before he might curl up on his mat and lose his misery in sleep. He sat down on the floor and wept loudly.

Anasuyabehn heard the noise and came swiftly back to the kitchen. 'What's up?' she asked her aunt.

'I've told this naughty boy that he can't have any dinner,' replied Aunt.

The sobs redoubled.

Anasuyabehn tried to look stern. 'You're right, of course,' she said, and then paused. 'Perhaps, tonight he could have his dinner, and, if he ever dawdles again, he could go without?'

Aunt got up to follow the others to the bathroom. Over her shoulder, she snapped, 'You spoil him.'

'I'm sure he's very sorry.'

The boy stopped crying, wiped his nose with the back of his hand and nodded vigorously.

'All right, if you wish,' replied Aunt and swept out of the kitchen, all injured dignity. The servant ran to Anasuyabehn and touched her feet.

'Eat quickly,' she told him. 'Wash the talis and clean the floor. You can do the saucepans in the morning.'

'Ji, hun,' he assented, still sniffing, while his eyes made an anxious inventory of the amount of food left in the saucepans. Obsessed by the need to eat, the note lay unremembered in his pocket.

Long ago, in the days of the East India Company, an Englishman had built himself a miniature palace by the river and, round it, had laid out a fine park with a wide promenade along the river bank, the whole surrounded by a high wall. His grandson, an irascible bachelor appalled by the overcrowding of Shahpur, had willed it to the city, to be a park forever, open to all castes and classes to walk and play in.

The people thronged into it, happy to be free of traffic and dust. Admittedly, the grass had worn a bit thin in places, and, at one point, the surrounding wall had broken down, yet it was still a blissful retreat on a hot evening. The palace was now a boys' school, sadly lacking in paint though high in reputation. Like the park, it was open to Untouchables, as long as they could pay their fees.

Beggars were kept outside the gate by an officious chowkidar. They gathered as near to the gate as they could get, however, exhibiting a horrible collection of deformities and lifting distorted hands to the passersby. Like some dreadful opera chorus, they chanted hopefully, 'Ram, Ram, Ram.'

Through this ghastly crew floated like petals on the wind girls and women in pastel coloured saris. They were closely escorted by their white-clad menfolk and were accompanied by a bevy of grave-eyed children. Amongst them, Anasuyabehn walked demurely behind her father and her uncle, a giggling cousin on either side of her, while the two aunts brought up the rear.

Though it was getting late, the park was far from gloomy; each path had its line of electric lights. The evening breeze blew coolly off the river, and the party walked the length of the promenade.

Anasuyabehn found it difficult to maintain her outward composure. Great gusts of fury kept sweeping over her. That Tilak should one day make protestations of love to her, and the next night be seen walking with an English lady was incredible. In this provincial town, nobody would walk alone with an English woman unless he had designs upon her. She forgot that Tilak was from Bombay.

'You're really so dull and depressing about your marriage,' complained one of her cousins. 'I'd give my eyes to be engaged to such a wealthy man – a man who sent me diamonds.' Her voice rose in sharp envy. 'And he looks so handsome in his photo.'

The reminder of Mahadev's generosity struck Anasuyabehn forcibly. She lifted her head proudly and her lips curled in a hard smile. At least her fiancé wanted her badly.

They came to the end of the promenade, and the older ladies sat down to rest for a few minutes on a stone bench, upon which they arranged themselves so that there was no room for anyone else. The two gentlemen walked slowly up and down the path in front of them, while the cousins stood patiently nearby. A lamp illuminated the bench, though it served only to deepen the shadows cast by a huge, drooping tree behind it. Faintly from the burning ghats on the other side of the river came the smell of burning wood, a sad warning of man's mortality.

The cousins grew tired of Anasuyabehn's long silences and ran across the walk to the balustrade, which divided the river shore from the park. Thankful to be alone, Anasuyabehn paced up and down on the grass behind her aunts. Under the shadow of the tree, her green sari made her almost invisible.

A husband and wife, who knew her family, stopped by the bench to pay their respects to the aunts, and Anasuyabehn stepped deeper into the shadow, rather than face another barrage of good-natured jokes about the joys of matrimony. Though very exhausted, she was still simmering with anger.

When she heard the very softest whisper behind her, she was shocked. Stifling a shriek, she turned. 'Go away,' she whispered back to Tilak. 'How dare you come near me? And how did you find me?'

Tilak's black jacket made him invisible against the tree's great trunk, as he breathed, 'Followed you from home. Now, listen. Quickly. Have you a passport?'

Indignation welled up. 'How dare you? How dare you?' she upbraided him.

149

'I'm sorry, I couldn't get away.'

'No? I imagine you were very pleasantly occupied.'

Puzzled at her attitude, he said irritably, 'Tell me, Rani. Your passport. I have to make plans for us.'

Anasuyabehn peered at him through the gloom. He was so close to her that she could feel his warmth. In the midst of her rage, her physical desire for this handsome man tore through her. One touch from his hand would have diverted the flood of jealousy into channels of self-recrimination and explanation.

'Sister, sister, where are you?' called one of her cousins, running back across the walk.

She whipped round, and, then, forcing herself to advance casually into the light, she called back, 'Here I am.'

Bewildered and frustrated, Tilak slunk into the darkness.

CHAPTER TWENTY-THREE

Old Desai sat on his wooden divan in his dismal counting house, his portable desk beside him. Sitting near him was his sister's husband, hastily summoned by telegram from Baroda. With him had come his sister's sons, aged fifteen and eighteen respectively.

Leaning against a battered filing cabinet and staring vacantly at the visitors was Mahadev's brother, his face showing none of the sense of panic within him. Mahadev and the Maharajah's jewels were missing and unusual decisions had to be made. He would probably have to go out to help with inquiries amongst dull Hindu clods in the villages, and he was not looking forward to it.

Why didn't his father leave the job to the police?

He knew the answer only too well. His father loved Mahadev above everyone; he would literally leave no stone unturned in order to find him.

The stout, plain man in his round black cap gave a small quivering sigh, and tried not to think of his wife's bitter tirade that morning. She had said she hoped that Mahadev would be found, since there had to be one brain in each generation of the family.

Old Desai turned to the one man in the room to whom he felt close, his Partner Brother, still spry in spite of his years and his sorrows, a man whose sons had died before him. He alone could truly appreciate his dread of losing Mahadev.

Partner Brother's small eyes gleamed behind his heavy, horn-rimmed glasses. 'Well, where shall we start?' he asked.

Baroda Brother took off his pince-nez and polished them, to indicate that he was getting ready for action. Since Mahadev, fleeced by the dacoits, had not arrived at Delhi, he was, in his opinion, lying dead somewhere along the railway track. He kept his belief to himself, however, and suggested briskly, 'We could search either bank of the railway track for some miles on each side of the site of the robbery.'

'The police will have already done that,' said Partner Brother.

The thorough, ponderous mind of Mahadev's own brother had not been idle. 'Father,' he said, with a trace of excitement, 'if there were anything dead within a couple of miles of the railway track, vultures would have come in clouds and would have been clearly visible; the police would have gone immediately to see what was attracting them.'

151

The other men looked at him in surprise. There was a stunned silence, and then everyone spoke at once.

'He *must* be alive,' said old Desai, his voice trembling.

Baroda Brother-in-law put his pince-nez firmly back on to his nose, and added, 'He must, since his body was not on the train.'

Mahadev's brother gritted his teeth. Even when he showed intelligence, he fumed, nobody really noticed. Even his name was forgotten by most; he was simply Husband or Brother or Son – or, worst of all, Mahadev's Brother – a simpleton in the background of other people's lives, lost in the shadow of a more brilliant brother and bullied by a shrewish wife.

Yet, who supervised all the account books of his father's great concerns? he asked himself. Who checked the incoming interest and made the first moves against those who failed to pay? Who sat up late at night, to comb carefully through each agreement, so that not once had they lost a court case when some outraged landowner took them before a magistrate?

He hoped, in the forefront of his mind, that Mahadev was safe. But, deep inside, he wished savagely that he was lost for good. He chewed again his already closely bitten fingernails.

His father's voice cut through his rumination. 'We'll first inquire of every Desai Society along the route, up to a distance of fifty miles from here. There is no great town to comb, unless he is, say, a hostage, in Shahpur itself – only villages.'

He then began to organize them. 'Dress plainly,' he advised. 'You are moneylenders going about your normal business. On no account mention the jewels. Go by bicycle or by horse carriage.' He tapped his fingers on his little desk, and then went on, 'Take a servant or one of the others with you – if we find the task too great, we'll close the office and use the clerks.' He wagged his finger warningly. 'Be careful to be courteous to the Headman or the Panchyat, when you inquire. And stop at isolated huts – and don't forget the Untouchable quarters.'

All the men nodded agreement.

'Should we inform Dean Mehta now?' asked Partner Brother.

Old Desai considered this question carefully. He would have preferred to keep the matter secret, but the Mehtas might hear a rumour.

A fresh fear struck him. Such rumours might well reach the dacoits. If Mahadev had been left for dead, if he had seen the robbers' faces and they realized that he was still alive, would not they also start to hunt for him?

He winced, as he foresaw a quick knife thrust under Mahadev's well-covered ribs, the moment he showed himself. Impatiently he pushed the unwelcome thought out of his mind, and answered his brother's question. 'I'll go to his office to tell him – so that, for the moment, his family does not have to know.'

He remembered grimly his Baroda Sister's remark, when she had first been asked to act as go-between. She had said, 'The girl is not lucky – she has already lost one fiancé.' He had snubbed her thoroughly as being superstitious and old-fashioned.

The men got up and stretched, and he clapped his hands. When his Chief Clerk came running, he told him to bring in the morning mail, together with his notebook and pencil. While he was doing this, old Desai turned to his younger son and instructed him to stay and mind the business. After he had dealt with his letters, old Desai tottered into the long, dark room which was his general office. His half dozen more junior employees all rose to salute him obsequiously. He made this round of the office daily, pausing to poke into every small detail that caught his eye. Occasionally, he left some young man trembling and ashen-faced, after being upbraided. All his employees were in some way related to him, and it was unlikely that he would ever discharge one of them; but he held the purse-strings tightly in his rheumaticky hands, and it took devoted service and slavelike hours of work to loosen them.

After having left a trail of moral destruction in the office, he returned to his younger son in a more amiable frame of mind. He wanted to compliment him on his deduction that Mahadev was probably alive, and he considered giving him the emerald ring he always wore. He half slipped it off his finger; then his lifetime habit of parsimony re-asserted itself, and he slipped it on again. Words, however, cost nothing, and he left his son considerably cheered up, when he finally climbed into his carriage to drive himself to the University.

From the depths of his dusty cubicle, Dean Mehta's secretary informed him that the Dean was at the Marwari Gate temple and would be a little late that morning. He looked at his watch, and said, 'He should be back in about ten minutes.'

'I'll wait,' Desai decided, and he was shown into the Dean's office.

The secretary returned to his work and Desai could hear him shouting down the telephone. Desai fretted that he should have telephoned before he came. He had a telephone in his office on which he received incoming calls, but he could never bring himself to make a call. Lines could be crossed, he worried, and the contents of very private agreements be overheard by outsiders; skeletons might rattle in family closets; thieves might overhear. The telephone was, indeed, not something to be used lightly. In fact, most telephone calls received by the Desais resulted in one or the other partner driving over to see the caller.

The Dean came in slowly, his ascetic face mirroring clearly his sharp abstinence from food that day and his lack of sleep.

He bade Desai welcome and sent for tea for him. He then sat, amazed, listening to his story. In the back of his mind, he wondered if Mahadev had absconded. Though Desai had not mentioned it, he guessed that Mahadev had been carrying valuables, probably jewellery. A fortune in jewels would be a great temptation to a young man who would know how to dispose of them and who seemed to like living in the West.

They discussed whether to tell Anasuyabehn and decided that she had better know. A rumour would disturb her almost more than knowing the truth of the matter.

The Dean asked what assistance he could give. His brother, he said, had already arrived to help with the wedding and was supervising the delivery of supplies for it.

'If you hear anything that might bear on my son's disappearance, would you let me know?'

'Naturally, I will.'

The Dean forced himself to stand up and see Desai out to his carriage. As they walked along the corridor, quiet except for the occasional burst of a lecturer's voice as they passed a half-closed door, Desai said that, if Mahadev was all right, he wished to bring forward the date of the wedding. He wanted to send the boy and his new wife to Paris again for a little while.

The Dean foresaw cries of objection from his sisters and his sister-in-law; women were always so fussy about ceremonies – and the astrologer would be full of forebodings, no doubt, at a change of date. He was, however, a little uneasy. Since her first outburst, Anasuyabehn had said no more to him about breaking the betrothal. Aunt had assured him that the girl now seemed quite reconciled to it.

155

Yet, he felt, he would be thankful when it was over; his last family responsibility would have been fulfilled.

As they paused at the top of the front steps, he said, 'The preliminary invitations have been sent out, but I'll hold back the second ones and the special invitation letters, until I hear from you.'

Desai smiled and saluted him. 'A-jo,' he said, and got back into his shabby, little carriage.

CHAPTER TWENTY-FOUR

'Where can a woman cry in peace?' Anasuyabehn asked herself miserably, as she went back home from the park. She felt that if she did not cry soon she would choke. Her last stronghold, her bedroom, was at present invaded by her two cousins. They would not leave until after her marriage – and, after that, she would cease to be a person in her own right and be an appendage of Mahadev's.

Apart from her grief at Tilak's behaviour and her approaching marriage, she was still haunted by memory of the fearsome monk. Her religion, with its ruthless rules for the purification of the jiva, the soul, during each rebirth, had re-asserted itself that morning in a most alarming way.

In betrothing her to Mahadev, her father had broken only a rule of caste, which had crept into the originally classless, casteless Jain belief. Jainism had, at first, been a movement of revolt against caste, she thought, and, to be honest, he was marrying her into a group which epitomized Jain life.

If she ran away with Tilak, she would commit the sin of

filial disobedience and would, in addition, marry a man of another religion, a high-caste Hindu. Even to love a man so much was in conflict with the teachings of her religion, she moaned to herself. To become too attached to anything or anybody was a prelude to suffering, and, as tears welled up in her, she knew the teaching had meaning.

'When are the merchants bringing wedding saris to show you?' broke in one of her cousins excitedly. 'I'm longing to see them.'

'Ask Aunt,' replied Anasuyabehn shortly. 'She has it all arranged.'

They turned hopefully to the old lady, to ask about everything to do with the marriage. 'When shall we visit the Desais? Can we go to a potter's yard? We want to mark his wheel with red powder and buy some pots for the marriage booth? And Lord Ganesh must get an offering of rice from us and have his elephant head specially marked, mustn't he, Aunt? Respected Aunt, do tell us?'

Aunt laughed and answered them amiably, while the object of all the preparations trailed slowly behind her and began to regret bitterly her sharpness with Tilak. Perhaps, she argued, he had been held up by his work, so that he could not meet her. And there simply had to be a reasonable explanation of his attendance on Miss Armstrong, if she could only think of one.

The servant had put out string beds on the roof for the gentlemen and on the veranda for the ladies, each bed swathed in a mosquito net.

On arriving home, the Dean immediately excused himself and went to his study to perform his evening devotions, while his more worldly brother betook himself to the roof with a copy of *Gone with the Wind* and a flashlight by which to see to read it. The older ladies retired to one end of the veranda to say their prayers and sink thankfully into their beds. The younger ones sat, cross-legged, on their beds and loosened their long plaits of hair, while they continued to whisper across to Anasuyabehn for some time. She was taciturn in her replies, however, and eventually feeling a little deflated they curled up and slept.

Anasuyabehn could not rest. For greater comfort, she took off her blouse and wrapped her sari loosely round herself. Her throat ached with suppressed tears.

Finally, she slipped out of bed and went into the house. There was no light under the study door, so she assumed her father had gone up to bed on the roof. She made her way to her own room and switched on the light. The heat of the house was almost intolerable, but the need to cry was urgent. She paced up and down restlessly; the tears, so long repressed, would not come.

Undeniably, Tilak still had the intention of marrying her; otherwise, he would not have bothered to follow her to ask about the passport. She understood the importance of the question; a large deposit was needed in order to obtain one, and government procedure was extremely slow.

Well, she had a passport, obtained when she had accompanied her father to a conference in Sri Lanka. The problem was how to get this information to Tilak and how to ask his forgiveness for her rudeness.

Her cotton sari was soaked with perspiration. She went to the window, opened it and leaned her head against the iron bars. There was not a breath of wind. She stared aimlessly out at the rural scene lit by a moon partially shrouded in dust. She hoped that houses would never be built behind her father's bungalow.

Then she remembered that, unless Tilak moved quickly, she would soon leave this pleasant home for the cramped and ugly Desai Society, behind high walls in the inner city.

158

She had not yet seen it, but she could well visualize its crumbling walls and worn steps, its wavery, tiled roofs, its lack of fresh air. Aunt had told her that not many people lived in its multitude of rooms, that the business took up a number of them. She thought of Mahadev's little girl wandering, solitary, through them. What was she like, after being pushed about by a spiteful aunt? Anasuyabehn felt suddenly cold at the thought of having to establish her seniority over her future sister-in-law — her aunt had warned her about this. And then there was the lonely, sad uncle whose wife and children were already dead. What was he like?

'I can't face it,' she cried softly. 'Tilak Sahib, how can I get a note to you?'

Her question was answered as if she had rubbed a magic lamp. From outside the window came an urgent whisper, 'Put the light out.'

Mouth half-open in surprise, she stood motionless, and then began to giggle almost hysterically.

'The light, Bahin.'

Still giggling, she went obediently and switched the light out.

'Come to the window,' pleaded Tilak.

She stood with her hand on the switch, trying to calm herself. She succeeded only in bursting into tears.

'Come, Rani.'

She ran to him, tears pouring down her face. Putting her arms through the bars, she clasped them round Tilak. A very delighted Tilak slipped his arms through the maddening bars to hold her as best he could. The bars bit into their flesh.

'My love, my dear love,' he murmured. Endearments and passionate kisses passed between them, and the passport was momentarily forgotten.

Suddenly, from the roof, Anasuyabehn's uncle shouted, 'Who's there?' Keener of hearing than his elder brother, he leaned over the parapet and swung his torch wildly about, the darting beam moving too fast to pick out any single detail.

Without a further word, Tilak slid away from the windowsill. Like a squirrel, he streaked along the backs of the bungalows, then cut across the field path into common land, where he lay panting in the dry grass, until the lights went out again in the Mehta home. Then he jogged back to his room, cursing under his breath.

CHAPTER TWENTY-FIVE

The following day, Dean Mehta asked his brother to come into his study. 'I must tell you something,' he said.

His brother had just washed his mouth out after lunch, and a few drops of water still clung to his chin. As he followed his brother into the stifling room, he dabbed his dripping face on his sleeve.

Contrary to the best advice of his guru, the Dean had an electric fan. Though he could not bring himself to stop using it altogether, he turned it off during his fast days.

'A fan,' the guru had said, 'injures the souls in the air. Yours, being electric, can also kill insects.'

Today, the fan was back in its cardboard box, and the windows were shut to keep out the onslaught of the afternoon sun. The heavy Western desk and chairs, the crowded bookcases, added to the oppressiveness of the atmosphere. Because of the extra people in the house, the boy servant had not had time to attend to the chattyas, the heavy copra mats which covered the outside of the windows and usually dripped comfortingly with water to cool the room. There was nothing to mitigate the sweltering weather.

The Dean's brother wondered how he was going to endure the house for a whole month. He deposited himself on one of the stuffed chairs, which immediately caused him to perspire even more.

The Dean told him briefly of Mahadev's disappearance. He did not mention his own suspicions that Mahadev might have absconded. He ended by saying, 'I shall, of course, tell Anasuyabehn. She has a right to know.'

'Anasuyabehn isn't very lucky, is she?' his brother responded glumly. 'If Mahadev turns up, we'd better hold the marriage as soon as possible, before anything else happens.' And then I can go home to an air-conditioned house, he added to himself.

'It's odd that you should say that. Desai said the same thing this morning. They have some business in France they want to send Mahadev to attend to; they want his wife to go with him.'

The younger Mehta scratched miserably at the sweat rash on his stomach. 'Certainly we can manage it, if Sister is agreeable.' He examined the backs of his hands thoughtfully; the skin was already dry and cracking from Shahpur's desert climate. 'Anasuyabehn was not very keen on this match, was she?'

'Not at first,' replied the Dean. 'It came as a surprise to her. Her aunt assures me that she's quite happy about it, now she knows more about the family.'

'It was a pity we could not find her a scholarly man.'

'Well, those we considered were either without prospects – and I wanted her to do better than our poor sister – or they were personally unprepossessing. And young Desai is

161

really keen on her. He sent her a superb diamond, you know.' He sighed, and then added a little defiantly, 'He's not ignorant either. He's a matriculate and has travelled a lot.'

The younger Mehta nodded. Then he suggested, 'Perhaps she should be a little more tightly chaperoned until her marriage – to avoid any hint of scandal.'

'Scandal?' The Dean looked shocked.

'Well, you know what people are,' his brother said defensively. 'She has a lot of freedom.'

'Well,' responded the Dean. 'We'll tell her aunts that she is not to go out of the house alone.'

Relieved that he had persuaded the Dean to have Anasuyabehn chaperoned, without having to mention to him vague suspicions aroused the previous night, he offered to send the girl in to see her father.

He found the ladies on the veranda. Each had a piece of needlework in her lap, but they, too, were wilting from the heat, and the needles were not being plied. When he came over to them, Anasuyabehn got up from the floor and her uncle could not help but observe the change in her from yesterday. The silence and the pinched look had gone from her. She was radiant, and when she spoke it was with the excitement of one in a fever.

He told her to go to her father and he watched her, as she vanished into the bungalow. He felt that she certainly had the strength of character to carry on an intrigue with a considerable amount of duplicity. Had he heard a man's voice last night or had he imagined it? he asked himself. Had she been saying her prayers, as she said she had? One did not pray in the dark, and, as he came down the stairs from the roof, he had distinctly heard a light being switched on. Her window had been shut, when his wife had gone into her room – he had asked particularly. Miss

162

Anasuyabehn was up to something, he was sure, but he could not accuse her without proof.

He was worried about a scandal for another reason. Soon his daughters would face the same shortage of marriageable men as Anasuyabehn had. He did not want the problem made worse by a scandal in the family. Some castes were short of women and a girl could take her choice of eager young men, but amongst the Mehtas, at the moment, there seemed to be a real dearth of males. He must tell his wife to watch their girls, he decided.

Further down the veranda, Aunt was watching *him* out of the corner of her eye, wondering why the Dean had sent for his daughter. She, too, was giving thought to possible husbands for her nieces, and was going over in her mind all the young men who might be eligible. Unlike their father, she had taken into account that they were nearly a decade younger than Anasuyabehn – a different generation. 'Ah,' she exclaimed, satisfied, as she managed to thread her needle and at the same time recollect a possible sixteen-year-old boy.

CHAPTER TWENTY-SIX

'This man you've sent me to work for, this Tilak Sahib, is very strange,' remarked Tilak's new servant to his uncle, Ranjit.

'He's no stranger than most modern people. Be thankful for a job. Now you can eat well – and, with care, you can make a little money,' Ranjit scolded.

They were seated on John's back veranda, sharing what

was left over of John's breakfast porridge. Having dispatched Tilak to his lectures, the nephew was on his way to the vegetable bazaar and had stopped for a minute or two to report to his uncle.

When he saw that Ranjit was cross with him, the boy immediately became obsequious. 'I'm grateful for the job, Uncle.'

'It isn't Tilak Sahib's fault that he has to cut up fish for a living,' Ranjit remarked. 'It's his father's fault for training him so.'

'Is he a fishmonger?' the boy asked, horror creeping into his voice. 'I thought you said he was a professor.'

'He is, he is,' replied Ranjit testily, as he collected up their dishes. 'He studies the insides of fish and frogs.'

The nephew's distaste, as he digested this information, was apparent on his ratlike face. Then he said uneasily, 'He went for a walk in the middle of the night – so late that the moon was beginning to set. What man in his senses would do that?'

Ranjit had the answer immediately. 'Perhaps he went to look at his experiment in the University.'

'What's an experiment?'

'I don't know,' said Ranjit truthfully, 'but I have heard from other University servants that, sometimes, professors go at night to check their experiments.'

'Oh,' said his nephew, and was satisfied.

Tilak was, however, news. Ranjit mentioned the late walk to another servant, joking that he might be hunting for another frog. This servant told the joke to someone else, and in due course it reached Miss Prasad's woman servant, who was one of Aunt's main sources of gossip, and Aunt learned that mad Dr Tilak went hunting frogs all through the night. She filed the information, with a lot of other more juicy titbits, for further use.

164

*

In the late afternoon, Ranjit went to town and ordered a tonga to come out to the house that evening, to take John to the home of Mr Lallubhai, one of the district's wealthier millowners.

Though Lallubhai was very rich, he was also a very conscientious man. His mills might hum with machinery forbidden by the Jain religion and turn out more cloth than any other works in India, but he combined in himself much that was good in a Jain gentleman. He provided housing for his workers which was the envy of other Shahpur citizens packed together in shocking slums. A small hospital, properly staffed, took care of the health of his workers, and a school for children up to the age of ten had recently been opened in his compounds. When building his house, he had installed outside his gates an extra water tap. This tap was considered miraculous because, no matter what the time of day, water ran out of it – and it ran fast, unlike the miserable trickle of the municipal supply. The tap was for public use, for all castes, and it was used with gratitude by Jain, Hindu and Muslim.

As John paid the tongawallah, and the chowkidar opened the gates for him, he watched the red-clad or white-clad women filling their water-pots. Amongst them stood Diana wiping her hands with her handkerchief. She smiled when she saw him, and the women all paused in their task, while they watched the couple.

She held out her hand to him, her discomposure at the end of their last meeting forgotten. 'My hands felt filthy from travelling on the bus, so I was washing them,' she explained.

John nodded, continuing to hold her hand and smile at her; she had four blue bracelets on her wrist, he noticed, and a hell of a lot of freckles.

165

A burst of giggles from the women, as they hoisted their water-pots on to their heads, made him drop her hand hastily. 'We should go in,' he said.

They turned and went through the heavy gates covered with beaten silver, and approached the huge, marble-trimmed bungalow. One broad picture window was lit up and they could see, on the inner wall of the room, a large copy of the famous painting of Gandhi and Nehru sitting together, a picture which graced many Indian homes. John grinned. The austerity of the great leader, clad only in his loin-cloth, seemed a bizarre comment on the ostentation of the house.

John's stick clicked across the terrazzo terrace. He could not think of anything to say to Diana and felt awkward in consequence. He thought she looked charming and he wondered that she had not been approached by someone like Lallubhai to become either his mistress or his wife. Diana could have told him, had he asked, that she had become quite adept at turning down such offers.

He found himself indulging in thoughts suspiciously close to jealousy, when Lallubhai seated her on a settee next to him. Lallubhai's wife also noticed the seating arrangements. She was an extraordinarily beautiful Madrasi woman, her red sari draped round her shoulders to make a frame for a face marred only by an expression of cynical boredom. John bowed to her and sat down himself. She may be beautiful, he brooded sourly, as he accepted glasses of water and fruit juice from a bearer, but in this provincial backwater, Diana, with her red hair, is unique.

Lallubhai cracked a joke with Diana and made her laugh. Then he called the meeting to order. He might enjoy dallying with a pretty woman, but he was, first and foremost, a businessman with little time at his disposal.

Within half an hour, John found himself with enough

mapmaking to last him through six months of spare time. A garrulous assistant from the City Engineer's Department, already overwhelmed at being amongst such wealthy people, was appointed to help John.

John was amused by the expressions on the faces of the remainder of the Committee, as Lallubhai apportioned to each of them a slum district to be visited, censused, as far as possible, and recommendations made regarding it. Since many of the slums were as horrifying as those of London in the eighteenth century, John was not altogether surprised at their sudden lack of enthusiasm. The police hardly ever visited such places and they were avoided by the health authorities, except at times of epidemics. The whole Committee quailed visibly and began to make excuses.

At last, a Christian missionary spoke up. He was a ghostlike, malaria-drained man from the American Middle West, white-haired, withdrawn. Though his voice was querulous, his white hairs demanded respectful attention.

'Gandhiji said that we *must* help ourselves,' he told them gently. 'If we can clean up and improve the city, we shall be acting on his behest. A healthier city benefits all of us – we shall have less to fear from disease, for one thing.' He paused, and put his hand on the back of John's chair for support.

John remembered when he had first come out to Shahpur, a brash, vulgar man with a text always on his lips. He had not had much success with his mission, but Shahpur had moulded him into a very fine person. Now, he put courage back into the Committee. He shamed them with Jain and Christian texts and his own eighteen years of work in the city. As they rose, they promised, resignedly, to do as Lallubhai had asked them.

The old missionary sank down into his chair again, and John shifted himself round so that he could shake his hand. At the same time, he became aware of Lallubhai's rumbling bass voice, accompanied by Diana's protesting contralto.

'Miss Armstrong, you cannot go home alone at this time of night, even in a tonga. I won't hear of it. I have ordered a car for you; it will be at the front door in a few minutes. Unfortunately, I cannot accompany you . . .' He looked round, and at the same moment John turned back from the missionary. 'Ah, my dear Dr Bennett, I wonder if you would take care of Miss Armstrong. My chauffeur will drive you both to your respective homes.'

Diana's green eyes twinkled momentarily, though she resented John's obvious alarm.

'Why – why – of course.' John leaned heavily on his stick, as he got up from his chair. 'Delighted.'

Snugly ensconced in the back of Lallubhai's air-conditioned Cadillac, the uniformed back of the chauffeur comfortably anonymous in the darkness, Diana sat quietly by John, her hands folded in her lap. Nothing indicated the dejection within her. He had not really wanted to escort her – and why should he? She felt, suddenly, despairingly lonely.

'Do you think this survey will ever be carried out?' John asked her. Her sweet and heavy perfume was from Lucknow, he guessed.

'Yes, it will,' she replied. 'Lallubhai will see to that. He is so powerful – and he has a most vindictive tongue at times.'

So she didn't like Lallubhai all that much. In case the chauffeur understood English, he quickly changed the subject.

He said cautiously, 'I wonder if you would like to walk for a little while in the Riverside Gardens?'

She sparkled immediately and said she would.

John redirected the chauffeur, much to the man's disappointment. He had been wondering what an Englishman did when he was left alone with a gorgeous woman, and now he would probably never know. He clicked his tongue irritably and swung the car around.

A Cadillac stopping by the park gates caused a rush of

beggars, each with his cry of woe. John had a busy moment or two while, with his stick, he kept them away from Diana. With good humour, he spoke to them in Gujerati, the homely language learned as a child from his beloved Ayah.

'Hey, Brothers,' he cried. 'Leave me enough so that I, too, may eat.'

They grinned at him, and whined, 'In the name of God, Sahib, you do not know the pain of an empty stomach.'

'I do know,' he said, and pushed pennies into sore-covered hands. The memory of his hunger in prison made him generous. 'Now, chelo,' he ordered them, and the chowkidar reinforced his order to them to go, by threatening them with his lathi.

Though she was not afraid, Diana kept close to him. So often, she had to face such people alone. Though their diseases, their starvation, their filth grieved her, one could get overwhelmed by sheer numbers.

They strolled into the nearly deserted park and John's stick thumped heavily on the asphalt path.

A man who had been leaning on the balustrade, his head buried in his hands, looked up suddenly. They were upon him before they realized he was there.

The light of a lamp fell full on Tilak's face, a face ravaged by weeping and lack of sleep, so filled with despair that it was hard to recognize the usually fretful, dogmatic man.

'Are you ill, old man?' John asked in concern, while Diana diplomatically stepped back a little.

'No, Bennett Sahib.' Tilak straightened up and made a great effort to appear calm. He rubbed his hands over his face. 'I may have a touch of fever, that's all. I thought it might be cooler down here. The servant you sent is very good – cooks quite well – and it hasn't dawned on him yet that the tradespeople pass our room by.' He rattled on, 'Ah, Miss Armstrong – it's pleasant down here, isn't it?'

Diana smiled shy acquiescence. Her nurse's eyes ran over the careworn face. Yes, probably fever – though, to her, he seemed terribly distressed mentally. Pity overcame her disappointment at not having John to herself.

John prepared to say goodbye and walk on with Diana, but Tilak was reluctant to let them go; it did not occur to him that there were times when John could do without him. When they moved, he moved with them, talking about odds and ends of campus news.

At first Diana left John to answer him. The serenity of the night enfolded her, a golden moon in its first quarter, a cloud of stars, the perfume of flowers ground to dust in the scorching daytime heat. Then, feeling that perhaps she should help John out, she interrupted the men to say brightly, 'Isn't the sky clear! No wonder poets praise the night.'

Tilak pounced on her remark and said, 'Poets create romantic illusions, Miss Armstrong. Romance has no place in India.'

His sharp response was unexpected, and she replied a little nervously, 'Come now, Dr Tilak. Indians are just as romantic as Westerners, and the winds of change have made them more able to express it, nowadays.'

'There *are* some of us who try to assist the wind, Miss Armstrong,' he admitted. He shivered, though there was no breeze to chill him.

John had listened uneasily to the exchange, and now he said, 'You're shivering. Perhaps you've a touch of malaria. You should get into bed soon.'

Tilak shrugged, as if to indicate that it did not matter if he had.

They returned to the gate. John gave up hope of having Diana to himself that evening; it would have to await another opportunity. 'Let's take a tonga between us,' he suggested. 'We can take Diana home first.' Tilak agreed absently and left John to bargain with the tongawallahs. A bargain was struck with a Muslim as thin and brown as an old pipe cleaner, and they climbed into the awkward little carriage.

In the enforced proximity, knees touching, bodies swaying together, the two Europeans could feel Tilak continuing to shake. They both expressed their concern.

Tilak shook his head. 'It's – how do you say in English – a goose walking over my grave. I'll feel better later on. Don't worry.'

As they passed under a street lamp, however, Diana saw that his eyes were fever-bright. He's terribly overwrought, she thought anxiously. She ventured to advise him, 'As a nurse, I prescribe three aspirins and bed.'

He agreed to do as she had said. How could he explain to her, he thought, that the shivering was caused by a fearful apprehension? A primitive scenting of danger to himself.

He was overwhelmed by worry that he would not be able to whisk Anasuyabehn safely away, before she was married to Mahadev, and that it was almost impossible to communicate with her. His nerves were screwed to breaking point and he did not know which way to turn.

At Mrs Jha's house, John got down to see Diana safely to her door. He waited patiently while Mrs Jha could be heard fiddling with the great brass bolts on the other side. He looked down at Diana. She smiled at him, and very gently he bent down and kissed her on the cheek. At that moment Mrs Jha was checking on them through her peephole. She was greatly shocked. Her thin lips were even thinner, as she let her lodger in.

Diana herself was agreeably surprised and gave him another smile, as he said goodbye.

He climbed back into the carriage and said to Tilak, 'We can go first to your hostel and the tongawallah can drop me on his way back to town.'

Tilak had been wrapped in his own thoughts, but he said that he would prefer to get down at John's bungalow and walk over to the hostel.

'But you've got fever,' protested John.

'It's a fever of the mind,' Tilak snapped, his voice full of wretchedness.

'All right,' agreed John, and at his bungalow they had an amiable argument as to who should pay the tongawallah. John won, on the grounds that he would have taken a tonga, anyway. He was worried enough about his friend to offer him a drink before he went to the hostel, and this was accepted by Tilak with evident relief.

Tilak sipped cautiously at his whisky and water. It did not taste quite as foul as he expected; he would rather have died than admit that he had never tasted whisky before. Shahpur was a prohibition area, and John obtained a small ration of whisky each month, on the grounds that he had drunk it all his life and was, therefore, an addict. He was much teased about it.

Troubled by the ravages wrought on his friend in a few distressing days, he watched Tilak thoughtfully, as he sipped his own drink.

The unaccustomed alcohol loosened Tilak's tongue. He spoke first of the English Fellowship and then, more slowly, about his desire to take Anasuyabehn with him as his wife.

When he heard this, John sat up in his chair, pain in his legs forgotten.

'Look here,' he said. 'The only way in which you can marry Anasuyabehn is by formally asking her father, or getting your uncle to ask for you.'

'If she has a passport, she could be married to me in a civil ceremony in Bombay and we could go straight on to the ship. The problem is that the Fellowship does not commence until October, and she is scheduled to marry this Desai fellow next month.'

'That would, anyway, be tantamount to an abduction in the eyes of the law, here. Dr Mehta is my old and trusted friend; I could never be party to the abduction of his daughter.'

'I'm not asking you to be.'

'Well, there's another point. I wouldn't like you to face a charge like that in a local court. Apart from its being a very serious charge, you're a Maratha – and they'd have your blood.'

Tilak made a face. 'Gujeratis are not very fond of us, are they? We are also not very fond of them.' He sighed heavily. 'You know perfectly well that the Dean wouldn't even give me a hearing. Every time I meet him in the corridor I can see him trying not to throw up again – and some of his Arts colleagues are positively insulting.'

John sat taut and attentive. Unless he was stopped quickly, Tilak might ruin himself, and end up being thrown out of the world of scholars – and out of his family, as well. He suggested gently, 'Look, Tilak. You've got this Fellowship. Take it. Go and work under Diamond – it's a chance in a thousand. Forget about Anasuyabehn. Mahadev is a decent man in his way, and her father, I believe, knows it.' He paused for breath, and then added persuasively, 'There are other women in the world, Tilak, women educated to your level. You'll find someone else in time.'

While John had been speaking, Tilak had left his chair and, with his hands clenched in his pockets, had been walking slowly up and down the room. Now, he went to

173

the door and flung it violently open. He glared out at the inky shadows in the compound.

He was furious; he dared not speak. One word would have loosed an avalanche of anger on to John – and in his heart he knew that John was the only true friend he had in Shahpur.

He ran down the steps into the darkness. The compound gate slammed after him.

CHAPTER TWENTY-SEVEN

Mrs Jha shut the door on John, replaced the padlock, and then turned to Diana. Beneath hooded lids, her black eyes were full of suspicion, and her lips were tight with disapproval; it was not seemly for a young woman to be seen home by a man. When previously Diana had been to meetings at Lallubhai's house, she had always been driven home with a number of guests, both ladies and gentlemen, in the car. Once she had arrived home having been driven in solitary grandeur by Lallubhai's chauffeur, which was bad enough; but after all a chauffeur was hardly a man at all. Now Mrs Jha awaited an explanation, while Diana stood in the hall in a half dream.

Mrs Jha rattled her keys, and Diana came out of her reverie. If she did not wish to lose her room, some explanation of John's presence was necessary.

'Mr Lallubhai asked Dr Bennett to bring me home,' she said. 'He's a very learned man – some people say he is a sage – who lives near the University. He writes history books about the Gujerati people.'

Mrs Jha's imagination was captured.

'Books about us?' she exclaimed.

'Yes,' replied Diana, with suitable gravity. 'He's made the Gujerat famous in America and England, as a place of learned and pious people.'

'Ramji! Fancy, books about us. And he is a sage, you say?'

Diana smiled.

'Well, not quite,' she said, 'but he lives a bit like a monk.'

Mrs Jha's face fell. Although she had disapproved of Diana's being accompanied home by a strange man, she was disappointed at being robbed of a secondary interest in a romance. A sage, indeed!

She moved down the passage, hitching her sari as she went, while Diana turned towards her room. Sages in ancient days were known to fall from grace, the old lady ruminated hopefully, and this one had certainly kissed the girl, which was quite shocking.

Diana took off her dress and wandered about her room in her cotton petticoat. With a mind hopelessly over-stimulated, she abandoned all thoughts of going to bed for some time and decided that, in spite of the noise it would make, she would do her washing.

She got out the wooden paddle with which to beat the wet clothes on the veranda floor, a bucket of water made warm by the sun, a bar of common soap and the cardboard box of dirty clothes. Methodically, she sorted the clothes, taking each garment carefully out with her fingertips and shaking it well away from her, in case a scorpion or a snake should have taken up residence. Then she went through her skirt and blouse pockets to remove dirty handkerchiefs.

And there it was.

Fluttering silently to the floor from a handkerchief, a minute piece of paper with a blue line across its creamy whiteness. Diana watched it fall, her brows knitted in perplexity.

'Now where did that come from?' she muttered, and bent down to pick the scrap up.

The movement reminded her. Of course, she had picked it up on the way to Pandipura. She smiled at the thought of how she had amused herself by wondering how it came to be at the foot of a cactus in the bush.

Then the smile died, her eyes widened. She knew what it was.

The dead donkey! Her patient's fear! The missing noise in the village! It all fell into place.

Her first thought was to run to the police. But, no. These were not like British policemen – she might find herself in a dreadful mess with them. Then go to ask John's advice? That was hardly practical at eleven at night.

Her heart pounded and she ran her fingers feverishly through her red hair, as she sought for the best way of dealing with the unnerving revelation.

'Perhaps I should do nothing at all,' she dithered uncertainly. Then she remembered the Englishwoman lying dead in her First Class carriage in the robbed train, and indignation rose in her.

'It might have been me,' she thought.

Absent-mindedly, she picked up a garment, damped it and began to scrub soap into it. She rubbed and scrubbed and beat the washing in a spreading sea of soapsuds on the veranda floor. Then, as she rinsed her clothes in a bucket of fresh water, she decided that Dr Ferozeshah would be the best person to consult. He was intimately bound up in the life of the city and would understand all the factors involved.

'I'll ask him as soon as I go on duty,' she decided, and shook out a towel so forcefully that it made a sound like the crack of a bullet.

CHAPTER TWENTY-EIGHT

Unwilling to take a tonga, which would draw too much attention to them, and having long since exhausted the limited bus service, the uncles of Mahadev trudged from village to village. Where there were Desai Societies in a settlement, they commenced their inquiries at them. Failing that, they went to a member of the Panchyat, the Village Council. They did not neglect the miserable corners in which lived the Untouchables; the weavers, the tanners, the lavatory cleaners. Though they tried to make their inquiries casual, the news flew from mouth to mouth and, at times, a train of curious children and officious, advice-giving elders trailed along with them.

Occasionally, their queries about a Bania they were to meet and had somehow missed, as they put it, caused an electrifying attention, and they discovered that police, on bicycles, had already been through some of the villages seeking clues to the train robbery and a missing man.

After he heard this, Partner Uncle hired bicycles from a small shop. He and his servant wobbled along sandy lanes, cursing the heat and the dust and the smells, but progressing at least a little faster that they had done previously.

Partner Uncle was not a young man and, by late afternoon, he was trembling so much from exhaustion that he could no longer balance on his bicycle. When they reached a small well, he bade his servant dismount.

A young Hindu shepherd was drawing water for his sheep. The flock baaed and swirled around him, as he filled a trough for them from the waterskin. He paused, and politely offered water to the weary travellers. They thankfully squatted down, and he poured water from the skin into their hands. Trickles of the cool liquid ran down to their elbows and splashed pleasantly on to their sandalled feet.

With a grunt of relief, Partner Uncle wiped his dripping chin on his sleeve and sat down, cross-legged, under a nearby tree which gave a straggling bit of shade. His servant sat with him.

Both shepherd and sheep eyed them doubtfully. Then the shepherd settled his plum-coloured turban more firmly on his head and returned to watering his flock. As he guided the rope quickly over the well wheel, he shouted above the noise of the sheep, 'Have you come far, Brother?'

'We have,' replied Partner Uncle. Then he asked, 'The railway must run quite near here?'

'Yes,' agreed the young man and gestured towards the horizon. 'You can see the telephone poles that run along the top of the cutting.'

Uncle scrambled up to have a look.

'That's where the train robbery took place,' went on the shepherd.

'Were you here when it happened?' asked Partner Uncle, with sudden interest.

'No, sir.' He bent over the trough to empty the skin, still looking at the Banias out of the corner of his almond-shaped eyes. 'I took the sheep home, because I felt a dust storm was coming. It was time for supper, anyway.'

'Yes?' encouraged Partner Uncle, sensing that there was more to come. A blankness crept across the shepherd's handsome face, however, and he silently let down the waterskin into the well again. The wheel squeaked mockingly.

Frustrated, Partner Uncle tried again. 'Have you seen another Bania going this way? We were to meet him at the village back there, and we have somehow missed him.'

This innocent question caused the shepherd to blench. His hand shook so much that the rope nearly came off the wheel.

Used to the evasions of bad payers, Partner Uncle suddenly roared at him, 'You *have* seen him. Has he been hurt – or robbed?'

The boy cringed. 'No, sir. No.' His eyes were wide with stark fright. 'No – no one's passed this way, today – except for the milkmaids going to and from town – and the vegetable sellers very early this morning.'

The sheep scattered uneasily at the sharp voices. Uncle's voice came like a trumpet. 'Perhaps not today – but a day ot two back. He did, didn't he?'

'Sir, I don't know your friend,' came the fearful reply. 'I've no remembrance of a stranger doing business in our village.'

Uncle's voice dropped, and he wheedled, 'Come, lad, I mean no harm – but I do need information about such a man. I'm sure no traveller would be assaulted in your village. You can, therefore, safely tell me what it is that you have seen.' He palmed a couple of rupees and let them show out of the corner of his hand.

Grey-faced, but with his eyes on the money, the boy began to babble. 'Sir, we stole nothing. We took good care of the stranger – yet, it's best when dacoits are about to say nothing.'

'Quite, quite,' agreed Uncle, trying to be patient. He made himself smile as he looked down at his plain, respectable white shirt and homespun dhoti. 'It's obvious, at least, that I'm not a dacoit – only a businessman from Shahpur. You can speak safely to me. I'll tell no one else.'

'True, Bhai,' replied the shepherd, trying to stop quivering.

'Well, what happened?'

The shepherd gulped. 'Sir, it was like this. My eldest brother was returning from market in our ox-cart – on the day of the storm. He knew a storm was coming, too, so he took the new road along by the railway – it's easier for a cart to travel on, though it takes a little longer.'

'This was on Monday afternoon?'

The boy counted on his fingers. 'Ji, hun,' he agreed. 'It was already dark by the time he reached the cutting and the storm was howling round him. Being alone, he was afraid and he stopped to light the lantern for the cart. In the darkness and the wind, he couldn't find his matches, and then he heard horses nickering and thought they must be tied to trees nearby. Now, horses are not much used here, sir. And my brother wondered who would stop in such a lonely place in a storm – they would surely press on to seek shelter in our village. My brother became too afraid to advance up the road, so, as quietly as he could, he drew the ox-cart off the road and tethered it, hoping that the cacti would mask his presence.'

Partner Uncle could well visualize the nervous, superstitious peasant caught in the storm and fearing devils, robbers, angry gods.

'Yes, yes,' he said impatiently.

'My brother crept away from the cart and lay in a hollow. He saw flashlights flick on and off, but the dust was so thick and the night so dark, he couldn't see who was holding them. Then, through the earth, he heard the vibrations of the Delhi Mail approaching. There was a big explosion – and rifle fire – and the train stopped, instead of roaring onwards.'

The shepherd had now forgotten his fear and was

absorbed by his story, embroidering in the details. 'He thought for a moment that the war with Pakistan had started – because we're only forty miles from the border, sir. Anyway, there were shrieks and cries – a woman screaming, and a rush of people, first down the cutting and then up again. Along the road and then across country the horses clattered, like devils sucked up into the sky.

'My brother lay perfectly still, quite safe, thanks to the storm – and, after a while, he heard the railwaymen shouting to each other, and the train started up.'

'The Bania?'

'I'm coming to that, sir. Did you say two rupees, sir?'

'Four, if you can tell me where he is now.'

'I don't know exactly where he is, sir.'

'Well, what *do* you know? Why are you telling me this long tale, which I can read in any newspaper, if you don't know?'

'Peace, Brother,' the shepherd's voice began to shake again. 'How will you understand if I don't tell you from beginning to end?'

Anger being a mortal sin, Partner Uncle did his best to swallow his. 'Well, what happened then?'

'My brother lay a long time in his hiding place. When nothing more happened, he crept back to the ox, listening intently. He got the cart back on to the road again and wrapped his turban round his face, because the sand was still blowing. He led the ox, for he still feared to show a lantern light, and continued slowly down the road. He had not gone very far, sir, when he heard a loud groan, right at his feet. Now, what would you have done, sir?'

With eyes closed, Partner Uncle stood up and stretched himself. 'I'd have fled,' he said sarcastically and then swore under his breath, mentally promising forty-eight minutes of penance to wash out the oath.

'Not my brother,' boasted the shepherd with pride. 'He looked about him, and, by the side of the road, saw a vague white bundle – like a fallen ghost.' He paused for effect. 'It moved a little. He advanced carefully, fearing it might be a wounded dacoit. It was a big, stout man weeping with pain – a townsman, he guessed.' The shepherd spread out his hands in a gesture of helplessness. 'My brother didn't know what to do. He went to the cart to get the lantern, however, and succeeded in lighting it.

'The man was a sorry sight, his face all covered with blood.'

Partner Uncle exclaimed in alarm.

The shepherd nodded, and went on, 'My brother wiped the blood from his nose and eyes. He tried to lift him up to put him on the cart and bring him home, but the man was too heavy for him and cried out in pain.'

Partner Uncle was, by this time, striding up and down in great apprehension. He stopped in front of the shepherd. 'Well, what next?'

'Brother took the blanket from round his own shoulders and covered the man with it – a good blanket, sir, now ruined by blood. He whispered to the man to try to keep quiet and he would bring help. He then tethered the ox again – because oxen are slow, sir – and ran home in the teeth of the storm.

'Five of us went out in that terrible storm, sir, and found the man and put him in the cart and brought him to my father's house. My mother washed away the blood and found he had two wounds, one on the top of his head and one in his shoulder. He was unconscious but mother said no bones had been broken. She bound him up – and all night we sat and wondered what to do. Ours is a very small village, sir, since the cholera killed so many, and my father is the eldest elder. The responsibility was his.' The

182

shepherd paused for breath, and then asked, 'He must have been a passenger on the train? Would he be your friend?'

'I believe so,' replied Partner Uncle, and then, as the shepherd showed no sign of continuing the story, he queried, 'Well?'

The shepherd evaded Partner Uncle's anxious glare. 'Sir, the sun is going down. I must take the sheep home.'

Partner Uncle swelled with sudden rage; the veins on his forehead stood out. He swept his arms above his head and shook his fists, like an avenging god. 'What is this?' he shouted. 'What happened to my nephew?'

The countryman cringed, and responded uncertainly, 'Your nephew? Sir, you *must* speak to – to father.'

Partner Uncle screamed again in rage, his voice echoing round the empty countryside. Pointing a finger at the unfortunate shepherd, he advanced threateningly towards him, only to be brought up short by milling sheep. The boy stammered, 'Come home with me, sir. Father will explain to you.'

The frightened sheep eddied between them. Afraid that his furious master would have a fit, the servant caught him by the arm, and implored, 'Master, keep calm.'

Partner Uncle shook off the restraining hand, but he did thereafter try to control himself. 'Very well,' he snarled. He picked up the hired bicycle and motioned to the servant to pick up his. The sheep were called and herded to the path. In the blinding dust raised by ninety-six little feet, Partner Uncle followed the flock and its shepherd.

Partner Uncle found little solace in being half-choked by dust, but his anger cooled and his quick brain went to work. It did not take him long to realize why the boy had stopped his tale where he had. After cleansing the wounds, the old father would naturally look to see if his unexpected guest had been robbed, by checking his money belt; and if it was indeed Mahadev and his money belt was still round his waist, the old man would have been faced with the terrible temptation of a fantastic fortune having arrived in his poverty-stricken hut. How easy to add to Mahadev's wounds, take him back to the cutting during the night and bury the money belt under the floor until such time as it seemed safe to remove himself, his family and the fortune to another part of India.

During the twenty minutes' uncomfortable walk, Partner Uncle felt it would be a miracle if Mahadev and the jewels were both safe.

Infinitely thin and wrinkled, Jivraj lay on his string bed. He struggled up to speak to Partner Uncle, however, and bade him sit beside him while he heard his business. Then with many a sly look over his shoulder, he confirmed his son's story of the robbery, and sent for his elder son, his nephews and his brothers, who all corroborated it. Though dreadfully afraid, not one of them said a word of how the robbers themselves had pounced on the village, uttering terrible threats and sweeping away all their donkeys with a promise of their safe return in a few days' time. In a matter of minutes in the dark night they had come and gone, leaving dismay and near panic behind them. And then, before the night was done, Jivraj had been faced with the problem of the wealthy, wounded stranger.

Now he must cope with this hard-faced Bania, just when it appeared that the train robbery was all but forgotten and all that remained was for the donkeys to be returned; he had no doubt that they would arrive home safely since their loss would cause comment all over the district, and the robbers would not wish to leave any indication of how they got out of the province.

'But where *is* my nephew?' demanded the frantic Uncle.

'Ah, Sahib, has no word come to you from the police?'

'No!'

Jivraj looked bewildered.

'But the doctor promised to find out who he was and inform the police, so that word might go out to his family.'

'Doctor?'

'Yes, Sahib. The morning after the robbery the stranger had high fever, and we feared he might die.' He looked helplessly at Partner Uncle, 'And then how would I explain away to the police a corpse with wounds?'

Another man pushed his way forward. 'I remembered that I had heard the white doctor was visiting a few villages away, so my son went for him.'

Partner Uncle took a large breath and relaxed a little. 'Did he come?' he asked.

'Oh, yes. He came with his big lorry. He said the Bania was very sick and had a bullet in his shoulder. He also needed medicine which the doctor didn't have with him. He asked what had happened, and we told him. Then he brought a cot from his lorry and we put the Bania on it and lifted him in. The doctor Sahib said he would take him to his hospital and inform the Shahpur police. We were deeply afraid of being implicated in the train robbery.' He stopped and looked uneasily round the group of anxious men who had gathered. 'The doctor said he would explain to the police for us – that he knew us to be honest men. He comes to the village occasionally.'

Partner Uncle stood up. 'Where's the hospital?'

The villagers looked at each other. Then one said, 'It's to the north – on the other side of Shahpur – ten or fifteen miles from here.'

'That side of Shahpur is desert. There couldn't be a hospital there.'

'That's where it is.'

185

A younger man bent down and whispered in Jivraj's ear, and Jivraj said to Partner Uncle, 'It's a God hospital – a Christ one.'

'Ah, a mission?'

Dusk was falling, and a woman of Jivraj's family came out of the hut with a lighted charcoal fire held in a pair of tongs. She put it down, put a covered bowl by it and began to slap rolls of dough between her hands to flatten them into rotis, preparatory to cooking them.

Jivraj looked at the exhausted old moneylender and was touched by the sadness in his face. 'Sir, if you can eat our food, one of my sons will serve you under the tree over there.'

Moneylenders are not popular in villages and Partner Uncle was surprised by the offer. He was glad to accept, however, and then he added, 'It's too late to find the hospital tonight. I'll return to Shahpur and set out again early in the morning.'

To his surprise, Jivraj said, 'To return to Shahpur from here is very simple. When they made the new road, they built a station for us at the nearby railway. In about an hour's time, a local train will come down the line. It's about a mile to the station.' He bridled with pride in the new facility.

So Partner Uncle found himself eating good millet bread and sag with a little yoghurt, under a tree in a strange village, and ruminating on the unexpected courtesy and kindness of country folk. Deep inside he felt a trifle ashamed of the many times he had, in years past, pounded money out of just such people.

'Ah, well, they owed it,' he thought, as he scraped the last bit of sag off the palm leaf on which it had been served.

'Not at 144 per cent interest,' said his conscience.

The young man who served him was the shepherd he

had met at the well, and he put the promised four rupees into his hand; the boy took them without protest, as his due. An older man then brought a lantern and led them, as they pushed their bicycles, over an almost invisible track down to the small railway station.

There are no words of thanks in the Gujerati language and Partner Uncle did not offer to pay for his meal, but the villagers knew and Uncle knew that a bond of hospitality had been forged between them. One day, when the opportunity arose, it would in some way be repaid.

Less than two hours later, Partner Uncle was reporting to old Desai, who himself had had a fruitless day.

'I know of the hospital,' said old Desai. 'It is called the Mission of Holiness. Once I met that doctor.' He picked his toes thoughtfully. 'I formed the opinion that he was not altogether trustworthy – you know how one senses it?'

Partner Uncle sighed, and nodded.

'Tomorrow, Baroda Brother and I will go to the hospital and inquire. You must rest.'

Partner Uncle agreed. It did not occur to either of them that the Mission of Holiness might be on the telephone – nor was it.

CHAPTER TWENTY-NINE

Tilak never remembered clearly how he got through the night and the following morning, after leaving John so precipitously. A veil seemed to be cast over his conscious mind and he was guided merely by habit.

Realizing that the Sahib was in some way ill, his servant made up his bed and suggested that he sleep. He helped Tilak off with his clothes and held back the mosquito net while his master silently clambered into bed. After a while, he slept.

Soon after daybreak, the servant brought him hot water for shaving and then a brass tray of breakfast. After he had laid out clean clothes, he sat down in a corner and wondered apprehensively what Uncle Ranjit would say if he ran away.

Tilak shaved mechanically, turning over his lecture notes as he did so. A plop of shaving soap fell on them and he wiped it carefully away with the towel. He continued to read while he ate wheaten porridge and drank some milk. Then he put the notes into his briefcase, dressed, gave the servant money for the day's food, and walked down to the University.

Though the sun was already well up, he shivered occasionally as though he were cold. It was not chill, however, but rather an inner perception that he faced a long, hard road to travel. He felt helpless, unable to accept the bitter facts regarding Anasuyabehn, which John had pointed out the previous evening.

When he arrived at the Arts and Science Building, some

of his students were hanging about outside it. They looked sullen and turned away from him, but he was too absorbed in his own problems to notice them. Inside, other students were hurrying to lecture rooms. They stared at him as he strode unseeingly to his own lecture room. He opened the door and walked in.

The room was empty.

Surprised, he looked at his watch. He was punctual. He put down his briefcase and took a few uncertain steps towards the window. Then he wheeled around and went out to the corridor again.

While the last students scurried through doors, like rabbits down their burrows, the Vice-Chancellor's secretary hurried up to him.

Tilak asked, 'Do you happen to know if they changed the room for my lecture? Is the Dean in yet?'

The secretary blinked excitedly from behind thick spectacles. 'The room? I don't know. The Dean has just gone over to the English Department. Dr Prasad, however, wishes to see you now.'

'I can't possibly see him now. I have a lecture – only all my students seem to be late or are in the wrong room.'

The secretary replied portentously, 'They are not late, Sahib.'

'What do you mean?' A fuming irritation at the fool standing before him began to invade him. 'Well?' he snapped.

'They're on strike, Sahib.'

'Strike?'

'Yes, Sahib. That's why Dr Prasad wants to see you.'

Seated in front of the Vice-Chancellor, Tilak looked at him amazed. He had not heard Dr Prasad's opening words, except that he realized that his tone was sympathetic. Now Dr Prasad was saying, 'This is a situation which I had not

189

foreseen. It will be the work of three or four hotheads. I have sent for Dean Mehta – he will know who are likely to be the miscreants, and I can assure you that disciplinary action will be taken.'

He waited for Tilak to say something, but Tilak was so taken aback that he was beyond words. All this because of a little dissecting? It was absurd. Yet, in his heart, he knew it was not absurd. He had struck at the roots of Jain belief.

'Would you like to take some leave while we deal with this?' asked Dr Prasad.

'Of course not,' Tilak assured him. Anger began to take the place of surprise and he felt like throwing something at the dolts who could not see that India, whether its inhabitants liked it or not, was a part of the twentieth century.

'I suggest leave, my dear Dr Tilak, because Dr Bennett mentioned to me, when I saw him recently, that you had had a brick thrown at you. It disturbed him because it happened on campus – and students are apt to be a little unstable.'

'Are you afraid of violence of some sort?'

Dr Prasad hesitated, and then said, 'I shall try to avoid it, of course.'

'Well, I'm not afraid of it – my mother and sister have gone back to Bombay, so I don't have to worry about them.' He laughed sardonically, and commented, 'It would be ironical if our Jain friends took to violence to defend non-violence!'

'It would, indeed,' agreed Dr Prasad sadly. 'But I hope it won't come to that. Meantime, I really think it best if you went on leave for two or three weeks.'

An hour later, the University's Head Peon was dispatched to town to make a reservation on the Bombay Express for that afternoon. Tilak's servant went scuttling down to the river, to rescue his master's shirts from the boiling vats of the washerman, and Tilak himself tried to deal with the chaos in his room.

Sheets, mosquito net, blankets, bedding roll, were spread all over the floor, as a result of his flustered servant's efforts at packing. Clucking with irritation, Tilak made up his own bedding roll and packed a trunk with his books and papers. As he worked, he considered how to let Anasuyabehn know of his impending absence. Dr Prasad had turned down the idea that he remain in the city, but not teach. 'It's better to be right out of it,' he had insisted. He felt physically weak and the sweat rolled down him, as he struggled with leather straps and recalcitrant buckles.

He began to weep helplessly and sat down suddenly on the bedding roll. Would it be better simply to walk out of Anasuyabehn's life? Go away to Bombay and never come back?

He gave a shuddering sigh. He couldn't do it; he must at least let her know what had happened. After a little consideration, he decided to ask John to deliver a note to her.

He scribbled a quick explanatory note to her, saying he hoped to return in two weeks, and enclosed it, unsealed, in another note to John. His servant could take it over to him.

Anasuyabehn, too, had spent a bad morning, wondering how to inform Tilak that Mahadev was missing, that there was a chance he had been killed, but that, if he were found, her wedding would take place sooner than expected.

She did not want to wish a man dead. This unexpected happening, however, made her hope that he would be missing long enough for the marriage to be deferred.

In the late afternoon, while the aunts and her cousins slept and Dean Mehta went back to the University, she sent the boy servant to the students' hostel, with a cryptic note giving some indication of her predicament.

191

'Go first with this,' she instructed him, as she handed him the chit, 'and, on the way back, buy some fresh pan leaves from the pan seller up the road. Give the note only to Dr Tilak. Nobody else. Do you understand?'

The little boy grinned slyly and slipped quietly out of the sweeper's door and up the field path. At the hostel, he found himself facing a padlocked door.

The wife of a student, baby on hip, was standing at the door of the next room, and she asked him what he wanted. He told her that he had brought a letter from Dean Mehta's daughter to Tilak Sahib.

'From Dean Mehta,' she corrected.

'No. Bahin wrote it herself.'

The woman looked thunderstruck. Then she said cunningly, 'Leave it with me, little Brother. I'll give it to him when he comes in.'

He held it behind his back and took a step or two away from her. 'No. It's for Tilak Sahib only. When will he be back?'

In a fury of curiosity, the woman answered him, 'He went away with all his luggage this afternoon. Perhaps he won't come back.' She started to advance towards him. The child turned, and ran helter-skelter down the stairs.

The middle-aged mother of another student opened her door further down the passage. 'What was that?' she asked the woman with the baby.

The woman told her, and so the story was sent on its way. Two days and several dozen gossips later, it was said on the campus that Dean Mehta's daughter was pregnant by Dr Tilak, who had fled to escape the consequences.

CHAPTER THIRTY

While Dr Ferozeshah was preparing to receive the morning rush of outpatients, Diana showed him the piece of paper she had found and told him of her deductions.

'Keep out of it,' Ferozeshah advised promptly.

'But the police might be able to trace the dacoits if they knew about this,' protested Diana. She was dressed in her white, nurse's uniform and was getting together the doctor's stethoscope, his thermometer, cotton wool and bottle of disinfectant and putting them ready on his desk.

In response to her protest, Ferozeshah said firmly, 'Never go near the police unless you have to.'

'I haven't done anything wrong!'

'Neither of us has. But once they are here, they'll hang around and expect to be fed – and if we really want anything done, they'll expect suitable baksheesh.' He finished buttoning up his white coat.

'Oh,' said Diana, immediately deflated.

'Cheer up. I'm sure you're right. But, at best, that piece of registered envelope you found is a clue; it's not concrete evidence against the dacoits. And, you know, the villagers will be punished – and the dacoits would still get away with it.'

That evening, after an early dinner, Diana went on the bus to see John and ask his opinion. Ranjit admitted her and managed a polite smile, a smile that faded immediately he returned to his back veranda; it was replaced by a look of great anxiety.

John agreed with Ferozeshah. 'I've heard that they have

193

sent a good man down from Delhi to investigate, because of the murder of that Englishwoman. Let *him* get on with it.'

Diana sighed. 'I suppose you're right – I felt so clever working it all out. But how will those poor people in Pandipura cope?'

'I bet the donkeys are back in the village by now. The villagers haven't suffered much and they'll all be as quiet as mice – they don't want the dacoits to burn the place flat next time they come this way.'

'That's awful! It's bullying!'

'We live in an awful world,' responded John almost flippantly.

His acceptance of human wickedness surprised her. It savoured of a Hindu outlook.

He continued. 'They probably had a plan to get the proceeds of the robbery out of the province and, because of the storm, it went wrong, so they pounced on the nearest village – they needed transport that fitted into the landscape and could carry, say, builder's sand, with the loot buried in it. Donkeys would be perfect. Horses stick out like sore toes, here.'

'Why use horses at all?'

'Speed – to get away from the scene, in the first instance. They probably had a string of camels waiting, and missed them in the dark and the dust.'

'My patient was so frightened and worried that she nearly died.'

'That's too bad. Is she all right now?'

'Yes. She'll be OK.'

'Good. I say, can you stay to dinner?' he asked shyly.

Diana looked up at him and smiled. 'I'd love to,' she said, and hoped she could eat a second meal.

John took up his stick and went to consult Ranjit. The bearer agreed morosely that he could provide enough food. John turned to go back into his room.

'Sahib . . .'

'Yes?'

Ranjit, seated on the floor in front of his precious Primus stove, looked up. He looked as sour as a piece of dried tamarind. 'Nothing, Sahib,' and he leaned forward to pick up his paring knife.

Really, John thought, Ranjit was a queer old stick sometimes.

As he re-entered, John asked Diana, 'Do you happen to know Anasuyabehn Mehta?'

'No. Who is she?'

'Dean Mehta's daughter. Lives a few doors down. I just wondered.' He did not like to say that in his cash box lay the love letter for her, left by Tilak's servant earlier that day, which he wanted delivered to her. He had read it. It said simply that Tilak had to return to Bombay and was consulting his uncle. It would mean the world to Anasuyabehn, and, even if Dean Mehta saw it, there was nothing dishonourable in it.

Diana watched him cross the room, leaning on his stick. 'I don't think that you need to use that stick all the time,' she said abruptly.

Startled out of his thoughts of Anasuyabehn, John glanced down at the offending stick.

'Do you have any pain now?'

'Not often, unless I've hit myself on something.'

'I don't think Ferozeshah has examined you for a long time. He's been rushed off his feet.'

'Oh, I only ask him for a sedative. In England, they told me not much more could be done.'

She gazed at John standing uncertainly before her, his face slowly reddening with embarrassment.

'Forgive me,' she said gently, 'for being so personal – but I saw a fair amount of similar injury during the war and

195

how it was treated. I believe you could learn to walk without a stick – and quite straight. It would mean that the rest of your body wouldn't ache so much from being out of position. I imagine it does ache?'

He nodded, and she got up and went to stand in front of him. 'Would you like to try?' she asked. 'I'll help you.'

She was not a tall person and seemed very diminutive to him. Her eyes crinkled up with humour, and she said, as if she had read his thoughts, 'I'm quite strong.'

'I wouldn't mind having a bash at it.'

'OK. I need first to see exactly how you put your feet down. Put your hands on my shoulders and I'll walk backwards, while I watch your feet.'

He laid his stick on the divan and shyly put his hands on her shoulders. It was so long since he had touched a woman that, at first, his thoughts were not about learning to walk. He stumbled, only to be steadied by a surprisingly strong arm round his waist.

Diana held him for a moment; then quickly let her arm drop, afraid that her instinctive movement might be misconstrued. John was thinking, 'She's too bloody innocent for words.'

'Let's try again,' she said in her bright, professional voice, and he glumly gave his attention to what she was saying.

He held on to her and advanced as she retreated.

Ranjit peeped through the half-open door and was horrified to see such abandoned behaviour. He went back to his cooking pots wagging his head in a hopeless fashion.

It was even worse when he went in to announce dinner. The copper and the dark heads were bent close together over the desk, while the Memsahib drew indecent pictures of men doing peculiar actions with their legs.

Ranjit hardly slept that night.

CHAPTER THIRTY-ONE

On a littered desk, lay Mahadev's money belt like a pallid, dead snake. Seated before it was a man leaning his head on his clenched fists. He had not moved for twenty minutes.

An increasing ruckus outside the window reminded him that patients were gathering there for morning surgery. He lifted his bald head wearily and rubbed his eyes with his knuckles, to look around his cluttered little office, where the few pieces of furniture were all piled high with dusty records. The corners of the room were festooned with cobwebs, and the uncurtained windows were opaque with dust, a myriad of smears and finger-marks. One window was open and, through it, he could see the dreary, flat, semi-desert landscape shimmering in remorseless heat.

The chatter outside the window increased; the Mission of Holiness was a very busy place, and the missionary himself felt tired to death.

He opened one fist.

On his soft, white palm glittered a beautifully cut ruby, its perfection undimmed by the gloom of the office.

It must be worth thousands, he thought, and glanced at the money belt in front of him. There must be a fortune in that!

The money belt was a plain strip of grubby white cotton, which had been folded and stitched down one side. Along the whole length of the belt, at about one and a half inch distance from each other, lines of stitching divided the belt into small compartments. Judging by the feel of it, each compartment held a stone at least as big as the ruby.

"Strewth, I wonder what it's all worth?' he muttered. 'I bet it'd buy a hundred new hospital beds, the salary of another doctor, two nurses and an operating room – and a stack of penicillin ceiling high. And bibles – dozens of them in Gujerati.'

He again looked at the ruby and smiled grimly.

'I could sell a gem like that in the jewellery market of Bombay or Delhi as easily as falling off a log – and who would know? I can simply say that he had no belt on him when he arrived here.'

As he ruminated, the waiting patients outside were being marshalled into a queue by a middle-aged Indian. The missionary had found him in a ditch, the sole survivor of a family of refugees from Pakistan who had died of starvation.

The whole queue would be suffering from malnutrition, thought the missionary despondently, apart from their heat boils, their venereal diseases, their tuberculosis and heaven only knew what else.

There was a knock on the door, and he hastily swept the belt into his desk drawer, and stood up.

It was only the woman sweeper coming to do the floor, and he walked up and down one side of the room while she swept the other side. The ruby was still clutched in his hand. What was he to do? And who was this man, anyway?

In the waist of his homespun dhoti had been knotted a return Interclass train ticket to Delhi. A small purse, pinned in the same place by a large safety-pin, had yielded twenty-three rupees and some change. His linen had, at one time or other, been marked with a D in Western script. Having found the money belt, the missionary could well understand why his patient had made such a frantic effort to escape from the train.

The sweeper opened the door to the passage and swept through it the dust she had collected. She began to sweep her way slowly and ineffectually towards the front door.

From beyond the door she faced, came the sound of loud, authoritative voices. A rifle butt was banged on the woodwork.

With lightning speed, the missionary shut the door of his office, snatched the money belt out of the drawer and bundled it and the ruby into the wall safe.

The sweeper opened the door and came flying into the room, at the same time trying to touch the feet of the police officers accompanying her. After them came the Mission's head nurse, protesting in Gujerati that the Doctor Sahib was very busy. It seemed suddenly that the room was filled with armed men, though, in fact, there were two police constables with rifles and one officer with a pistol in his holster.

Calmly and benignly, the missionary rose from his desk chair, one hand raised as if to bless. On the desk lay his bible, open as if he had been studying. 'Good morning, gentlemen. What can I do for you?'

The belligerent attitude of the police gave way to faint respect. The small man with the pistol stepped forward and answered him in good English. He said that they were looking for a missing Bania and that they had heard that he had recently had a Bania as patient. Before he could be answered, he turned to the constables and told them to wait outside.

The missionary answered calmly, 'Please sit down,' and motioned his unwelcome visitor to a chair. With his eyes on the doctor, he sat down with a rattle of accoutrement.

On his part, the missionary weighed up his visitor. A Bengali by the accent, supremely shrewd, a very senior police officer judging by the good cut of his khaki uniform.

From a corner, the head nurse watched them both, and tried to stop his teeth chattering.

'We do have a man here, who by his dress appears to be a Gujerati Bania,' agreed the missionary.

'I believe he arrived here under unusual circumstances and that he had a bullet in him.'

'Yes. He has had high fever for three days, so we have no idea who he is. Had his temperature not gone down during the night, you would have heard from us today. He is now under sedation. He is obviously exhausted and needs to sleep.'

'I'd like to see him,' said the officer, still watching the missionary.

'He won't wake for at least two more hours. You could try waking him now, of course, but I doubt whether you would get any coherent response from him.'

'You should know that in circumstances such as these, the police should be informed immediately.'

'Ah, yes, of course, quite,' the missionary was at his vaguest, with a gentle smile. 'We have no telephone – and we are so busy – you have seen the queue outside. I could not spare anyone to go to town. I knew he would recover. It was not a question of murder.'

'It's a question of attempted murder,' replied the Bengali tartly. 'I'll leave a constable to sit by his bed, and I'll return in about two hours; I've other business in the neighbourhood.' He stood up, ready to leave. 'Exactly how did this man come to you?' He had already heard the story from the Mission's lorry driver, who had been roughly questioned a few minutes before, but he wanted to hear the American's version.

Now, he found that it tallied quite well with what he already knew.

'The Pandipura villagers saved his life, of that there is no doubt,' the missionary told him. 'They are to be commended.'

'It would seem so,' grunted the officer.

After the officer had gone, the American took out the money belt and carefully eased the ruby back into it. Then he went to see his patient.

Mahadev was sleeping quite relaxedly and his colour was good. By the bed, sat a police constable, his rifle across his hairy knees. He was already dozing.

'Are you ready, Doctor Sahib?' his nurse inquired. 'There's a long queue.' He had his hand on the door latch of the dispensary.

The American sighed and said he was ready. How much penicillin would a ruby buy, he wondered?

CHAPTER THIRTY-TWO

That morning, old Desai was so anxious that, for the first time in his life, he missed reading his morning mail. After drinking a glass of milk, he set out at daybreak for the Mission of Holiness. A servant drove the carriage, and Desai snarled at him unceasingly to hurry.

The old man had a brass box of lunch on his knee and a full water-jar on the seat beside him. Next to the water-jar, sat Baroda Brother. He was placidly polishing his spectacles on his shirt end; the morning was relatively cool, and he was enjoying the drive through the half-awakened city. By the driver sat his son, thrilled at the adventure.

The narrow city streets gave way to wide gravel boulevards, lined with trees shading the graceful houses and bungalows of the city's well-to-do millowners. These petered out to become a rough track; and the last mile was little more than lorry wheelmarks in the sand, through which the horse could hardly drag the carriage. Finally, the passengers got down and walked along beside the vehicle and made better progress.

Meanwhile, Mahadev lay in his hospital bed, under a mosquito net, and listened. His head ached so intolerably that he could not bear to open his eyes. When he tried to shift himself slightly, the pain in his back made his senses reel. One of his arms seemed to be tied to his chest. A short distance from him a number of voices made a steady hum — he wondered if it were the dacoits and lay very still, so as not to betray his presence.

Then he realized that he was in a bed of sorts, and made himself open his eyes for a second. He caught a glimpse of an old-fashioned English screen making a wall around him. Above the wall, he could see a shelf with glass containers sitting on it; over them a squirrel scampered.

He tried to think.

That was it! The trip to Delhi, to return the Maharaja's jewels. He had borrowed against them to set up a radio factory and now he wished to pay his debt.

The jewels!

With his unconfined hand, Mahadev felt round his waist. The belt was gone.

The shock was so alarming that he tried to sit up, only to fall back as rivets of pain went through him.

'Doctor Sahib,' called a voice beside him, and he forced himself to open his eyes again.

He did not know what he had expected, but the sight of a constable gaping down at him was a further shock. Apprehension about the loss of the stones gave way to fear for his personal safety. What had he done that he should be under arrest? In a split second, Mahadev saw himself flung into a filthy prison or, at best, reduced to utter poverty, a lender of single rupees.

In response to the call, a man came round the screen. An Englishman! The sense of lunatic nightmare increased.

'Ah, I see we are better,' the missionary said, his professional smile covering his own despair. 'I'm probably damned if I steal that belt,' his thoughts ran, 'and, if I don't, I'm condemned to this unmerciful round of watching patients suffer for the lack of simple drugs. Why, O Lord, why?'

He took the patient's wrist in pudgy, capable fingers, and added to himself, 'And if this guy pays his bill, I'll be lucky.'

'How's the head?'

Mahadev ignored the question. 'Where am I?' he asked.

'You're in the Mission of Holiness Hospital. I brought you in from Pandipura, near Ambawadi.'

'How badly am I hurt?'

'Bullet lodged in your shoulder – I've got it out, and a neat furrow across your skull where another one hit you – that was a near thing.' He turned and asked the constable to help him prop up Mahadev, while he looked at the head wound. The constable, who had never been in a hospital before, was fascinated, and did what the doctor ordered very carefully. Mahadev cried out with pain, however.

The doctor was undoing the bandages round his head. 'You'll be OK,' he assured the shattered moneylender, who was certain nothing would ever be OK again. The conversation was in Gujerati and the police constable watched and listened attentively. 'What happened? Do you know?' the doctor asked.

'The dacoits must've been short of men, because none of them caught hold of my carriage door, so I opened it and slipped down on to the track and ran for the embankment. A huge dust storm was raging – confusion – horses – screams. I started to climb further up the embankment where there were trees and bushes. They must have seen the movement.' He sighed and winced. 'When I came round, the train had gone.' He stopped; the effort of talking was too great. The missionary removed the dressing, and when the pain of it subsided, he went on, 'I remember trying to crawl to the new main road – and a woman washing me.'

The constable spoke. 'It's better to stay in the train in a raid by dacoits. If you hand everything over quickly, you're usually all right. Not so with Muslims, of course.'

Mahadev looked at him sourly and nearly shrieked when the missionary muttered, 'Ah, healing nicely,' and clapped a new dressing on to his head. When he had replaced the bandages, he said, 'Well, sir, you've had a lucky escape. Later on today, you could try moving around a little. But, first, I want to look at your shoulder. And I want to know who you are, so that I can inform your family.'

Sulkily, Mahadev told him. He wanted to ask where his money belt was, but was frustrated by the presence of the constable. Never tell the police anything, had been drilled into him from childhood. Of course, he thought miserably, the police themselves might have the belt, in which case he would leave to his father the delicate negotiations to get it back.

'What day is it?' he asked, and was thoroughly perturbed to hear that it was Friday morning. The raid had taken place on Monday evening.

As the doctor worked, he chatted, partly to cover his own worries and partly to reassure his patient. 'A police bigwig will be here in about half an hour, to question you,' he informed his patient.

'A *Delhi* police chief,' interjected the constable reverently. He had parked his rifle against the bed, so that he could see better what the doctor was doing.

Mahadev closed his eyes and tried not to feel too bitter. A Jain gentleman was forgiving, patient under affliction. He did not feel like that – only cross and petulant and dreadfully weak.

He realized that the glass bottles ranged around the wall contained pickled specimens of foetuses, and his empty stomach began to heave. Fortunately, a woman in a white sari brought him some water to drink and distracted his attention. She was followed rapidly by the tramp of boots across the floor, heralding the return of the tiny police chief.

A little later, a triumphant and much relieved old Desai was shown into the dispensary. He stumped across the room, muttering that private initiative had been better than the perfidious police force. Had he not found his son himself?

He was much chagrined when, rounding the screen, he saw a very yellow and shrunken Mahadev lying on a bed and an obviously frustrated and fuming police chief sitting cross-legged on the chair beside him; Mahadev was not going to be much use as a witness.

The police chief looked up, as the old man entered, followed by his brother-in-law and nephew. He understood something of what was passing through old Desai's mind. The police had, in finding Mahadev first, scored over him. He immediately felt better and rose politely to salute him. 'Here is your son, sir. You may take him home as soon as you wish.'

Driving back from the Mission of Holiness in the early afternoon, old Desai was very quiet. It had been agreed that Mahadev should remain in the hospital for two more days. Baroda Brother-in-law asked him, 'Are you worrying about Mahadev?'

'No, the boy is obviously recovering. That English

doctor knows what he is doing.' Old Desai could never remember that Americans were not English.

'It's what he was carrying?'

'Yes. We couldn't ask him with the police all round him.'

'Where do you think it is?'

'It's not with Mahadev. He touched his waist and made a tiny gesture to indicate that.'

'It'll be a frightful loss.'

'We shall have to pay. It's our reputation which is at stake. We've never failed to return securities lodged with us.'

'Do you think the train robbers took it?' asked Baroda Brother, thankful he did not have any share in Desai's business.

Desai replied slowly, 'I suspect that the English doctor has it.'

'What? He would've told us.'

'Not all English people are so honest.'

'It couldn't be. Anybody could've taken it when he was unconscious.'

Old Desai did not agree. He had not built up his enormous business without acquiring a profound knowledge of human nature. Like the Bengali detective, he sensed that the Mission doctor was hiding something. The man was disturbed in some way, and such a fortune would tempt the holiest of men.

'Have you told the Maharaja anything yet?'

'I sent a telegram saying that our representative would be with him in a few days' time.' He chewed his lower lip. 'I don't know yet *what* we send him, however.'

Their gate was opened by the chowkidar, who had been watching for them, and the whole family and staff swooped upon them.

Old Desai creaked slowly down from the carriage. He

picked up his silent, wide-eyed, little granddaughter. 'Papa is coming home in two days' time,' he announced to her, 'and I think Aunt should get the tailor to stitch you a new dress for the occasion.'

The child smiled and relaxed, her head on his shoulder. Dear Grandpapa.

CHAPTER THIRTY-THREE

'I wish your father would make up his mind when the marriage is to take place. Everything is upset. The astrologer says he can't find a better day than was originally arranged. Now it's got to be changed, and the wedding invitations have the wrong date on them,' Aunt grumbled to Anasuyabehn.

Anasuyabehn hardly heard her. The boy servant had just returned from his visit to the hostel. She could see him through the window, cowering in a corner of the compound, apparently afraid to enter the house.

'Your father said that it was your future father-in-law who wanted the date brought forward,' chimed in the visiting aunt.

'I should imagine that the tailors will need at least another three weeks to finish the stitching,' interpolated the eldest cousin. She was stroking, with avaricious fingers, a gift of three silk saris still sitting amid its wrappings on the floor.

Aunt pursued the subject of the change of date. 'I don't quite know what the fuss is about,' she admitted. 'Mahadev has not yet returned from Delhi.' She wondered if there were any truth in the rumour she had heard that he had disappeared, but felt it wise to keep that to herself. She turned again to Anasuyabehn. 'Immediately after your marriage you are to go to a place called Paris in England – very strange to me – in my day, you would have remained at your father-in-law's house.'

'Ji, hun,' agreed Anasuyabehn. She went to the window. 'Bhai,' she called to the servant. 'Hurry up, now. Light the stove on the veranda for me, and put some water on for the lentils. I'll be out in a minute.'

'Let me help,' offered a younger cousin, who had taken a great liking to Anasuyabehn.

'No, no. The boy will do most of the work – I must just guide him.' She made an effort to smile at the golden-faced girl, and, after a little while, made her escape to the side veranda, where she could already hear the fire crackling in its little stove.

'Gone away?' she exclaimed to the boy, as he handed back her note.

'Yes.'

'Who told you?'

'A lady next door.'

'Did she see the letter?'

'No, Bahin.'

'Good boy.' Her whole body trembled with fear and, again, before her eyes danced the calm face of the monk, the all-seeing eyes ripping her secrets from her. Bad actions brought bad results. Had Tilak fled because she was already affianced? How cruel could men be? He had promised – and he had failed her.

She held on to an old water-pot stand for support, as the veranda whirled around her. She felt trapped, like a ground squirrel cornered by dogs. Until Tilak came striding into it, her life had seemed useless and empty. Now, he was gone like fluff on the wind, without a word to her. Spasms of pain shot through her and perspiration poured down her face.

Her cousin wandered through the door from the kitchen. 'Bahin!' she cried in alarm and ran to her. She put her arms round the swaying girl, while the servant squatting by the fire watched nervously.

'I'm all right,' murmured Anasuyabehn through clenched teeth, ' . . . heat made me faint.'

'I'll get mother,' said the girl.

'No,' cried Anasuyabehn sharply. 'I'll sit down – it's only heat.'

Her cousin lowered her carefully to the floor and she leaned her head against the cool stone of the water-pot stand. Her cousin took the water-ladle from its hook and filled a brass jar with water. She then dipped her sari end into it and, kneeling down by her, she dabbed Anasuyabehn's face with it.

The cold water revived her and she surreptitiously slipped her note to Tilak into her waistband, under cover of her sari. Then she very gratefully put her arms round her cousin and leaned her head on her shoulder. Her cousin, mystified but sympathetic, held the trembling bride-to-be, and instructed the servant to get on with his work.

'Let me ask mother to come,' she begged Anasuyabehn, after a few minutes.

'Don't worry. I stayed too long in the sun this morning, talking to Savitri.' Her courage came slowly back to her and she again was able to put on her armour of patient amiability, so that her cousin was finally convinced that, indeed, nothing much was wrong.

CHAPTER THIRTY-FOUR

A week later, Mahadev Desai, accompanied by several members of his family, came to the Dean's home for a little ceremony. Some fruit and a green stick were solemnly buried in a hole which was to hold one of the supporting poles of the wedding tent. The story of his adventures had preceded him and, with his arm in a sling, he was looked upon as something of a hero. He was unusually pale and moved about very carefully. He was allowed to see his bride-to-be at the ceremony, but did not get much chance to speak to her. After the visitors had had tea and departed, three carpenters took over the compound and proceeded to dig holes all over it for the remainder of the supporting poles.

Their activities impeded the delivery of sacks of grain, sugar and pulses and tins of vegetable oil, all of which the Dean had had to buy on the black market, because some were rationed and some were in very short supply. He and Aunt, therefore, went to the big storeroom to see the stuff weighed. They already had a house full of guests and, closer to the wedding day, would have to feed many more, including the Desai contingent. To accommodate everybody, a house down the road had been rented.

There was a lot of gossip amongst his current guests on the pros and cons of the marriage; such things were always picked over and examined in detail in families. But it was public gossip which was worrying Aunt, as she scolded the coolies for being clumsy.

That morning, the Vice-Chancellor's ayah had dropped

in to pay her respects. The ayah always knew a lot about the doings on campus, so Aunt had edged her away from the visitors and back to the compound gate, while they talked. The ayah was simply breathless to confirm with her that what she had just heard was not true and that the wedding was, indeed, going forward. She felt it her duty to inform Aunt that there was a rumour that Anasuyabehn was expecting by Dr Tilak and that he would be forced to marry her. Aunt had been shocked to her very sandals, had scolded her and sent her packing with instructions to deny such a calumny everywhere.

Anasuyabehn was not with child, that, at least, Aunt was sure of. Only last week she had kept the three days of retirement from cooking and other household tasks, which she had kept ever since she was fourteen. And Aunt had herself dispatched the bloody clouts to the Untouchable washerman. As for her virginity, that was another matter. And Aunt was very apprehensive about this.

Anasuyabehn had done obediently everything she was required to do in connection with the marriage. The whole family had, on Mahadev's return, been to dinner at his house and the girl had sat quietly with the women who would be her in-laws. Mahadev's little daughter had been brought to her during the meal, and she had persuaded the child to sit with her and had fed her with food from her own tali. According to the Dean, this had pleased old Desai greatly when he heard about it. Mahadev had put in a limited appearance because he was still quite weak, but he had smiled on his bride when she arrived. But would he, quaked Aunt, smile if he had been cheated?

She picked up a paper which was being blown about in the draught, her mind elsewhere. She could not read, so she handed it to the Dean. 'Is this a receipt we should keep?' she inquired.

211

The Dean, who was tired, unfolded it impatiently and glanced down at it. His expression changed and he closed his hand over it quickly. 'Come into the study,' he commanded Aunt. Puzzled, she followed him. 'What's up?' she asked.

The Dean closed the door after them. 'Where did you find this?'

Aunt shrugged. 'It was on the floor. What is it?'

'Beloved,' read the Dean, a break in his voice. 'Meet me at the far end of Riverside Park tonight. I will wait from 9 till 11.'

Aunt felt sick. On top of what she had heard that morning, this was too much to bear. What could she say? The hope of being regarded as the family's finest matchmaker suddenly vanished, with all the delights that such a reputation would bring. Instead, she heard the sniggers of the womenfolk and the dirty jokes of the young men. Somehow the Desai marriage had to be saved.

'Is it signed?' she asked, to give herself time to think.

'No. I know the handwriting, though. It's quite distinctive.'

'Whose is it?'

The Dean looked very grim. 'It's Professor Tilak's. He and Anasuyabehn – I would never have dreamed of it!'

I might have done, thought Aunt, if I'd thought about it. With an effort, she asked, 'Is it addressed to her?'

'No.'

'Then it may belong to one of her cousins.'

The Dean disagreed. 'I doubt if they've even met him.' Suddenly he pounded his desk with his fist. 'The stupid girl!' he shouted. 'Bring her to me *quietly* – before that mob outside realizes that anything is wrong.'

Aunt hurried to Anasuyabehn's room. Before opening the door, she slowed to her usual shuffle. Anasuyabehn was seated cross-legged on her bed with three cousins and Savitri. Curled up together, they were chattering amiably. Anasuyabehn was listening, her deepset eyes ringed with black, her mouth drooping.

How ill she looks, thought Aunt. Not at all like a girl about to be a bride. And all Aunt's misgivings returned.

As she approached the girls, she forced herself to smile. 'Your father wants you in his study, niece. Run along, now.'

Anasuyabehn slipped off the bed and hastily smoothed her hair and hitched up her sari. Since the safe return of Mahadev, she had steeled herself to face the fact that Tilak had deserted her and that she must marry the big, widowed moneylender.

The pain of Tilak's leaving her was almost more than she could bear. It ate into her like an acid, an unbelievable anguish. She felt removed from events around her; everything seemed distant and unreal. The slightly smutty jokes her cousins had been making seemed sickening to her; she could not laugh.

The only person who impinged upon her understanding was Mahadev himself. His first task upon his return had been to call upon her, despite the agony of being jolted along in his carriage. They had faced each other, not knowing what to say in front of their relations, she resentful, he longing. Through her misery, she had realized that within him lay a powerful personality; he was not to be trifled with.

When she had been to dinner at the Desai Society, he had found a moment in the bustle of departure to hold her hand. She had looked up in astonishment at the firm, warm touch, her first physical contact with him. He had laughed down at her and she had caught a glimpse of a man instead of a moneylender. She had been afraid.

As she entered her father's study, closely followed by Aunt, she inquired politely, 'Ji?'

She was shocked, when he shouted at her, 'What's the meaning of this?' and thrust a sheet of paper at her.

Bewildered, she took it from him. It was worn at the corners and must have been lying about for days. She bent her head and read it.

Her first reaction was one of overwhelming joy. So he had tried to communicate with her. A singing happiness made her giddy for a moment. She kept her eyes on the missive. The paper was much handled. When had it been written? Of course! He had been in the Riverside Gardens with her. The joy faded, but she held on to the paper tightly – it was part of him.

'Well,' snapped her father.

The desire to protect Tilak was instantaneous, and with elaborate care she lifted her eyes to her father. She made her eyes twinkle and her lips curve in a smile. 'We seem to have stumbled on somebody's little romance – where did it come from?'

Aunt was watching her intently. She's clever, she thought, but not quite clever enough. That letter is hers, all right.

She continued to stare out of the corner in which she squatted, as the Dean, his burst of temper unexpectedly checked, asked, 'Well, isn't it yours?'

'I've never seen it before,' replied Anasuyabehn quite truthfully. 'It's very old. I wonder where it came from – it isn't even signed.'

'Oh, I know who wrote it – the writing is unmistakable.'

'Who?' asked Anasuyabehn, ignoring her father's angry frustration.

'That doesn't concern you, daughter, since you say it is not a letter to you. If it's not yours . . .' He glared at her. 'Then the wind must have blown it in.'

'We've had a great many visitors, including the Desai family,' Anasuyabehn pointed out. 'Any of the younger women could have dropped it.'

The Dean was stopped in his tracks. 'Of course,' he muttered. 'Of course.' He sat down in his chair and tapped his fingers on the desk, while Anasuyabehn waited politely. 'I'm glad that you have not done anything despicable.'

'What she says is very likely,' Aunt interjected, and Anasuyabehn was grateful for the unexpected support.

The distant buzz of talk from relations on the veranda suddenly ceased, as if it had been switched off. Aunt looked towards the door of the room, as if she would love to go to investigate.

Outside, an English voice asked for Dean Mehta.

'Dr Bennett!' exclaimed the Dean. Then he sighed. 'This note is not yours?'

'No, father.' Anasuyabehn hated to lie to her father, but could not find any other safe answer. She turned to go.

There was a knock on the study door. The servant showed John in. He was carrying a parcel and stood diffidently blocking the doorway, not realizing Anasuyabehn's frantic need to escape.

'I've . . . er . . . um,' he began, and looked down at Anasuyabehn. God, how ill the girl looked and almost as if she were going to cry. 'I've brought a little something for Anasuyabehn, if she may accept it. I – er brought it myself, because I was afraid any other carrier might drop it.'

He did not add that he had in his pocket a letter which had far more import to her. Tilak was a damned pest to leave him such a job. He had racked his brains for days to find a way to get the letter to Anasuyabehn, but no opportunity had presented itself. If he had posted it, he knew that the Dean would automatically open it and read it himself, before giving it to his daughter.

Now, on his desk at home, lay his invitation to her wedding reception. And he did not know what else to do, other than buy her a present and watch her marry a man she did not want to marry. Poor kid. She would get over it, he supposed; Mahadev was no fool and presumably knew a bit about managing a woman. He hoped that when Tilak heard the news of the wedding being hastened, he would not blow out his brains.

Caught between loyalty to his old mentor, the Dean, and affection for Tilak, he now stood in the middle of the Dean's study, a box of fine English china in his arms, sensing that he had stumbled in on some kind of domestic crisis.

Dean Mehta was the first to regain his equilibrium. 'Come in, come in. You shouldn't put yourself out on our behalf.' He watched, with growing astonishment, as John walked slowly, but quite straightly, to his desk to put the parcel down. 'You're not using your stick,' he exclaimed.

John grinned with satisfaction. 'Trying to manage without it. I left it parked on the veranda.'

'Well, well. That's excellent. Anasuyabehn, bring a chair for Dr Bennett.'

Anasuyabehn pushed a chair up behind him, and John sat down rather suddenly.

He smiled up at the careworn girl. 'I've brought you an English tea service,' he told her. 'I know the family will shower you with all kinds of beautiful things, but I thought you might enjoy some china – something different.'

Anasuyabehn shyly thanked him.

'May I wish you much happiness,' he said gently.

As if in unbearable pain, her creamy eyelids half-closed, while she nodded a polite acquiescence. John cursed himself for being a clumsy clod; yet he knew that he could not tell her father. Either she or Tilak must speak up.

Anasuyabehn had turned back to her father, 'May I be excused, father? Savitri is waiting for me.'

Her father, his hands clasped on his desk, nodded absently. She said thank you in English to John and went quietly out of the room. Aunt slid after her, making a polite namuste towards John as she passed him. He jumped, not having noticed her presence.

Savitri! Why hadn't he thought of her before? A thoroughly modern woman, who drove her own car and was liable to shock everybody by talking about trial marriages. He was certain she was tolerated in the Dean's house only because her father was a Professor Emeritus. She and Anasuyabehn were great friends – and she was smart.

Whether Anasuyabehn was actually married to Mahadev or whether she was not, she was, John argued, entitled to receive any correspondence addressed to her. Thin, bespectacled Savitri would enjoy being the messenger. Who knows? he reflected. Tilak just might be able to turn the tables, in an honourable and decent way.

And in Bombay, Tilak pleaded for Anasuyabehn before a sardonically amused uncle and a bewildered, affectionate mother. 'You could telephone the Dean at the University,' he begged.

CHAPTER THIRTY-FIVE

The Desai business was too large to be totally neglected during the week before the wedding. Old Desai, Partner Uncle and Mahadev, therefore, stayed in the Desai Society, while the rest of the family moved over to the house rented by Dr Mehta for his guests.

Mahadev had had a trying time commuting between the Society and the Mehtas' home, to attend the various ceremonies preceding the actual wedding day. Though his head ached abominably and his left arm was still in a sling to protect the shoulder while it healed, his paternal aunt had insisted, at one of the ceremonies, that he must have the traditional iron ring tied into his hair. It seemed that every time he lay down, he lay on the ring. He wished passionately that the Mission doctor had shaved his head completely, when preparing to stitch up his wound; instead the doctor had considered that he might be a Hindu and had, therefore, kindly left one longish tuft, to which the ring had been appended.

His father and his Partner Uncle had spent weary hours with him discussing the expansion of the French business. They were all agreed that, in these uncertain times, they should have some money invested outside India.

In one of the earlier marriage ceremonies, he had sat in the flapping marriage tent, with a silent, veiled Anasuyabehn beside him, and had hardly glanced at Ganesh, the benign elephant-headed god, remover of hindrances, who was being worshipped. His mind had been filled with the legal difficulties of the French investment, so much so that he had jumped when a lucky woman, taking four pieces of wood and dipping them in oil, had touched his forehead with them. Then the ring had been tied into his hair.

Ceremonial gifts of rupees had been given to him and to Anasuyabehn. Other money gifts had also been presented by relatives, to be kept until after the ceremony, when they would be divided between his and Anasuyabehn's paternal aunts.

A company of elderly Jains had been specially invited for the later ceremonies; they would inspect the quality and the quantity of the wedding gifts.

Mahadev sighed frequently. Though the marriage festivities would be briefer than those for his first marriage, they were time consuming. It was well that he had been able to get plane reservations for Paris for the second day after the vows had been completed.

Gradually, however, as the day of the actual wedding came closer and his health improved, his mind turned towards his bride and he began to think of the pleasures of again having a wife. He dearly wished to please her and to see her eventually installed in a modern house of her own, where his little daughter might thrive better and have brothers and sisters. He never doubted that Anasuyabehn would care for the child, and in this he was correct.

One morning, he had to compose convincing arguments to persuade the Government of India to allow an overseas investment, and when he finally put down his pen, it was with a feeling of relief that he had done it skilfully. He sat in his dreary office, feeling wells of hopeful anticipation rise in him. He collected up his papers and at the same time began to sing a morning raga. The clerks in the counting house lifted their heads in amazement, as the strains of this devotional hymn came rolling out of the private office.

With a fine disregard for his comfort, Mahadev's brother had been ordered to oversee the wedding party at Dean Mehta's rented house and to travel back and forth daily to supervise the counting house. Now, while Mahadev carolled away in his room, in another little office his younger brother was inquiring of his father, 'What are we going to do about the Maharaja's jewels? I sent a telegram saying we would send another messenger. But what are we to do now?' His plump face creased with anxiety.

His father leaned back on the sausage-shaped pillows of his divan. 'Humph. Didn't Partner Uncle tell you? We shall indeed dispatch another messenger. You're going to go – and take the stones with you.'

He watched in quiet amusement, as his son's weak mouth opened in surprise. There was also a gleam of fear in the younger man's eyes – he knew he was no hero, and he dreaded violence of any kind.

'You'll go by plane – in spite of the cost,' his father assured him.

'But we haven't got the jewels?'

'Oh, yes, we have,' the old man chuckled. 'I put them in the strongroom myself.'

Relief replaced anxiety. 'But . . . but . . .'

Old Desai wagged his finger at his son. 'Your brother's sagacity is something to emulate.'

The younger man appeared to shrink into himself. The small button eyes almost vanished amid the folds of fat. The chin sank down to the chest and the chubby fingers were clenched. So the almighty Mahadev had done something wonderful again.

'What did he do?' he inquired dully.

Old Desai clasped his hands over his stomach. 'Well, it was interesting. Your uncle and I were sitting by the bed at the Mission, wondering how to broach the subject of the missing money belt in front of a constable, who was still there. We didn't want to accuse anyone of taking it, and find we had a libel suit on our hands. Anyway, when Mahadev was dressed and ready to be discharged from the hospital, he sat on the edge of the bed, to rest himself before making the further effort of going to the carriage.' Desai ran his tongue round his few remaining teeth, while he looked at his dejected younger son.

'Well?'

'He was quite clever. When the Mission doctor entered the room, he looked at him and said, "I'm ready to put on my money belt now. Will you kindly fetch it for me?"'

The younger brother was intrigued. 'What happened?'

'The doctor replied, "Certainly." And then he went to get it.'

'How extraordinary!'

'Yes, it was. If he had not intended to keep it – if he could – the Mission doctor would surely have mentioned to Mahadev that his valuables were being kept in safety. With his simple request, Mahadev gave the impression that he remembered the belt being removed from him by the doctor.'

The brother sighed, and old Desai glanced again at him. In comparison with Mahadev, the boy was dull. He was, however, extremely useful; he dealt with all the irritating details of the business. Old Desai thought suddenly of the Maharaja and his brand new radio factory. The Maharaja might be willing to pay an experienced accountant very well, to come to him. And all over India new enterprises were springing up which needed more than an abacus-rattling clerk to keep their accounts; his younger son might easily plunge into a new life, away from his family.

Old Desai did not like these ideas; the boy was flesh of his flesh; he did not want to lose him.

He picked up a memo pad from the portable desk beside him on the divan, and unscrewed his fountain pen. As he addressed his son, he wrote down each point. 'Now that you have reached years of discretion,' he said, as if he had been patiently waiting for his younger offspring to grow up, 'I shall put more responsibilities on your shoulders. I can no longer travel, as I used to, and your uncle is also feeling the strain. This Delhi trip will be the first of many for you, for Mahadev has, in addition to his other responsibilities, to watch the Paris and Bombay businesses.'

He could almost feel the relief shooting through his son's

veins. Just to get away from his wife, thought the old man grimly, would probably cheer him up. And to travel on a plane was definitely prestigious. Though it pained him to say it, he added, 'And you will need to draw more money in future.'

The plump figure ceased to slump. It expanded to its full girth. Dignity descended upon him like a new garment slipped over his head. As a trusted representative of the family, always bustling off to new places, he would at last be able to patronize his wife.

As expected, the Desais had not yet paid their hospital bill. The medical missionary, however, knelt by his bed and thanked the Lord for removing the temptation of the money belt. The muttered prayers ceased for a minute or two, while the sorely tried worshipper rested his head on his string bed. Then, in an almost businesslike voice, he again addressed his God, 'And now, Lord, about some funds. The need of your children is terrible. Must they suffer so?'

Perhaps God heard, for about that time some ladies in California met together and, for the sake of something to do to fill their spare time, decided to have a fund-raising drive to extend the Mission of Holiness near Shahpur in India.

CHAPTER THIRTY-SIX

Though Savitri and her parents, being Hindus, had not been asked to Anasuyabehn's wedding, they were, like John Bennett, invited to a reception to be held after it. Because she was a close friend, however, Savitri came and went freely in the house. Her thin scornful voice mocked the ancient ceremonies, until Anasuyabehn asked her wearily to cease.

Though Savitri's eyes were myopic, they missed little. She had guessed from Anasuyabehn's lack of enthusiasm that her friend was not very keen on the marriage. She had suggested that if Anasuyabehn was not happy she should refuse the offer. Anasuyabehn had said dryly that she had not been given much opportunity to do so; everything had been fixed before she was consulted. When Savitri mentioned this to her own parents, they had ordered her to hold her tongue; Dean Mehta knew what he was doing. Rather cowed by her parents' joint outrage at her attempted intervention, she had obeyed.

Her spirits crushed by Tilak's apparent desertion, Anasuyabehn wanted to curl up in some secret lair and never come out again. But she was being carried along by events and had no one to trust, except her father. She clung to the idea that the reward of filial obedience was a well-ordered and contented life. Clutching at this frail hope, she complied with all her aunt's requests. In any case, what use was there in fighting when there was no one for whom to fight?

She had spent one night seething with rage and frustration, asking herself madly why Tilak should so suddenly vanish. Involved in the preparations of the marriage within the two families, she had not heard the rumours as to the cause of his quick departure. It had naturally not occurred to her father or the Vice-Chancellor to tell her the exact reasons.

The white light of morning had brought a dawn of commonsense. Tilak was an honourable man. Perhaps he had left her because she was already affianced and, anyway, of another religion and caste. The furious temper was curbed, the burning desire held down. She bowed her head and told herself, without much hope, that true happiness was to be found in a loyal partnership with a man chosen by one's parents.

On her wedding morning, she submitted quietly to the

ministrations of her cousins and aunts. They bathed her, washed and oiled her hair and plaited it with flowers. With great care, her eldest cousin knelt before her and painted her face with delicate flower designs. Another one stained the palms of her hands and the soles of her feet a soft orange. Finally, they wrapped her in a fine red silk sari embroidered with gold thread.

Before they pulled the sari end down over her face, they brought her a mirror, so that she could admire herself. She looked into its shiny depths and saw a stranger, a very glamorous one. She looked at the image expressionlessly; then she thought of Tilak seeing her when the veil would be lifted, and her lips curved in a gentle smile. The smile faded. Bitter tears welled up and coursed unrestrainedly down her cheeks, to spoil the paint and to trickle over the large, glittering nose-ring and fall like small diamonds into her lap.

The cousins laughed and mopped up the tears. They touched up the painted flowers and agreed that everybody cried when they had to leave their home.

'When you've got a little son in your arms, you'll be truly happy,' Aunt assured her.

Dressed in their best, the families were waiting in the compound. She had, therefore, to compose herself and join them in worship, her face mercifully veiled.

Fourteen young girls were merrily feasted. Armed with gifts of wheat, dates and coconuts, they then streamed down the lane, where a potter awaited them. He cheerfully supplied them with four water-pots.

The fun of a wedding overflowed the compound and spread around the neighbourhood. Little groups of servants, sweepers and village people on their way to town stood in the lane, to glimpse what they could of the fine clothes and jewellery. At the side of the house, the caterers built up their great charcoal fires again and again, and sweated and shouted and turned out innumerable sweetmeats and savouries.

In the storeroom, the Dean's younger brother, with a couple of nephews to assist him, doled out sugar, nuts, flour, spices, oil and vegetables, with a sure hand, seeing that nothing was wasted or stolen, and that yoghurt and water were kept cool and not spilled.

A small band of musicians drummed and squeaked in a corner, their well-practised efforts often lost under the babble of dozens of voices.

The Brahmin, who would officiate at the actual marriage rites after sunset, was fed and fussed over, his shaven head and gnarled hands gesturing a polite 'No', as his palm leaf plate was heaped higher and higher.

The Dean wished that his daughter's wedding should be a joyous occasion. He sailed amongst his guests, greeting them jovially, giving no hint of his inward worry about Anasuyabehn, with whom he had spent an uncomfortable half-hour the evening before. In response to his forecasts of a happy family life, she had responded sadly with a simple, 'Yes, father.' He hoped sincerely that Mahadev knew enough to make her happy.

Meanwhile, in the rented house, a slightly abashed Mahadev was submitting to other ceremonies. Still clucking about the mess his shorn head was in, his paternal aunt replaced the iron ring attached to his topknot with a silver one. With suggestive jokes, the barber washed and powdered one of his toes. A group of giggling young women swooped on him and fed him with sweets.

His friends then helped him mount a decorated horse. His shoulder objected strongly to the exercise, and he winced. As they rode to the temple to worship, they chaffed him that he was lucky the dacoits had left him able to consummate the marriage.

In a splendid procession of cars, horses and pedestrians, he was taken from the temple to Anasuyabehn's home. His heart beat furiously under his silk shirt, and he hoped the girl would like the jewellery he had bought her.

The sun was going down, as they went through the streets. Women and children lolled on the little verandas above the shop fronts, as they waited for the evening breeze to come rippling down the ovenlike, smelly streets. On the pavements, their menfolk squatted idly, smoking and gossiping after their evening meal.

The flickering lights of the procession brought everyone to their feet. At one corner, a beggar in the crowd stood and cursed. He shook his fist at the bridegroom. The bystanders laughed at him; they knew him well. He was harmlessly crazy. They knew he hated the Desais because they had foreclosed on his little shoe shop and forced him into beggary; but, then, none of them liked moneylenders.

As gold and silver trimmed saris, gold bracelets and jewelled necklaces glimmered in the beams of the car headlights, the watchers admired unrestrainedly. They sniffed appreciatively, as waves of flower perfume passed over them from the multitude of garlands carried in the procession. The men admired the horses and the shining cars. Except for that of the beggar, there was no animosity at the display of wealth; they enjoyed the spectacle and never thought of it in relation to their own pressing needs. The Desais, however, were not very trusting. The walking ladies were confined within heavy ropes carried on either side of the procession by their servants and younger male members of the family. Nobody was given the chance to snatch at so much as an earring.

In the centre of it, Mahadev, his pain soothed by aspirin,

his spirits high, enjoyed the pomp of his wedding day. Un-haunted by thoughts of his first wife, for whom he had gone through the same performance, it was as if he went to his first marriage. This time, he told himself, he was marrying for love, and he knew a great content from the thought of it.

The compound had seemed quite full before the advent of the Desai party. Now it was jammed. Space was somehow made, however, for the bridegroom to make his way to the bungalow, where a crushed Anasuyabehn sat dully behind a curtain.

As required, she spat betel juice at him, while her maternal aunt, in lieu of her dead mother, marked him with auspicious marks and threw little balls of rice and ashes over him. The aunt then waved a vessel of water over his head, managing not to splash his magnificent, flower-bedecked, silk turban.

From behind the thin curtain and her shrouding red sari, Anasuyabehn watched him out of the corner of her eye. He looked very fine in his bridegroom's clothes, and there was nothing about him to which she could truthfully object, except that he was not Tilak.

Escorted by their relations, the couple were now taken through the stifling March heat, to the marriage tent. There, a committee of leading Jains awaited them in festive mood. Mahadev's friends brought forward his gifts to the bride and laid them before these gentlemen, who rapidly totted up their value, were greatly impressed by it and announced that the gifts were most generous. The gifts were then handed over to the bride's friends.

Mahadev and Anasuyabehn were seated side by side and shook hands with each other. Under the stare of so many witnesses, Mahadev did not dare give Anasuyabehn's hand a hearty squeeze; he had to content himself with a light shake. The end of her sari was then tied to his scarf.

One of his friends brought him a box, which he handed to

Anasuyabehn. When she opened it, her aunts leaned forward eagerly to view its contents. Rings and bracelets of solid gold made them gasp enviously.

With his face aglow, Dean Mehta brought his offering for his beloved daughter. Iridescent saris, blouse lengths and petticoat lengths to match, a finely-wrought gold necklace, more gold bracelets. Anasuyabehn had never owned so much in all her life. Father has spent too much, she fretted, and wondered if he would have enough money to retire on; then she remembered that he would need no money. As a monk he would need nothing, not even her. She would have no one to turn to – except her husband. She sighed a little sobbing sigh. Hearing her, Mahadev turned quickly towards her but could see nothing but the vague glimmer of her face behind the silk.

In the half-light of the oil lamps, old Desai seemed to float towards his son. Aided by an ancient cousin, he washed one of his son's hands; Anasuyabehn's maternal aunt did the same for her. She then placed Anasuyabehn's hand in that of the groom. Mahadev cheerfully held on firmly and, despite her depression, Anasuyabehn was forced to take cognisance of the fact that the man sitting by her was real, with needs to which she must give attention. She began to tremble and Mahadev, feeling it, massaged her palm gently with his fingers. He tugged her to her feet and they solemnly circumvented the flickering fire before which they had been sitting. Four times, left to right, they paced together, while lucky women pressed forward to receive sopari nuts from Mahadev; thus must husband and wife walk together equally, like oxen, pulling the wagon of life.

Sweets cooked by a Brahmin were offered to the couple and were formally refused.

They walked together into the house, where worship

was offered to Anasuyabehn's gotrija, her kinsmen of lineal and collateral descent from a common ancestor.

The couple were, next, to go in procession to the rented house for a similar ceremony in honour of the bridegroom's ancestry. The day had been a long one and, before setting out, Anasuyabehn whispered rather frantically to her maternal aunt, and was given permission to go to the bathroom, escorted by her favourite young cousin.

The sweeper's door into the bathroom had been left open for ventilation and, when she went to close it, she saw to her astonishment Savitri standing hesitantly on the field path.

'Hey, Bahin,' cried Savitri, stumbling towards her along the rough path.

'Hurry up,' whispered her cousin, from the other side of the door which led into the house.

'Anasuyabehn,' panted Savitri, keeping her voice low. 'I've been trying for two days to get you alone – and now I don't know what to do – it's the letter.'

'What letter?' Anasuyabehn pushed her veil back from her eyes, so as to see her friend's troubled face more clearly.

'From you know whom – John Bennett gave it to me – he couldn't deliver it himself – though he said he called on you.'

Anasuyabehn remembered John bringing the box of china himself. By all the gods who ever reigned, he had had a letter to deliver! The trembling which had begun in the compound became a helpless shake.

'Give it me.'

'Come on,' urged her cousin and opened the other door.

Savitri ignored the young girl and took the letter from

229

under her sari. It smelled faintly of her perfume and Dr Bennett's tobacco, and the envelope was quite dirty.

Ignoring her watching cousin, Anasuyabehn tore open the envelope, her fingers clumsy. The cousin pressed forward, but a glare from behind Savitri's heavy spectacles made her shrink back.

And so the screw was turned once more.

The gentle, courteous words and promises, so quickly penned, seemed to hit her under the heart. The pain was so intense that she cried out, before she fell fainting into Savitri's skinny arms.

The shocked little cousin rushed forward and together they half dragged, half lifted, Anasuyabehn into the passage. The younger girl opened her mouth to call her mother, but Savitri was made of sterner stuff, and whispered, 'Shut up. Wet your hankie under the lavatory tap – quick.'

The cousin obeyed.

The touch of the water on Anasuyabehn's face failed to bring her round. Her aunts could be heard calling to her to hurry. There was a shuffle of footsteps on the veranda. Savitri rose, and ran towards the footsteps, while the frightened cousin pillowed Anasuyabehn's head in her lap.

A bevy of ladies hurried into the passage, calling, 'Hurry up!' In the background, Mahadev inquired if anything was wrong.

Savitri composed herself and said quietly to the first lady, 'Anasuyabehn has fainted. It must have been the heat and the excitement.'

The little cousin discreetly slipped the note from under Anasuyabehn's trailing veil and stuffed it down her blouse. She had no idea what the letter was about, except that it must be most important to Anasuyabehn. With thumping heart, she gave way to Aunt and wrapped her sari loosely round herself, to hide the telltale bulge.

Between them, the ladies got Anasuyabehn on to her bed and crowded round her, chattering anxiously, while word spread in the compound that the bride had been taken ill. 'A bad omen,' muttered one old lady to another.

Dean Mehta, old Desai and Mahadev pushed their way into the crowded room. To give the patient air, the Dean ordered that the room be cleared, except for the three gentlemen, Aunt and Mahadev's aunt. This was done, though the little cousin continued to stand, unremarked, by the head of the bed. Savitri had considered it prudent to sidle quietly out of the house through the sweeper's door.

A lota of water was brought by the boy servant and Aunt sponged her face. After a few minutes, the eyelids fluttered under their smudged paint – and closed again, as she realized her predicament. She was now legally married to Mahadev – and, far away in Bombay, Tilak was trying to start negotiations to marry her; he had not deserted her, he had not run away. He loved her and she loved him. Waves of grief broke over her, as if someone had died, and she sobbed helplessly before her astonished relatives.

How many times do we die in our lives, she wondered, our spirits crushed and broken? And yet the body lives on.

The marriage garland round his neck withering in the heat, Mahadev could bear the sobs no longer. Regardless of convention, he pushed Aunt away. Kneeling by her bedside, he took her hand and himself massaged it gently to get the circulation going. At first Anasuyabehn neither knew nor cared whose hand held hers, whose fingers carefully rubbed her wrists. It was, nevertheless, comforting, as if someone, at least, realized her suffering. Eventually, the weeping ceased. She lay with eyes closed, while Aunt leaned over and gently wiped the wet cheeks.

Her eyelids felt heavy, too heavy to open, but Mahadev waited patiently, and, finally, she did open them, to come face to face with the anxiety and fear clearly mirrored in his usually cold, intelligent eyes. Dimly she knew that, of all the people gathered round her, Mahadev cared the most – and Mahadev was innocent – he had not done anything that contributed to her predicament; she had received nothing but kindnesses from him. 'I'm sorry,' she said, and closed her eyes again.

Old Desai and Dr Mehta were relieved to see her come round, and began in hurried whispers to debate what they should do. Aunt interposed to say that the wedding must go on, as soon as Anasuyabehn was a little recovered; it would be too unlucky otherwise.

Anasuyabehn felt so tired that all she wanted was to be left alone. But Mahadev was there, still rubbing her hands. With a great effort, she swallowed her tears, opened her eyes again, and said that, if she could have a very hot, strong cup of tea, she thought she could go on – the time taken to prepare it, she argued, would give her a few minutes of rest.

Mahadev laughed out loud with relief. He whispered that she could have the whole of Gujerat if she wanted it. She made her lips smile.

The tea was made, the guests reassured, and, by the light of the moon, they set out in procession for the house rented by Dean Mehta. Laden with sweets, dates, money and the kernels of four coconuts, the Mehtas returned home exhausted, to go to bed for the remainder of the night.

The following evening, shaken but composed, Anasuyabehn sat quietly amongst her cousins, while the committee of eminent Jains inspected further gifts from her family. Then alms were distributed to an eager crowd of beggars and saddhus waiting at the compound gate.

Normally, the guests would have been feasted for several more days, but Mahadev had to go to Paris, so, to the sound of steady drum beats, Anasuyabehn dipped her hand in red powder and marked the house walls with the imprint of her palm. In the marriage tent, she impressed an auspicious mark on Mahadev's brother's forehead, making the gesture very respectful and leaving him beaming contentedly. Someone handed her yet another sari, and she wondered vaguely how many dozen she now owned. A coconut was put into her hand and, with Mahadev smiling down at her, she stepped into his carriage. Another coconut was put under the wheels of the carriage and the vehicle jolted over it to break it. The pieces were then offered to her, with four sweetmeats and two brass vessels.

The driver whipped up the horse. Cars and carriages slid out before and behind them. In procession, they made their way into the old part of the town to the Desai Society.

'This is it,' she thought numbly. 'In that old house they will have prepared a bed covered with rose petals and I will sit on it and Mahadev Desai and I will be alone for the first time.' She knew what to expect and she felt dull and lifeless. She could feel the warmth of her husband's thigh against hers, and she turned towards him instinctively. 'Don't be afraid,' he told her gently. 'Everything will be all right.'

At home, the Dean looked at the imprint of his daughter's hand and prayed for her. Then he went to say farewell to most of the guests, pressing some to stay a few days more. He did not yet want to be alone.

In the hopelessly untidy kitchen, deserted for the moment, Anasuyabehn's faithful little cousin surreptitiously read Tilak's letter. Through the crumpled paper, she saw Anasuyabehn's face, so colourless, so dead, her lips hardly moving as she forced herself to say, 'Burn it.' To the young girl it was as if something in the new bride had burned with a mighty flame and was now cold ashes, and the youngster trembled with fear of love not yet experienced.

She struck a match, lit the letter and held it in her hand until it was reduced to a tiny corner of paper attached to curling, black embers. Then she dropped it into the ash-choked charcoal brazier.

CHAPTER THIRTY-SEVEN

On the morning after Anasuyabehn's departure, Aunt stood on the veranda and surveyed the appalling muddle. Pieces of tissue paper, palm leaves, withered flowers and garlands, two pieces of cloth flapping loose from the marriage tent, a pair of chuppells abandoned on the steps; behind her, in the kitchen, a mass of teacups and glasses to be washed, and unsorted laundry to be dealt with, seven house guests still to be fed, and a reception for some thirty people to be arranged for that evening. The last item, thank goodness, would be dealt with by the caterers and her younger brother; she could already hear him talking to two of the cooks; and Dean Mehta, she supposed rather sourly, was probably at his devotions. Lucky for some people that they had so much time for prayer and meditation; she herself had to be content with hastily repeated mantras as she made the morning fire.

The postman, his khaki uniform already black with sweat, picked his way through the debris and handed her the morning's letters.

Although she could not read, she recognized amongst them the handwriting of a great-uncle who had been invited to the wedding. What a mercy that old windbag was too old to travel, a walking gossip column, who would have smelled out the rumour about Anasuyabehn and would have retailed it on every veranda between Shahpur and Calcutta. She sighed, when she thought about this, and hoped that Anasuyabehn's first child would not arrive before ten months – in fact, twelve months would be better.

When she knocked at the study door and opened it, the Dean still had his rosary in his hand. She put the letters on his desk and retreated to the kitchen.

After he had put his rosary into its box, the Dean mechanically opened his letters. It was with considerable shock that he read Tilak's uncle's preliminary inquiry regarding a match between his nephew and Anasuyabehn.

It seemed to him, at first, that he must have misread, and he perused again the careful description of Tilak's assets, both physical and monetary. But there was no doubt that it was an offer for his daughter.

Here was proof that the girl had lied to him. His little daughter had lied. He was engulfed in wretchedness. What had she been doing?

As he stared at the letter, his fear and disappointment at his daughter gave way to anger against the hapless Tilak. He tore the letter up and flung it into his wastepaper basket.

If he heard so much as a breath of scandal about Tilak and his daughter, the man should go. If it were the last thing he did as Dean, Tilak should be made to rue the day he ever tampered with Anasuyabehn.

The letter from Bombay crossed with one from John to Tilak, in which he told of entrusting Tilak's letter to Savitri for delivery. He wrote also of the haste with which the marriage was being solemnized, and that he hoped that Tilak would find someone else and be happy with her.

When the servant brought John's letter to Tilak, he was

sitting by his mother's couch while she had her morning tea. As he read the missive, a fearful numbness crept over him, and his mind refused to accept the news it contained. He continued to sit, the letter in his hand resting on his knee, while the numbness gave way to a ghastly emptiness.

It seemed to him that he had been stripped of his clothing and walked by himself through a vast empty space, a cold wind beating upon his bare flesh. It seemed that he walked for a long time, ignoring the wind, refusing to be afraid, and gradually his senses returned.

When he opened his eyes, he did it carefully and slowly, as if letting in the light would also let in something horrible; but it was only his mother's troubled eyes which met his.

She had put down her cup in her saucer, and she asked, 'What's the matter?'

Tilak was unable to speak. He handed the letter to her and she read it, her English being quite adequate to the task.

'Your friend in Shahpur – the Englishman?'

'Yes.' With that single word, all the emotion which he had tried to control since he left Shahpur suddenly erupted. He fell to his knees by the couch and buried his head in the Kashmir shawl draped over it. He hammered the couch with clenched fists. 'Why couldn't Uncle get through on the telephone?' he almost screamed.

His mother put down her cup and saucer with a clatter, and leaned forward to put her arms round her wilful, dreadfully hurt son. 'The lines to Shahpur were simply choked by calls, my dear child. Uncle couldn't help that – it'll be years before we get a proper service.'

CHAPTER THIRTY-EIGHT

Because both Tilak's uncle and his mother feared a nervous breakdown, they did their best to dissuade Tilak from returning to Shahpur.

'There's nothing you can do, my son.'

'I know that, mother. But I want to see the Vice-Chancellor and find out how things are in the University, and I would like to hear from John Bennett exactly what happened.'

Though he was obviously distraught, he was, they felt, trying to be rational, so they reluctantly agreed to the journey. The following morning, he and his servant arrived at Shahpur station. In the vast Victorian waiting-room there, he took a shower and changed his clothes. He was calm enough to eat a little breakfast in the empty first-class dining-room, while his servant ate in less sumptuous surroundings at a platform stall.

He had an overwhelming desire to see Anasuyabehn once again, just to look upon her face. He told himself sardonically that one is permitted to look on the face of one's dead. He did not wish to call on her; apart from it being too modern an idea for the Desais to accept, it would awaken again in her the despair she must have felt at having to go through with her marriage. But just to see her passing by was a gnawing need.

The servant came into the dining-room to inquire what he should do next, and Tilak instructed him to take his luggage to his rooms in the students' hostel.

The servant looked scared, and whispered that perhaps the Sahib should not show himself there for the present. Wouldn't a hotel be safer?'

Tilak told him roughly not to be a fool. The students

were not going to hurt him. 'For myself, I may stay a night or two with Bennett Sahib. I have to see him.'

Satisfied, the servant went away to find a porter.

After giving up his ticket, Tilak went through the barrier. He hesitated on the steps outside, and a motorcycle rickshaw drew up quickly by him. 'Sahib?' the man queried hopefully, revving his engine.

'Do you know the Desai Society – the one in the city centre?'

'Ji, hun. Everybody knows it.'

'Right. Put me down fifty yards before you get to it.'

They drove through narrow alleyways thronged with people, then into an area where the alleys were little more than passages lined with the high boundary walls of various Societies. They came at last to a square which held the goldsmiths' bazaar, and there the rickshaw wallah stopped.

He pointed to an archway on the other side of the square. 'Through there, Sahib, is a vegetable bazaar. Opposite it, is the Desai Society's gate.'

Tilak paid the man without comment. He had a shrewd suspicion that he had been taken on a tour of the old city and that probably there was a much shorter route from the station, but he could not be bothered to bargain; his mind was on Anasuyabehn.

Uncertain what to do, he walked through the archway and found the compound gate without difficulty. A few women and children were standing near the gate, sweepers or the very poor, and one or two professional beggars squatted with their backs against the Desais' wall, their begging bowls in front of them. Tilak hastily crossed the tiny square and pretended to look through the vegetable bazaar.

'What are the people waiting for?' he asked a stallholder.

The stallholder told him of the great marriage just performed. Today, the rumour was that the bridegroom was going to take his bride on an aeroplane. He thought that the women were waiting, in case, at the time of departure, the Desais felt like giving a little more in charity.

As he was talking, a taxi came from the further side of the little square and drew up at the gate.

The compound gate was opened by a chowkidar, who immediately kicked one of the beggars to make him move out of the way. The grumbling beggar moved about six inches and then was forced to his feet by the rush of onlookers who closed in on the entrance. Tilak himself was propelled, not unwillingly, towards the gate by a couple of eager youths and three giggling country girls, and was soon hemmed in by a small crowd.

A servant put two suitcases into the taxi. Then a very old man in horn-rimmed spectacles was assisted in, while the crowd murmured in nervous awe; everyone knew of old Desai.

Surely, the bride would come now. The women pushed forward and Tilak, to his consternation, found himself to the front of the crowd with the beggar who had been so ignominiously kicked, and rows of women pushing behind.

A murmur of women's voices came from within the Society. Anasuyabehn, her face half obscured by her flowered silk sari, stepped on to the street, followed closely by a man in white khadi, who, Tilak presumed, was her husband. They were followed by several ladies and gentlemen who stood around the gateway. Anasuyabehn turned her head, as if to say goodbye to one of the ladies – and then she saw him.

For a moment she stood transfixed, the words of farewell unspoken. She lifted her sari further over her face to shield herself from the gaze of the jostling relations.

Oblivious of the reason for her momentary pause, Mahadev put his arm gently round her back to move her towards the taxi, and in the self-same second the beggar, knife in hand, lunged forward as if to stab her.

239

Tilak saw the knife flash as it was drawn and he leaped between them, taking the knife in his own back, as he and Anasuyabehn crashed to the ground.

She screamed as she fell and, in the rush of people towards her, the beggar turned and ran for his life.

A shocked Mahadev beheld a man with a knife in his back lying over his new bride. The crowd began to move hastily away, while the chowkidar lifted Tilak up slightly so that Mahadev could get at his wife. He pulled her free and lifted her to her feet. She was dust-covered and bruised, but was able to stand on her feet, one hand to her mouth, as Partner Uncle bent and very carefully withdrew the knife. He tore a light cotton shawl from round his neck and pressed it on the wound, while he shouted for someone to bring a string bed to carry the man into the compound.

From his more elevated position in the old-fashioned taxi, old Desai had watched with horror. Now he scrambled out and went to Mahadev. 'Is she hurt?' he asked anxiously.

Mahadev was gently wiping his wife's bruised cheek. 'No bones broken,' he said. 'The man seems to have taken most of the fall, somehow.'

Old Desai whipped round to look at his Partner Brother kneeling by Tilak. Partner Brother looked up and said, 'He's dead.'

Anasuyabehn turned her face into her husband's shoulder, while a Desai aunt tried to persuade her back into the compound. Mahadev, his face deadly pale, held the shuddering young woman. 'Wait a minute,' he urged the aunt.

Old Desai turned back to his son. 'Take your wife and go to the airport. Catch the plane. This is a police matter, and they'll keep you here for weeks as a material witness. Your wife can tend her bruises and change her sari in the airport.'

Mahadev stared at him, overwhelmed for the moment by the sight of murder.

'Go, boy, go,' his father urged. 'That knife was meant for *you*. Your wife nearly died instead of you, because just at the very second he struck, she moved in front of you. Seated in the taxi, I saw exactly what happened, and I fear there may be other dacoits nearby who will make a second attempt.' He paused for breath, an old man fearing the loss of his eldest son. He caught at Mahadev's sleeve. 'Wake up, boy, and get into the taxi, quickly.'

Mahadev forced himself to speak firmly, as he wrapped Anasuyabehn's sari end round her bruised arm. She was not weeping, only breathing heavily, her face almost colourless. He half-lifted her into the taxi and, when he followed her, she clung to him, burying her face in his shoulder. During the nights he had spent with her, he had been very gentle, making sure that she was pleasured. Last night, he thought with a sudden glow, she had turned willingly to him and had responded to his overtures.

Despite the shocked looks of two older ladies, who had scrambled into the taxi after him, he continued to hold her and to whisper to her not to be afraid; he would protect her.

Thankful to get away, the taxi driver hooted to persuade the stallholders, who had replaced the original crowd, to get out of his way while he turned in the small space.

At a point where the narrow street he was travelling debouched into a main thoroughfare, he was stopped by an armed policeman. The constable flung open all the doors, took a good look at the passengers, made sure no one was hiding under the seats, and then motioned them onwards.

Through his mirror, the driver saw a police jeep ease its way into the rabbit warren he had just left.

241

CHAPTER THIRTY-NINE

Immediately the police jeep was noticed coming down the lane, the stallholders shot back to their vegetables and began assiduously to rearrange them; the open-mouthed women pulled their plain white saris over their heads and became anonymous bundles hurrying through the far archway, following their menfolk. After them ran a bunch of little urchins afraid of being left behind.

The old American army jeep slid to a stop on its smooth tyres, and the Bengali police chief leaped out. A constable dropped off the back of the vehicle and hammered on the door with his rifle butt. The iron bar across the inner side squeaked as it was turned, and the nervous chowkidar let in both the police chief and three constables.

Despite the melting away of possible witnesses, which he had observed as he came into the small bazaar, the Bengali was hopeful that he might now get a lead on the dacoits. In the back of his mind, he had rather expected that an attack might be made on Mahadev. The passengers in the held-up train would have seen only a vague collection of men with their faces covered; Mahadev had left his carriage and might easily have seen how they moved the loot.

Old Desai was amazed to see the police arrive so fast. He was in the process of going through Tilak's pocket book, so that he could identify him when he himself telephoned the police.

'I telephoned them as soon as I saw what had happened,' his younger son told him.

The Bengali, as he approached and heard his remark,

smiled with approbation on the stout accountant. 'Very wise,' he told him. 'There are not many entrances to this area, and I sent men on bicycles to block them immediately.' He shrugged, as he approached Tilak's body, lying on a narrow bed in the shade of a loggia. 'Of course, if the man climbed a wall and went through one of the Societies, we might not be lucky.'

Chairs and glasses of water were brought and, while his men lounged on the other side of the compound, the Bengali got down to detail. The contents of Tilak's wallet had hardly yielded the letters about the Fellowship, which gave his name and Bombay address, before old Desai's office telephone rang. A nervous clerk came to say that the police chief was wanted on the line.

The Bengali listened intently and said, 'Charge him.' He slammed the receiver down and came crossly back to the waiting Desais. While they waited, he sat down and lit a cigarette. At last, he addressed old Desai.

'We've got the man. He ran into the arms of one of our men on his usual beat, struck the constable and was arrested for assaulting a police officer. He fits your description.'

Everybody present sighed with relief. The Bengali continued to stare at the body. Then he added, 'He's not a dacoit. He's known to the beat constable. He was a shoe merchant on whom you foreclosed, and he's been known to utter threats against you.'

'I didn't recognize him,' said old Desai.

'There's a lot of difference between a well-to-do merchant and a mad, starving beggar,' replied the Bengali and swung off his chair and on to his feet.

The group of men in front of him stiffened visibly, as they realized his contempt for them, in spite of their wealth.

The detective called his men over, and told them to bring a stretcher and remove the body.

He had seen a lot of death, had this small Bengali; yet it angered him that a man clever enough to obtain an English scholarship had died instead of one of these accursed moneylenders. His small, snakelike eyes regarded Desai. 'You were fortunate that such a brave man was near. Otherwise, you would undoubtedly have lost your son.'

'Yes,' said Desai, who by this time was feeling that he had had as much as he could endure, 'I am grateful to him – very grateful.'

Remorselessly, the Bengali then went on to upbraid him for allowing a material witness like Mahadev to depart from the country.

Old Desai was nearly sulky when he replied, 'I was afraid there might be other dacoits in the crowd; they might have struck again. How was I to know he was only a debtor of ours?'

After warning old Desai to hold himself in readiness to attend the inquest and the subsequent trial, the detective followed his men swiftly out of the compound, and left the demoralized Desais to their own consciences.

As the stretcher-bearers lifted the stretcher to put it into a small van which had drawn up behind the jeep, the Bengali stopped them. He lifted the cloth laid over Tilak's face and looked down at the beautiful, calm features. He was remembering a remark of one of the older ladies, when he asked if anyone knew the victim. She had said, 'Our new daughter seemed to know him – she turned to look at him, before he was struck down.'

As he let the cloth drop, he muttered, 'I wonder why you were in this unlikely part of town this morning? Was there a connection between you and the new bride?'

244

The puzzled bearers pushed the stretcher into the vehicle and slammed and locked the doors.

The Bengali returned to his jeep and climbed in beside the driver. He wondered if he had stumbled on a love affair as well as a murder, and, with all a Bengali's understanding of the passions of human nature, he decided it was unnecessary to intercept the younger Desais at the airport; he could get a conviction without them. In his own mind he was certain that the victim had given his life for the sake of the girl – old Desai's exact description of the movements of his son and his wife and the beggar at the moment of the tragedy made that fairly clear.

As his driver took him slowly through the ancient streets, he thought about Mahadev Desai and his new wife, and then about the fine scholar whose life had been so summarily ended. There was a story there, he was sure of it.

He threw his cigarette end out of the window and it was immediately pounced upon by a beggar. Who am I to muddy the water further, he asked himself angrily. Tilak Sahib, rest in peace; I'm going to hang the bastard that killed you; but it's one of those cursed moneylenders who should be at the end of the rope – they drove him mad.

CHAPTER FORTY

The news of Tilak's murder came too late for that day's newspapers, and the Bengali police chief, taking his address from the letters found on him, informed only his family in Bombay. Neither John nor the barber who had come to cut his hair that afternoon, were, therefore, aware of it. John, however, was not in the best of tempers; he felt indescribably petulant and he had been unable to concentrate on his writings. The arrival of the barber had been a relief, and he limped out on to the veranda and sat down in his basket chair.

The barber wrapped a clean towel round his neck.

'Have you got my comb and shaving brush?' asked John. 'I prefer them to yours.' And he looked with distaste at the grubby shopping bag of barbering necessities lying on the veranda floor.

The barber looked pained and his beautifully waxed moustache twitched with irritation, but he answered, with a slight bow, 'Of course, Sahib. Ranjit has brought everything, including hot water in your own lota.' He pointed to the little brass vessel sitting on the veranda rail.

'Good,' grunted John. 'Very well.'

The barber began to comb. Since all Englishmen have an unnatural interest in the weather, he talked about the weather. Diplomat, gossip, messenger, the barber studied all his customers, and, as he went from house to house and village to village, he retailed the news, views and scandal of the district, slanted according to the views he supposed his customer of the moment held.

'Getting a little thin just here,' he announced, planting an accusing finger on a non-existent bald patch amid the thick thatch on John's head. He put down his comb and rummaged in his shopping bag.

'To avoid losing one's hair it's important to oil it daily. Now I have here a new oil which many of my customers are finding most efficacious . . .' and he waved a bottle in front of John's nose.

John blinked as the bottle sailed dangerously near, but managed to read *Asoka Medicinal Hair Tonic* on a flower-decked label.

'What does it smell like?' he asked doubtfully.

The barber whipped out the cork and a tremendous perfume immediately enveloped them both.

'I'd rather be bald,' said John decisively.

The barber bit his lower lip and looked hurt, then he surveyed John's head from the front, cocking his own head first on one side and then on the other. 'Well, of course, it doesn't show in front,' he said at last, 'but it won't be long.'

'I couldn't stand it,' said John, all his sales resistance hastily marshalled. 'Perfumes – er – perfumes make me sneeze,' and he sneezed to demonstrate the fact.

The barber leaped out of range of any droplets, and said with a regretful sigh, 'Pure mustard oil might help, though I think it's really too far gone for that.'

Frown lines on John's forehead warned him that his customer was getting irate.

'Well, well, never mind,' he said. 'I expect you would like a shave, as usual, Sahib.'

'Yes,' John replied.

'Ears cleaned? They need it – you've got hairs growing in them.'

'Very well,' his customer agreed resignedly.

247

'Nice wedding Mehta Sahib had for his daughter,' said the barber as his scissors clipped merrily.

'I expect so,' said John. 'I didn't go to the wedding – only to the reception for friends the next day.'

'Oh, it was very fine indeed, though the number of guests was limited by the size of the compound. She has married a very fine gentleman – his toenails were clean and well clipped,' he added as a professional detail.

'Did you get the toe powdering job?'

'Yes, indeed. I did his brother, too, when he was married.'

'Decent tip?'

'Fair, fair.' The barber did a rapid run round John's left ear with the scissors. 'Of course, they're moneylenders – but so rich, Sahib, it is unbelievable. You should have seen the gifts.'

'I can imagine them.' John ducked as the scissors shot across his forehead.

'Keep still, please, Sahib.'

The barber stepped back in order to view his handiwork, and then said coyly to John, 'I hear you're considering marriage, too, Sahib.'

'What?' shouted John, sitting up in his chair so suddenly that he nearly lost an eye to the advancing scissors.

The barber jumped backwards, scissors held engarde, his professional aplomb severely shaken. 'I – I – er just heard a little word about it,' he said, eyeing John nervously.

John laughed at him and relaxed again into his basket chair.

'Wherever did you hear it?'

The barber took up his comb and combed furiously, while he considered his reply. He bent his head to look at the hairline he had trimmed. 'I think that'll do,' he muttered, and whipped a hand mirror out of his shopping bag.

John glanced at himself in the tiny mirror. 'OK,' he said. 'No oil. Where did you hear it and who is to be the bride?'

248

'Aren't you going to be married, Sahib? I must say I thought it unlikely, in spite of other rumours to the contrary.'

He looked down at John's spare body and the hurt legs.

John was irritated by the look. 'Well? I want to know who I'm to marry – Miss Prasad?'

The barber ventured a snigger at the mention of this prim, dedicated female. 'No, no, Sahib. The English lady with the copper-coloured hair, Sahib. She's often in the villages, working with Dr Ferozeshah. I don't know her name.'

'Oh, Miss Armstrong. Well, she's a friend of mine. I wonder why anyone should think I'm about to marry her, though.'

'It was your inquiry about the house which Dean Mehta rented temporarily for his daughter's marriage. It's to let again. A good house, Sahib, with its own well.'

Despite being smothered in shaving soap, John sat bolt upright in his chair.

'Look here,' he almost shouted, 'I haven't made any inquiries about that house.'

The barber tut-tutted and wiped soapsuds off John's eyebrows.

'The landlord himself told me, Sahib; I came straight from him to you. He said you had asked about repairs and rent, so naturally he assumed you were about to marry – the lady comes to see you regularly.' The barber waved his razor in the air rather hopelessly. 'It seemed quite natural, Sahib.'

John sniffed. 'I've made no inquiries and I don't intend to get married just to please my neighbours. The man must be out of his mind.'

'Just bend your head a little to the left, please, Sahib. That's better.' The fearsome razor swept gracefully round

249

his neck. 'Your skin is not what it might be, Sahib. The sun is very hard on white skins. Now, I have here . . .'

'No,' snapped John resolutely. 'My old red hide is doing quite well, thank you. Married, indeed.'

'Well, Ranjit said it would be quite soon.'

'He did, did he? Hmm. I suppose it was he who actually saw the landlord?'

'Of course, Sahib.' The barber was by now completely bewildered, and silently tackled the cleaning of John's ears, while John sat and fumed.

The mirror was again produced and John looked at himself.

For the first time for years he really considered what he looked like. Heavens, his face was seamed and weatherbeaten, and was that really grey hair at his temples? Surely, at thirty-four he should not be grey?

The crushed barber saw his client's fingers stray up over the offending skin and hair and hastened to pay a compliment.

He smiled ingratiatingly and said, 'Most distinguished-looking, Sahib.'

'Humph,' said John, nonetheless slightly comforted. 'How much?'

The barber was paid, packed his shopping bag and retreated down the path to the compound gate, promising to come again in two weeks' time.

'Ranjit!' roared John, and, at the tone of voice, Ranjit appeared with the speed of a rabbit, hastily wiping his wet hands on his sweat cloth.

'Just what have you been doing? That lunatic of a barber said you were inquiring about the house for rent down the road.'

Ranjit swallowed, considered what he should say and only succeeded in looking very guilty.

250

'Well, Sahib, it . . . er.'

'The wretch suggested I was going to be married . . . now I'll be bothered by everybody asking me if I am, blast it, and every tradesman in the district will try to sell me things. What on earth have you been doing?'

'I happened to meet the landlord, Sahib, and I asked him – er, out of general interest, Sahib. You will remember that we were talking about the need for you to have a better house a little while ago?'

John took a large breath and reminded himself that Ranjit was his most devoted friend.

'And getting married?'

This question in Ranjit's opinion demanded a straight answer. It was obvious that his young master – John was permanently about eighteen in Ranjit's mind – did not know what he was doing. Otherwise he would not ask such a silly question.

'Sahib, even in England, if you favour a young woman with your interest and she eats with you and you sit close to her, doesn't that mean that you'll marry her?'

Despite his indignation, John's eyes began to twinkle. 'It depends on your intentions.'

'A man such as yourself could not possibly have any intentions, except marriage,' declared Ranjit stalwartly, but wondering suddenly if Englishmen were, perhaps, a little like Indians in some respects.

John's temper had cooled. He took out his pipe and lit it, putting the dead match carefully back into the box, before he answered.

'I've no intentions at all, Ranjit. You know that my legs are a mess. They don't work very well and they are scarred. I'm also no longer young. I wouldn't like to ask a woman to marry such an old crock.'

Seeing that the storm had passed, Ranjit ventured to sit

down on the top step. He rubbed the grey stubble on his chin, as he considered John's last remark. He loved his master, as if he were his own son, and enjoyed serving a bachelor, but lately the Sahib had been fretful without reason. He had seen him watch the little Memsahib go down the path to the gate, and then turn back to his desk, to sit silently staring at the papers before him, unable to work.

It was the law of all Hindu families that parents should marry off their children. Men and women should enjoy their spouses and only in age turn to asceticism. The Sahib had never known the joys of marriage and this was not normal.

Few servants liked to serve a married couple – wives had a habit of poking their noses into every domestic detail – but Ranjit was prepared to do this, if it made his master content. He, therefore, cleared his throat, blew his nose, and went into battle.

'Women, Sahib,' he began, 'are peculiar creatures. When they care for us, it is frequently because of our deficiencies and stupidities.'

John blew a cloud of smoke, and laughed.

Ranjit looked indignant. 'You laugh, Sahib, because you have no experience. The little Memsahib . . .'

The laugh died in John's throat. 'Well, what about her?' he asked quite sharply.

Determinedly, Ranjit plunged on. 'The little Memsahib doesn't see that you are a little older than some. She does not *see* your sick legs, though she will help you to cure them. She sees only you, Sahib.'

John looked silently out over the shabby compound. Ranjit had the eyes of a vulture, missing nothing.

At last he said, 'Have you asked the lady for me, Ranjit?'

'There is no need, Sahib. It is in every look she gives you.'

'Do you like her, Ranjit?'

'Yes, Sahib.' He searched for words, pulling nervously at

his little pigtail at the back of his head as if to stimulate the brains within. 'More than other English ladies I have served.'

'Ah, well, Ranjit. Cats can look at kings, and I suppose I can look at a pretty woman sometimes. Now I am going to think about this map I am to draw for Shri Lallubhai. Go away and make me some dinner.'

'Ji, hun,' assented Ranjit, heaving himself to his feet and wondering if he had done any good at all with his attempt at matchmaking.

Dusk came while John was still working on the map. Lacking a large table, he had pinned big sheets of paper to the walls of his room. Propped up by the end of his table, he stood in front of these, pencil in one hand and ruler in the other, while he roughed in the districts that he knew. He hoped that his assistant from the City Engineer's Department would be able to add more details to his work.

He had turned to pick up a fresh pencil and to switch on another light, when he thought he heard the compound gate click. He paused, took up his stick and went towards his open front door.

It was much darker than he had realized, the stars already lay like brilliants on indigo velvet and the world was quiet with after-dinner hush.

She saw him before he saw her, his spare figure silhouetted against the light of the lamp, and she came towards him like a drifting ghost.

'Diana,' he exclaimed.

The sound of her first name made her pause, then she came swiftly up the steps, her arms full of rolls of paper, her face aglow.

He took the rolls from her and tossed them on to his couch, then took her arm and drew her into the softly lit room. He did not let go of her arm, but stood looking down at her.

253

'This is a pleasure,' he said.

'Ranjit said in the bazaar this morning that you wanted to show me the map, so I came as soon as I could and brought that stuff from the City Engineer.' She pointed to the pile of papers, and then realized that he was still holding her bare arm. She faltered, and looked up at him a little beseechingly.

'Ranjit is apt to be a trifle premature,' he said rather grimly, and continued to hold her arm and look at her, until her pulses quickened and she dropped her own gaze, lest he realize how disconcerted she was.

'Come and sit down,' he said, and led her to the couch. He moved the blueprints and sat down beside her. He had never done this before, and she looked at him out of the corner of her eye. He caught the look and she smiled at him. The tight, withdrawn expression on his face faded, but he continued to look at her as if he had never really seen her before. He knew suddenly that he wanted her like he had never wanted anything for years. Not only did he desperately want her in his bed, but he wanted her to be opposite him at breakfast, to listen to his hopes and fears – and even to his very bad jokes. He slowly let go of her arm. Dare he ask her?

His eyes moved over the short, red-gold hair to the little, freckled triangle of skin under her throat, burned red by the sun, and he realized that she had on a different dress, the neckline of which plunged and curved delicately over full, white breasts. It was a dress meant for dinner dates and moonlit evenings, not for hard work on maps. He chuckled, and grinned at her engagingly.

'Could you stay to dinner once more?' he asked hopefully. 'I don't have enough company these days.'

To his further amusement, she blushed furiously, scarlet running up to her hairline. She fingered her glass bangles nervously, before she answered.

'Ranjit said you would expect me to stay to dinner

whenever I came. He said you always asked people because you didn't like eating by yourself.' She said it teasingly, as if to belie the telltale blush.

It will be a marvel if he hasn't asked her to stay to breakfast as well, he thought, but he answered without hesitation, 'Ranjit is quite right.'

'Then I shall be delighted to stay.'

John stood up and went to the window.

A well burnished moon was rising. The University gardens would be a pretty haven tonight, he thought, and he turned back into the room, his mind made up.

'Ranjit,' he roared. 'Make dinner for two. Armstrong Memsahib has come.'

Ranjit came through the door from the back veranda. He had shaved and had on a clean shirt. He grinned toothlessly, as he announced, 'Dinner is ready now, Sahib, and there is plenty for two.'

'Ranjit, you are a genius.'

And Ranjit viewed the rather self-conscious couple and replied contentedly, 'Yes, Sahib.'

By Helen Forrester

Fiction

THURSDAY'S CHILD
THE LATCHKEY KID
LIVERPOOL DAISY
THREE WOMEN OF LIVERPOOL
THE MONEYLENDERS OF SHAHPUR
YES, MAMA
THE LEMON TREE
THE LIVERPOOL BASQUE
MOURNING DOVES
MADAME BARBARA

Non-fiction

TWOPENCE TO CROSS THE MERSEY
LIVERPOOL MISS
BY THE WATERS OF LIVERPOOL
LIME STREET AT TWO

Helen Forrester was born in Hoylake, Cheshire, the eldest of seven children. For many years, until she married, her home was Liverpool – a city that features prominently in her work. For the past forty years she has lived in Alberta, Canada.

Helen Forrester is the author of four best-selling volumes of autobiography and a number of equally successful novels, the latest of which is *Madame Barbara*. In 1988 she was awarded an honorary D.Litt by the University of Liverpool in recognition of her achievements as an author. The University of Alberta conferred on her the same honour in 1993.